Aurora

Julie Bertagna was born in Ayrshire and grew up near Glasgow. After an English degree at Glasgow University she worked as the editor of a small magazine, a teacher and then a freelance journalist. She has written many award-winning novels for teenagers and younger children and speaks in schools, libraries and at book festivals across the UK. Her books have also sold all over the world. *Exodus*, her first novel for Macmillan, was shortlisted for the Whitbread Award and was described by the *Guardian* as 'a miracle of a novel'. Julie writes full-time and lives in Glasgow with her family.

Visit Julie Bertagna's website at
www.juliebertagna.com

Books by Julie Bertagna

EXODUS

Shortlisted for the
Whitbread Children's Book of the Year 2002

Winner of the Lancashire Children's
Book of the Year Award 2002

Best Scottish Book of the 21st Century (*The List*)

Highly Commended for the
Eco Prize for Creativity 2005

Winner of a Santa Monica Green Literature Prize (US)

The story continues in

ZENITH

Shortlisted for the Angus Award in Scotland

Winner of the Catalyst Children's Book Award

And concludes in

AURORA

Julie Bertagna

Aurora

MACMILLAN

First published 2011 by Macmillan Children's Books
a division of Macmillan Publishers Limited
20 New Wharf Road, London N1 9RR
Basingstoke and Oxford
Associated companies throughout the world
www.panmacmillan.com

ISBN 978-0-330-43564-2

1 3 5 7 9 8 6 4 2

A CIP catalogue record for this book is available from
the British Library.

Printed and bound in the UK by CPI Mackays, Chatham ME5 8TD

For the Kiribati Islanders whose plight inspired
Exodus, Zenith *and* Aurora *and for everyone who has*
accompanied the characters of these stories,
and me, on our epic journey.

'To be part of a nation that might be under the sea gives
me a feeling that I am from nowhere.'

i-Kiribati native

CONTENTS

SURGE

SEEK

The untold want, by life and land ne'er granted,
Now, Voyager, sail thou forth, to seek and find.

Walt Whitman

WINTER'S END
The year 2116

THE WIND OF WAR

The world's wind blasts the old steeple tower as if it will tear it apart stone by stone – and hurl Pandora to her death.

Rain lashes the girl's fierce, wind-burned face. Her green eyes steal sparks from the lightning storm. Pandora scrapes away dripping tangles of hair, scrubs her eyes with a sodden lace sleeve and squints into the howling darkness.

Where is Fox?

He must be up here, somewhere.

Pandora was rummaging through her hoard of old weapons in the museum when the crash of his axe echoed through the dank, storm-raked halls. *Who!* demanded a startled owl as it swooped from a headless statue to fly through one of the tall, shattered windows out into the storm.

'Fox?' Pandora called, as startled as the owl by the violent axe.

Who else could it be? There was no other human presence, only their two selves, in all the netherworld.

Yet she grabbed a shield and a sword along with her moonmoth lantern and raced through the clutter of the museum into the adjoining tower, following the noise of the axe. Up a thousand twisting stairs she ran, through scared flutterings and slitherings and scuttlings of netherworld creatures, pausing only to skewer a fat rat with her sword – she'd roast it later for supper. Gasping for breath, she stopped as she reached an open door at the top of the stairs.

The crashing axe had stopped.

Pandora crept through the doorway. Her moonmoth lantern cast a fluttery glow upon tumbledown bookstacks, hillocks of mildewed pages and storm-shuttered windows that rattled in the hammer of the wind. As she stepped through the litter of lost centuries she spied a strange, dark gap. Tiptoeing towards it, sword at the ready, she saw that part of a bookcase was tugged out from the wall.

'Fox?' she whispered, and poked her sword, tentatively, into the gap.

The thin blade shivered in a gust of wind. Pandora squeezed into the gap and lifted her lantern.

The mothlight revealed a smashed door.

A secret door! Pandora had thought she knew every secret of this old tower.

She looked at the rusty key stuck fast in the lock, at Fox's axe still wedged in the wood. *He knew there was a secret door here? And never told me?* Furious now, she scrambled through the gash in the door, ripping her gown on jagged splinters.

Pandora climbed up into storm-blasted darkness. The wind roared through a stark geometry of archways that rose all around and above her, in a vast cone of stone and air. Amazed, she saw that she stood *inside* the great spire that topped the old tower like a spiky hat.

Now Pandora clings to an archway and battles the wind that wants to send her crashing down to the drowned city in the netherworld waters, down on to the seaweedy roofs that rise at low tide like the helms of sunken ships. Even she, with webbed hands and feet and the soft gills on her neck, might not survive such a fall.

Raindrops as big as frogs splat upon her head. Pandora curses her dress, one of the museum's ancient hoard, its drenched skirts a dragging weight as she tries to move across the slimy stone.

'Fox!'

The wind snatches his name from her lips and the sword from her hand. The sword *clangs* as it tumbles from the tower – yet another treasure lost to the flooded world.

Something has been happening the last few days. Something big. Pandora has seen it in Fox's eyes, breathed danger in the scent of his sweat. And now he's smashed his way up into the spire in the teeth of the storm.

Pandora raises her face to the battering rain and peers up through the soaring archways of the spire to the city of New Mungo, looming high above. Its skyscrapers dwarf the old netherworld tower like a crowd of giants. *Police patrols?* She scans the enormous towers and their network of connecting sky tunnels. *Is that why Fox is up here? Surely they wouldn't swoop on a night like this!*

Skybikers can swarm down without warning like wasps from a poked nest. Pandora and Fox have a hundred hiding places from the searchlights and guns that sweep the netherworld, hunting fugitives from the boat camp beyond the city wall – though none have made it through in years.

Sky patrols have been rare this winter. The ferocious storms have kept them at bay. And the sky empire is sunk too deep in new dreams and nightmares, says Fox, to feel the tremors of revolution gathering in the world beyond its walls.

A sensation of hot goosebumps prickles Pandora's skin as

9

a spindly finger of lightning reaches down towards the spire. All around her, the devilish stone faces of the gargoyles in the nooks of the old tower seem electrified into demonic life. The lightning jabs at a figure perched on the strange little stairway that twists up inside the spire, past the bell that never rings, right to the innermost tip of the huge cone.

'*Fox!*'

Pandora shouts with all her might to the one who has been everything since he found her as a tiny mud urchin, abandoned in the ruins. No longer that sad and scraggy waif, Pandora has stared at her reflection in the slime pools of the museum and seen a young woman grown tall and lithe and beautiful. Now she is the warrior queen of the netherworld, dressed in the jewelled gowns and armour of lost ages, with a lustrous tangle of hair and green eyes that glow like moonmoths when she looks at Fox.

Soon she and Fox will have so much more than this kingdom of drowned ruins. When war smashes through the city wall, they will leap into the future together and rebuild a world where the sky empire's brutal grip on the flooded Earth is broken at last.

The rain pelts harder and Pandora raises her shield as if to a hail of bullets, imagining herself battling alongside Fox in the coming war. She loves him so endlessly she'd *die* for him, she vows, as she lunges towards the precarious stairway.

Thunder rips through the world, a sound so immense it might be one of the sky towers tumbling down. Pandora unhooks the little brass bugle she keeps on her belt, waits for the thunder to fade, then blows the hardest blast she can muster.

At last, Fox looks down.

'The boats,' he shouts. 'Pan, come and see!'

10

Pandora pulls dripping locks of hair from amazed green eyes. The great wall that makes an ocean fortress of the sky city, and traps the netherworld in gloom, is the only horizon she has ever known. She has never seen the boat camp beyond, only imagined it clinging like a crop of barnacles to the other side of the wall.

Over the years she and Fox have listened to the crackling voices on the soundwaves: flood refugees telling desperate stories of their survival on the oceans. They are *her* people, thinks Pandora, because her lost family must have been boat refugees. Fox chose his netherworld exile; he fled his home in the sky city above to launch the revolution that will soon shake the world. But how did *she* come to be here? Pandora has no memory of family or a life beyond the wall.

For now, the boat people cling in wretched anchorage around the Earth's sky cities, barricaded under gun shields, crafting weapons from sea junk for the battle ahead. At least, Pandora hopes so. Their communications with the boat camps died in the mighty winter storms. Searching the hissing desolation of the soundwaves, listening for a pulsebeat of the outside world, Pandora has imagined the boat people all swept away.

Step by trembling step, she now begins to climb up the precarious, twisting stairway towards Fox – who takes a sudden leap across empty space and vanishes through an archway.

Pandora searches the darkness. A tiny parapet encircles the top of the spire. *Is that where he went?* The wind pounds her, fear drums inside, but she climbs on.

'Here.'

His voice is suddenly close. Sheet lightning turns the sky as bright as the moon and Pandora glimpses his ghostly figure in an archway, just above. One last heart-stopping twist of the stairway . . . a few more terrifying steps . . .

'Take my hand,' shouts Fox. Rain streams from his outstretched arm. Sweat steams from his skin.

If she misjudges the jump, Pandora will follow her lost sword down into the netherworld sea. But she grabs Fox's hand, leaps through the archway – and lands on the narrow parapet at the top of the spire, safe in his grasp.

Lightning flickers across their drowned kingdom, illuminating the cathedral that seems to float as an ark in the netherworld sea and the broken bridge that lunges from the water like a lagoon monster, draped in seaweed and barnacled with ancient rust-heaps. All around the old steeple tower and the water-glugged museum, scattered among the massive trunks of the sky towers, lie the last scraps of a city lost to the sea: tiny mud-banked land-scraps, crammed with trees and ruins, teeming with animal life. Enclosing it all is the vast city wall.

'Look,' urges Fox.

Beyond the wall, as far as she can see, is an immense heaving darkness.

The world's ocean!

And out on that violent ocean are the jostling shadows of the boats. Lightning turns their metal gun shields into the scales of slumbering sea dragons.

'So many!'

A smile breaks on Fox's drenched face. 'Not just here. Outside every sky city in the world . . .'

A silver pathway stretches out across the ocean and ends abruptly in the darkness.

'The eastern sea bridge,' murmurs Pandora. Fox has schooled her well in the workings of the sky empire.

The bridge project to link the sky cities of Eurosea was abandoned after the slave breakout of 2100 that brought Fox to the netherworld. That was when the gates in the city wall were sealed. No ship or refugee has breached the walls since. Now, food supplies from the vast ocean farms and floating greenhouses and all trade between cities comes by the airships that land on the roofs of the sky towers.

'I heard whispers on the soundwaves,' says Fox, his voice a warm huskiness in her ear. 'Voices so faint they might have come from the stars. It was our boat people. I had to see them, just once, with my own eyes.'

Pandora looks up at the billowing darkness that has smothered all the stars. Never have they known a winter so wild. Barricaded in the tower, she couldn't see how the boat people out on the wild ocean could survive.

Somehow, they have.

Fox grips her hand as they gaze out at the seething black ocean. 'Whatever happens now, whatever we have to do, Pan, remember this moment. *This* is what we're fighting for, all those people out there.' He pauses for a heartbeat. 'And for the others, wherever they are.'

His last words are almost lost in the howl of the storm. But Pandora hears the break in his voice and knows he's thinking not only of the refugees around the sky cities of the world, but of those who fled in the 2100 exodus of ships that went North. The memory of that day is burned into Pandora, as it is also in Fox.

She remembers swimming towards the fleet of white ships, too small to keep up with the other urchins. Seaweed clung to her, clamping her legs. She couldn't break free. The netherworld would not let her go. By the time she crawled on to a mudbank, choking on seawater, the ships were surging out through the gates in the wall. And she was left behind, a lone little urchin, grubbing around in the mud and ruins. But then Fox, with the soft face of a man-boy and eyes full of fire and broken dreams, found her and brought her to live in the crumbling tower with the wise old woman, Candleriggs, who mothered Pandora and guided Fox in his revolution, until she died.

Pandora drags her gaze from the mass of boats to Fox's handsome, rain-streamed face. Her heart leaps as she understands why he has smashed his way up into the spire and why he speaks, now, of the ones who fled North.

Fox is as charged as the electric wind.

'Is this it? Is it all beginning, Fox? Now, at last?'

Excitement jolts through her, as if a bolt of lightning has hit the tip of the spire.

'As soon as the storms settle and the soundwaves clear. Once the radios are back up and running . . .' Fox pulls her close in a rare, fierce embrace that Pandora yearns for more than anything in the world. 'Then the global Surge begins.'

THE HOME OF THE WIND

A scream tears across the great lake at the top of the world.

The North Wind hurls the sound upon the ancient faces of the mountains, scattering echoes into the forest of Candlewood. The scream is neither animal nor human. Yet as they settle for the night in their earthy burrows under the forest floor, the people of Candlewood greet it like the voice of a long-awaited friend.

Pine needles crackle like excitement under Lily's deerskin boots. Beyond the tree lamps the forest is a dense darkness, the cold as fierce as fire, and the wind is everywhere.

'Lily!'

Lily pushes on through the scaly trunks of the pine trees and pretends not to hear.

The icebergs are dying. Far out on the lake, the scream of rupturing ice climaxes with a *crack* that seems to split the night apart. Winter's harsh reign is ending. At last.

'Lily Longhope, come back *right* now – or else!'

Lily hesitates. She's in trouble if she doesn't turn back. A quick glance over her shoulder shows the slim, dark-haired figure of Mara, her mother, haloed by the light of a tree lamp.

'I just want to *see*,' Lily yells back.

It's all right for *her*, Lily sighs, kicking a tree. She's had all the adventures anyone could ever want. Her mother has no idea what it's like to be cooped up in the family burrow for the fifteenth winter of her life, aching to be out in the world again and pent up with a restlessness that makes her feel ready to explode like a pine cone in a flame. She is desperate for some excitement. The icebergs crashing into the lake will do.

'Take a tree lamp, at least. Lily, the *wolves*!'

Lily smiles to herself. She knows all about the wolves. There's a boy in wolf's clothing she's hoping to find. Nevertheless, she runs back and grabs a flickering tree lamp from a branch.

'Just to keep you happy.' She gives her mother a cheeky grin.

'I'll only be happy once you're back safe and sound in the burrow,' says Mara, fastening a wind-shield around the lamp, 'so don't be long. Stay on the shore and don't dare go looking for Wing in the dark.'

Oh, shutupshutup, Lily thinks as she plants a kiss on her mother's cheek to pretend that she'll do as she says.

Soon the trees crowd so densely that Lily must push her way through the scratchy pine trunks and branches like big, icy feathers. It's easy to lose yourself in this patch of the forest, but the trees will help her. Lily casts the lamp around to seek out the glinting eyes of the forest: amber firestones set in the trunks to mark pathways through the trees. She swings the lamp up and follows the firestone trail.

Time is against her. Any moment now the icebergs might disappear with an almighty crash into the lake. It often happens like this: a sudden meltdown, a tumultuous mass death, soon after the best day of the year when the forest dwellers rush from their winter burrows to greet the new sun as it clambers on to the shoulders of the eastern mountains after months of polar darkness.

Lily pushes forward, then stops. She cannot find the next firestone. But there's another kind of fire that can guide her through the night. She throws her head back and gazes up beyond the wavering tips of the pines.

A lone star glistens; a cool blue light.

Lily scrapes and squeezes through tree trunks, keeping her eyes on the blue light. Now she can see a sprinkle of stars. She pushes on. And there, right above her head, is the star crown of Queen Cass. Lily lowers her gaze, lifts the lamp. The trees are thinning out. Just a few more trunks and branches to push past . . .

All at once the night opens up. Lily steps out of the forest, dazzled by a sky of hot stars. The North Wind shakes them until they fall from the heavens and gust down to sizzle upon the icy lake.

Far out on Lake Longhope, the world is changing fast. Great pillars and towers tumble as the huge ice cathedrals crumble into thundering whiteness. Lily blinks, eyes tingling in the blast of ice-wind. Ice crystals land in the waves of tawny hair that frame her soft, bright-eyed face. She puffs out a cloud of a sigh. Winter is ending, yet it's impossible not to feel a stab of sadness at such a spectacular death. Icy shock-waves crash all along the shore. Slowly, slowly, the lake settles into stillness. Lily blinks again. Apart from chunks of icy debris, it's as if the armada of icebergs had never been.

A wolf howl makes the girl's skin prickle. She listens intently, chewing her lip. Her heartbeat quickens as she crunches across an expanse of frosted ferns and runs on to the rocky lake shore. That howl, Lily is sure, does not belong to a true wolf.

'Wing!'

She swings the lamp to cast its light across the rocky shore. A second howl fills the night. But this one is not Wing. There is something awful in this wolf cry, as if it carries all the loneliness of the world.

The cry tears at Lily's insides. Some animal part of her understands the wolf's dread song. She calls for Wing once again, as loud as she dares, scanning the dark shore, hearing her own cry roam across Lake Longhope.

On Candlewood Spire, a huge spike of granite resembling a giant finger fossilized in rock, a wolfish figure leaps from a perch and lands, on all fours, on the shore. Starlight glistens on its long snout and coat of silvery fur. The figure stands upright. Brash echoes of its heavy tread on the pebble shore clatter across the lake as it runs towards her.

The smell of Wing's wolf coat, musky and rank, reaches her before he does. The head of his dead wolf brother lolls on one shoulder, still attached to the thick fur he wears like a second skin. The wolf's eyes have been replaced by amber firestones; Wing's own eyes burn with the blue fire of the stars.

'I've missed you,' Lily bursts out. 'Winter felt like forever!'

She wants to bury herself in his wolfskin as she would when she was small. Something stops her now. But Wing laughs away her awkwardness, hugging her tight in the deep fur of his wolf coat and it's as if he has never been away.

'Mountain thunder!' he gasps, his breath hot in her hair.

Lily looks up at a face chiselled by winter. His lean, strong features and sleek-haired skin make Wing seem more wolfish than ever. He is more man than boy now. *A wolfman*, thinks Lily, though no wolf has webbed hands and feet and soft neck gills and swims all summer long in the lake, like a

18

fish. Wolfman or human fish? Lily has no idea what he is and she doesn't care. He is Wing.

She breaks free of a hug that's full of the new strength she sensed in him as he ran towards her. The strange shyness sweeps through Lily once again as she absorbs all his subtle changes and huddles into her deerskin parka, sharply aware of the bewildering body she has grown during her winter hibernation; all the curves and softnesses where there had been skinny straight lines.

Wing is studying her in the starlight, nuzzling her hair as if to memorize her subtly changed scent, absorbing all *her* changes with a slow smile.

'Wasn't thunder – it was the icebergs,' Lily says, to divert him. 'You were on the spire, you saw them crash!'

'Icebergs,' Wing nods, '*and* mountain thunder.'

He points to the starlit crests of the southern mountains and mimics the roar that he heard. Fluent in the language of the wild, Wing stumbles with human words, even more so after a long winter with the wolves. But Lily has known him forever and can patch together the bare scraps of his speech.

'When I is cub,' Wing measures the height of a small child with his hands, 'we cross sea. On ship.' Lily watches Wing's webbed fingers form pictures in the cold air to illustrate his bare words. He makes a tunnelling motion. 'Go through mountain.'

Lily lifts her head to look beyond the head of the lake to the mountain pass where she was born at the end of that desperate journey to find a home in the high lands of the flooded world.

'Earth *roar*.' Wing crouches and smashes a fist on to the pebbles at Lily's feet. 'Mountain *thunder*. Mountain *crash* on Tuck.'

19

Wing rarely speaks so much, so intensely, at least not in words. Lily stares, amazed, absorbing what he has said.

'Tuck?' Her mouth falls open. 'Tuck is a *person*?'

Lily has only ever known the words *Tuck Culpy* as a curse.

'A dead person,' Wing elaborates.

'Why has no one ever told his story?' Lily is bewildered.

How often has she heard the stories of her people? Tales of Granny Mary, her great-grandmother, who fought to save the people of the North Atlantic islands when the seas first rose; the exodus across the ocean, led by Mara, her mother, when the island drowned; her parents' great escape from the the sky city and its netherworld, with the Treenesters and Wing's band of urchins; and the tragic loss of Broomielaw and her baby at the end of their journey across the world's ocean . . .

Yet no one has ever breathed a word of this mysterious Tuck – except as a curse.

Wing scratches the dead snout of his brother wolf, frowning, avoiding her eyes. Lily prods him.

'Why is his name cursed?' she demands.

'Tuck take globe,' says Wing at last. 'Mara's globe.'

Again, his hands help him tell the story and from his own breath cloud Wing seems to magic up the forms of a globe and a tiny wand – and the strange halo that Lily knows lies inside the little wooden box covered in tree-like patterns that once belonged to Granny Mary and is kept zipped away in her mother's tattered old backpack.

'The globe,' whispers Lily, remembering the tales she loved her mother to tell when she was small. Tales of a magical world inside a globe . . .

Wing nods. 'Mara's magic wizz.'

'Tuck stole the globe?' Lily chews on a tail of her tawny

20

hair, frowning, trying to piece together the mystery. 'But the mountain crashed down on Tuck?' She sucks in a breath, understanding now. 'So the globe is . . .'

'Under mountain,' says Wing. 'Tuck too.'

'*Oh.*'

Then Tuck's crime was so hateful that her people did not want to tell his story. But he hasn't been forgotten. Mara flinches on the rare occasions that Lily's father, Rowan, mutters the name in anger.

'Earth *roar* again,' Wing repeats.

'Tonight, you mean? That's what you heard?'

Wing nods.

Lily stares at the southern mountains.

In the hungriest heart of winter, when the wolves howl ever closer to Candlewood, the forest dwellers huddle around crackling fires in the earth burrows, watching the smoke puff up through the chimneys in the forest floor. Then, Lily will sink into all the old tales of the world that lies beyond the lake and the mountains. A world of drowned lands and boat people where cities are as tall as the sky and ramshackle pirate fleets rampage across the oceans.

The stories help battle the long months in the winter burrow when Lily is so bored and restless she can barely live with herself, never mind anyone else. She might be stirring soup or squabbling with her small brothers, but in her mind's eye she's crossing mountain ranges, adventuring across the ocean, sailing to towering cities with a band of imagined friends. Just as her mother once did, for real.

'Let's see why Earth roared.' Lily grabs Wing's hand. 'What if we found a way back through to the ocean world? Wing, it's been so long since we had an adventure. I thought I'd die of boredom this winter.'

She yelps with excitement as she sees the longing in Wing's eyes. The ocean beyond the mountains is his lost home. Does she dare go? She'd have a hundred punishment chores on her return, but so what? It'd be worth it for a glimpse of the ocean she has never seen.

In her mind's eye she is already scribbling a charcoaled *Don't worry* note on a scrap of wood-pulp paper and creeping out of the burrow in the dead of night. Just herself and Wing. Just for a day or so. Just to see . . .

A long howl from Wolf Mountain interrupts Lily's magnificent dream. Wing tenses, all instincts attuned in an instant to the wolf call. Before Lily can stop him, he is running full pelt across the wide shore towards the fierce, beckoning cry.

WOLF MOUNTAIN

The cry ignites a hot ball of jealousy in the pit of Lily's stomach. It's the wolfwoman, Scarwell, calling Wing home. Furious, Lily races across the shore towards the mountain, where Wing has vanished into the dark.

The lone howl is joined by another, then another and still more. The bone-chilling wolfsong pours down into the vast bowl of the lake. Lily's heart thuds, every hair on her body raised in fright.

'Great Skua!' she cries. '*Wing!* Where are you?'

In the shadow of the mountain, the night deepens around her. She's left her lamp back at the lake and can hardly see a thing. She gasps as something moves through the darkness towards her. Then the familiar cold, leathery skin of Wing's hand clasps hers. He gives a loud, harsh bark and the howling fades.

'Scar's birthing,' he announces.

Lily snatches her hand from Wing's.

'Scarwell's having a baby?'

Her voice quavers. Her mind races. She feels sick.

Lily was a small child when Scarwell was thrown out of Candlewood. No one would ever say exactly why, but the pack of unruly urchins from the netherworld were always causing trouble – and Scarwell was more trouble than all of them put together. Their wild natures, along with their sleek-haired skins, webbed fingers and toes and, most of all, their unnervingly fish-like gills meant they were not human, said the wary forest dwellers. There was a great sigh of relief in Candlewood when they left with the outcast Scarwell.

Only Little Wing stayed, because he was Mara's special urchin; he had saved her life once. He became Lily's older guardian as she toddled about the forest, her only playmate as she grew into a mischievous sprite of a girl, scrambling up trees and splashing about on logs on the lake. No other forest children had yet been born. Yet the call of the wild world was stronger even than his bond with Lily and when Scarwell came back for Wing he too followed her to live on Wolf Mountain.

But guilt engulfed Candlewood as the summer sun died and the long polar night descended on the top of the world. Lily's tears for her beloved Wing were answered when the forest dwellers decided that the urchins could not be left to perish in the teeth of winter or the jaws of a wolf. The hunters Pollock and Possil were sent to search the mountains, though even they dared not venture into the wolf caves.

The urchins who had survived both the onset of winter and the wolves were brought back to live in the safety of Candlewood. But Wing wouldn't come. The pulse of the wild world beat too fiercely in him, as it did in Scarwell. Together, they took to the world of the wolves. Lily's only consolation was that Wing always came back to her, to the human world and to the lake, when the sun returned.

Scarwell was never seen again.

The wolfwoman is close to no other human except Wing.

If she is birthing, Lily knows the baby must be his.

But Wing is chuckling softly.

'Not Scar! The she-wolf called Lunder. Scar births the pups.' His voice turns sombre. 'They come before sun, they die.'

A wolf birth! Relief sweeps through Lily. Feeling foolish, she laughs, but a jittery feeling remains. What *is* between Wing and Scarwell? She can never tell and cannot bear to think of them so close together all winter in the wolf caves.

'The sun is back now,' Lily reminds him, though it's only an ember sun as yet.

He pauses as they reach the huge tumble of boulders at the foot of the mountain.

'Don't go,' Lily murmurs. 'She's had you all winter.'

His eyes linger on her face. Lily feels her skin burn in his gaze.

'Come,' he says.

Lily reads the mischievous glint in Wing's eyes. 'To Scarwell's cave? She'd have me for supper!'

'*My* cave too,' Wing insists. 'Come.'

She should go home. Hungry winter wolves are killers. But gnawing curiosity about Wing's life with Scarwell overcomes her sense. And Lily cannot bear one more suffocating night in the burrow with her brothers bothering her and her parents bickering with each other, as they always do. Wing will keep her safe.

He pulls her deep into his musky wolfskin again, rubbing the fur all over her, covering her in its scent so that the wolves won't rip her to shreds, until Lily crackles with static.

'Keep close,' he tells her.

Wing climbs as if a secret trail leads him up through channels in the steep rockways. But Wolf Mountain has cruel tricks to repel strangers. Rocks as sharp as fangs tear at Lily's deerskin clothing as she scrambles to keep up. She doesn't care about scrapes and bruises. Winter is behind her. There's a starwind in her hair, the vast magic of the universe sparkles in her eyes, and she feels tinglingly alive.

All of a sudden the hairs on the back of her neck warn of a danger she can't see. A deep vibration in the air. A granite sound, like the voice of the mountain itself.

Lily looks up. A host of terrifying eyes, the vivid orange of firestones, stare down from a ledge above. Wolf breaths steam in the darkness.

Too late, Lily wishes she were back home in the cosy burrow. Anywhere but here.

SCARWELL'S CAVE

Lily has never been so close to a lone wolf, never mind a whole pack. Their noise shakes the walls of her heart. She slips under Wing's wolf coat and clings to him, feeling *his* galloping heart through the ragged deer hide wrappings he wears under his furs, wishing she could leap off the mountain and land safely among the branches of Candlewood. What a fool she's been!

Wing is growling his own warning in wolf-tongue. The noise of the pack grows a notch less ferocious. Lily peeks out from under Wing's arm and gasps as vivid eyes meet her own, the dark pupils wells of distilled danger.

'Be slow,' says Wing. 'Don't fright 'em.'

Frighten *them*? Lily is abuzz with terror as Wing eases her out from under his wolf coat and the pack erupt into slavering excitement.

At the fire at the mouth of a cave a wolf rises up on to its hind legs and struts forward. Wing reaches out and wraps his arms around it.

Lily lets out a shuddering breath. It's Scarwell, of course.

A patchwork of furs cover the wiry figure of the young woman. Wolf tails hang around her, knotted into her knee-length straggle of hair. With all the battle scars on her downy skin, she is well-named.

Wing plants himself between Lily and the wolves as Scarwell speaks to the animals in a low snarl. The pack quietens into unnerving stillness.

What is the power she holds over the wolves? Is Wing, Lily wonders, also captured in Scarwell's fierce spell?

'Mara's pup.' Scarwell paces around Lily, her dark eyes narrowing through locks of matted hair. 'Not brave like Mara?'

'Well, my mother's a *legend*,' Lily retorts, with fake bravado. 'Just like *you*.'

Scarwell stops dead, head tilted to one side.

'Legend?'

'The Woman Who Turned Wolf,' says Lily.

Scarwell has become as still as her wolves. So feral is she that Lily cannot judge her age in human time. There is a searing quality in her, a wolfish sensuality as she absorbs Lily's presence that makes the younger girl huddle into her parka, slammed back into awkward girlhood. The jealousy that has smouldered in Lily all the long winter months when Wing is alone here in the caves with this wild young woman now flares into desperation. She is no match for Scarwell.

'I am a story?' Scarwell demands. 'The forest people make *me* a story?'

'Gorbals did,' Lily affirms.

Scarwell smirks. Then reaches out, grabs a handful of the tawny hair that Lily likes to hide behind, and studies her young rival's face. The wolfwoman's lips draw back from her teeth in a silent snarl. She throws the hair back across Lily's face like a slap and struts away. But Lily saw something in the older girl's face that brings a sudden awareness of her own power. She sidles up close to Wing and they follow Scarwell into her cave.

It stinks.

The cave reeks of wolf and rotting flesh. The floor is littered with furs and skins and bones; some gnawed white and clean, others blackening, with shreds of flesh still stuck to them. Wing peers into a dark nook of the cave where an exhausted wolf mother is licking clean her new litter. The fond look he exchanges with Scarwell as he croons over the pups makes Lily turn away.

She yelps in fright as she finds herself face to face with a beast. It stands upright like a man. But it's only a stuffed beast, Lily sees, long dead; yet unlike any ever hunted around Lake Longhope. There is something uncannily human about its cheeky, clever face. Lily strokes the beast's hairy hand; he has five fingers, unwebbed, like hers.

'What is he?' she asks Wing.

'Nederwuld beast.'

'Netherworld?'

Wing crouches beside her and begins to draw in the dirt of the cave floor. Lily watches him sketch the lines of a structure as majestic as the ice cathedrals that have collapsed into Lake Longhope and remembers her people's tales of the drowned netherworld they once fled.

'The tower full of books? The ruined cathedral? The museum of old things?'

''Zeeum!' says Wing triumphantly. 'Beast from 'zeeum. Scar bring him on ship.'

Once again, Lily feels excluded from all that they share. The dead beast, Wing and Scarwell come from a world that for Lily is as distant and mystifying as the moon. Knowing Scarwell is watching her every move, Lily takes Wing's hand in hers and strokes his webbed fingers.

'And what kind of beast are *you*?' she teases.

'He's *mine*,' Scarwell hisses.

He might be yours all winter, thinks Lily, *but he's mine the long sun nights of summer.*

But as Scarwell moves towards her, the firelight revealing all her battle scars and bloodstains, Lily backs away, remembering last summer when she and Wing watched a pair of she-wolves tear at each other's throats.

Scarwell and Mara, whispered Wing.

Lily could only stare and wonder, thinking of her smiling mother now playing with the little ones, Corey and Coll, in the garden of the summer tree hut.

Scarwell's lips draw back from small, discoloured teeth in a silent snarl. 'Go!'

Lily edges towards the mouth of the cave. She halts and looks back at Wing as the pack outside slaver and whine, but he and Scarwell seem to be having a silent battle of wills.

'We're going on a – an adventure,' Lily announces as a clumsy parting shot. 'Tell her, Wing.'

Scarwell shoots Wing a burning look. 'Stay here. With *me*.'

'He's coming with *me*,' Lily insists. 'To the *ocean*.'

She knows how Wing craves the sea, his first home. He tries to satisfy that craving every summer, living down by the water. But Lake Longhope is not the world's seas.

Scarwell draws in a breath as the ocean-hunger trembles all through Wing.

'To . . . *ocean*?' The wolfwoman turns to Lily with a dangerous smile. 'Lily go find father?'

Lily shrugs at the senseless comment, then hears a growl from Wing that is almost too low for human ears.

'My father's at home in Candlewood,' Lily retorts, looking quizzically from one to the other.

'Rowan?' Scarwell's smile is as sharp as a blade. 'Rowan not Lily's *father*.'

30

THE FOX FATHER

'*Scar*,' hisses Wing.

'Of course Rowan's my father,' Lily insists, bewildered, but a shiver of dread runs down her spine.

'Your *father*,' says Scarwell, 'is across ocean. In sky city. Your father is *Fox*.'

Her wind-scraped voice seems to reach inside Lily and rake at a long-buried hurt. Forgetting the wolves, Lily's only thought is to get away from Scarwell and run for home. She darts for the mouth of the cave.

'Lil! No!'

Wing catches her arm, yanking her back into his protection as the pack outside the cave rises to its feet with an unearthly noise.

'I want to go h—'

Lily falters on the word, on the idea of home.

She presses her face into Wing, overcome by a strange, unravelling fear. He and Scarwell are muttering to each other in their wild language; a throaty wolfspeak, barely human words that Lily cannot understand. But she knows some furious pact is being made.

Scarwell strides to the entrance of her cave and lashes the

pack with her voice. The wolves calm into sulky whimpers and slink away. Lily takes her chance. She breaks free from Wing's grasp and rushes from the cave to scramble down the mountain, too desperate to escape to care about the bruising rocks. When at last she stumbles on to the boulders on the lake shore, she finds Wing is close behind. They face each other in the darkness, wrapped in clouds of steamy breath.

'Rowan is my father,' Lily bursts out. 'What did Scar mean?'

Wing's silence fills her with a churning dread. But she has to know.

'Who – who is *Fox*?'

Wing takes her face in his hands and Lily reads in his eyes, in his touch, an answer he can't give her in words.

ON THE HINTERLAND

Lily runs from Wing until the trees stop her, tripping her up on a knobbly root. She crashes on to the forest floor and sits up, spitting pine needles from her mouth – then is yanked to her feet by strong arms.

'Found!' says the familiar deep voice of Pollock, the hunter. He sniffs her hair and snorts. 'Been with wolf-boy?'

'So?'

'I don't trust him or the wolfwoman,' Pollock growls. But his eyes twinkle at her in the light of an approaching lamp. 'You can come bear-trapping if you need some excitement.'

The lamp makes a radiant circle in the dark forest and illuminates a worried face peering out from thick plaits of hair.

'Lily!' cries Molendinar. 'Your mother's been searching for you – we all have. Where have you been?' She raises the lamp and groans at Lily's defiant face. 'Oh, let me guess. Wing is *trouble*, Lily. Best leave him to Scarwell.' Mol shakes her head despairingly. 'Thanks, Pollock, I'll see her home. We're not standing here in the freezing cold a moment longer. Back to your burrow, Lily Longhope!'

Lily plants herself in front of Molendinar.

'Why is my name Longhope?' she asks.

The question bursts from her, almost against her will.

'It's Mara's name, of course,' says Mol, grabbing Lily's hand and pulling her through the trees.

'But why don't I have my fath— Rowan's name?'

'Your mother saved our people. You should be proud to have her name,' Mol retorts.

'But my brothers have Rowan's name,' Lily points out.

'You have Mara's name, they have their father's,' Mol says. 'That's fair, isn't it?'

Lily ponders that – and sees, in the glow of the lantern, the strange glance that shoots between Mol, her mother's friend, and Pollock the hunter, as they push through the low-hanging branches of the pines.

'So why didn't you give your little Broom *your* name?' Lily persists, as they reach the clearing in the forest that is the heart of Candlewood.

Mol sets down her lamp on one of the log seats by the communal fire, struggling for an answer. The weary figures around the fire greet their arrival with relief.

'Just like her mother,' Mol exclaims, her patience breaking when she can't seem to find an answer. 'Trouble on two legs!'

The others burst out laughing.

'Now, now,' Ibrox chides, handing Mol their squirming baby to feed. 'All's safe and sound.'

'Without Mara's troublemaking,' Candlewood's story-master, Gorbals, reminds Mol in a dry voice, 'we'd still be stuck in the netherworld.'

Some of the wild urchins once rescued from Wolf Mountain, tamer in nature now and grown, gather around Lily, drawn to the musky wolf scent on her skin, hair and clothes.

'You saw Wing?' Skye whispers enviously.

'And Scarwell?' asks Stroma, wide-eyed.

'The wolves let you live?' marvels Hoy.

A soulful howl resounds through the forest. The men grab flaming sticks from the fire and stride towards the trees. Mol tucks her baby into her fur parka and pushes Lily towards one of the wooden doors set in the forest floor.

'Burrow! Now! Before the wolves have us all for supper – go!'

'I'm gone,' Lily says, but she lingers till the wolfsong ends. Only the urchins, who grin at Lily as they jump into their burrows, have guessed that it's only Wing.

His goodnight call emboldens her as she lifts the door of her own earth burrow to descend into a warm fug of fire smoke and her mother's furious blast of relief.

THE EMBERS OF THE TRUTH

Lily creeps down the wooden steps that lead into the heart of the burrow. She ducks the damp washing that hangs from a tree root and heads straight for her snug: a dug-out at the far end of the burrow, blocked by heavy deerskin drapes, to give her some blessed privacy.

'Well?' Mara steps in front of the snug, hands on hips, blocking Lily's escape.

'I'm *tired*,' says Lily, avoiding her mother's eyes.

'Your father's out looking for you. Where have you been?'

'Nowhere,' Lily mutters.

She lifts the lid of the pot on the stone stove in the centre of the burrow, and wrinkles her face at the mush of leftover root stew.

'I trusted you to go to the lake and straight back,' says Mara. 'If I find out you were on Wolf Mountain with Wing, in the dark—'

Lily slams the lid back down. 'Tuck's sake, can't I have a *life*?'

'Don't use that curse in here,' says Mara, edgily.

'It's just a *word*,' Lily retorts. 'Some dead person's *name*.'

Mara's dark, steady gaze flinches at that.

'It's a name I don't want to hear,' she says firmly, after a pause.

The burrow door rattles above them and Rowan bounds down the wooden stairs.

'Back all in one piece then?' He blows out a great sigh of relief, then glances from Lily to Mara, reading the fraught silence between them.

'We were worried.' Rowan puts a calm hand on Lily's shoulder. 'There are winter-starved wolves out there, you know that. What were you thinking?'

'I've been thinking about – about – if – if you're . . .' The words stutter out before she can stop them. 'Who is *Fox*?'

Rowan's hand drops from her shoulder. Mara steps backwards, stricken. As soon as she's spoken Lily wishes she could swallow her own words.

No, she thinks. *It isn't true. It can't be.*

One of her small brothers lets out a wail. Mara turns away and pulls back the fur curtain of the snug where the little ones sleep. She lifts the toddler to soothe him and as he wraps his arms and legs around his mother, Mara sinks her face into the blond curls that are so akin to Rowan's.

A thought slices through Lily. There is nothing about *her* that is like Rowan.

She is akin to Mara in many ways: her quick-eyed curiosity and daredevil nature; her lithe limbs, even her hands and feet, down to the shape of her fingernails and toes. But the tawny waves that ripple down her back are nothing like the silky darkness of Mara's hair. That belongs all to herself. Or so Lily thought.

'Bedtime,' says Rowan, watching Lily with an expression she can't read. 'We'll talk tomorrow. It's the middle of the night and everyone's tired and upset.'

He gives Lily a hug, warm and tight as ever, and his usual goodnight kiss.

Lily huddles into her nook of the burrow and listens to the moan of the wind in the trees above ground. Under the warm heap of bear furs her body surrenders to exhaustion, though her mind and thoughts whirl. But on the hinterland of sleep she hears Mara whisper; the first words she has spoken since Lily left for bed.

'You heard what she said?'

There is a long pause. Lily feels her scalp prickle.

'I always told you it would come out,' Rowan murmurs at last. 'She was bound to hear something one day. We should have told her long ago.'

The words bolt through Lily. Her eyes spring open.

Not another word is said. There is only the hiss of the stove fire as it is dampened for the night and the sounds of Mara and Rowan preparing for bed. The burrow falls quiet and still.

Lily stares into the darkness.

Can it be true? That her real father is a stranger across the world's ocean?

She will not believe it. Rowan *is* her father. And they wouldn't – they just couldn't – have hidden such a thing from her all this time. If it were true, her whole life would be a lie.

Yet she knows what she saw in Wing's face, what he told her without words. A terrible truth shone in Scarwell's eyes too. Didn't she glimpse it again in the uneasy glance between Molendinar and Pollock, when Lily asked about her name? And she heard it just now in the strained whispers between the two people she thought were her parents.

Does everyone else know? Even Scarwell? Everyone except herself?

But Rowan *is* her dad. He must be. No father could be more loving. Lily thinks of the special tenderness between them that always makes her feel precious, different to his rough-and-tumble love of the boys. She always thought it was because she was his only daughter. A horrible dread engulfs her now as she wonders if that gentle love might be the care you give to something that doesn't truly belong to you.

Lily huddles deep into the bearskin and shuts her eyes tight. She never knew it was possible to feel so alone.

SIGNALS IN THE SKY

Lily rubs her cold nose and snuggles deeper under her fur quilt, trying to settle back to sleep. But something keeps niggling her, as if there's a jaggy pine needle in her sock.

It's not a pine needle. It's a painful, stabbing thought.

Rowan is not my father.

Lily wakens with a nasty jolt and stares into the darkness. After a while she throws off her quilt and creeps out of her snug into the main room of the earth burrow. Stepping over wooden toys, she hears the sleepy breaths and snores of her family behind the deerskin curtains of their snugs. Easing on her furred parka, as quietly as she can, she climbs up the wooden steps set steeply in the earth and pushes open the door in the forest floor.

Outside, stars still prickle the tops of the pines. The night sky is lightening but the sun is not yet up. Lily avoids the other forest dwellers who are emerging from their burrows and runs towards the lake. Dawn mist tumbles down through the branches and when she reaches the end of the trees there is no lake or mountains, the world is blank. The mist keeps tumbling and it seems to Lily as if the sky is falling down.

*

'Why did you never tell me?' Lily demands, when Mara finds her later, shivering by the lake. 'Why did you *lie*?'

Mara sits down on the rock beside her. Lily, furious, turns away.

'I did try to tell you – when you were little. Don't you remember?'

Lily shakes her head, wanting to block her ears to Mara's low, shaky voice.

'You got upset. You didn't want to hear. You were such a happy little thing and Rowan was such a good dad to you. It was just –' Mara breaks off with a guilty sigh, 'oh, *easier* to let things be. And when you never brought it up again I thought you wanted to forget. Like I did,' she adds, softly. 'I only wanted us all to be happy. Time flew and you've grown up so fast. Last year you were still a little girl and suddenly you're not . . . I'm sorry, Lily. I got it all wrong.'

The guilt in Mara's voice maddens Lily. The last thing she can deal with right now is her mother's emotions. Her own are churned up like the lake in a storm.

And there *is* a memory of running away, a long time ago, from something she didn't want to hear. Lily remembers hiding deep in the trees, listening to Mara endlessly calling her name. It was Rowan who found her and gathered her up in his arms and brought her back home where everything was the same as it had always been. He was still her dad and the strange hurt was left buried and forgotten among the trees.

'You were never going to mention it again?' Lily wrenches away as Mara reaches out to her. 'I was to live my whole life never knowing who I really am?'

'I always thought we'd talk about it properly one day,' says Mara. 'I always meant to, when the time felt right. But these days your moods are all over the place and—'

'So it's *my* fault you never told me!'

'That's not what I mean!'

Now Mara's voice is rising. Usually when they flare into a row Rowan will cut in with a joke and they'll end up laughing instead of squabbling. But he's not here, and now the thought of the man she loves like a father makes Lily feel strange.

'What's that?' says Mara, and the abrupt change in her voice makes Lily look at her mother at last.

All around the lake the mountains have shrugged off the early mist. Mara is staring at the sky above the southern peaks.

'What?'

'*That.*'

Now Lily sees a glint of silver moving across the pale sky.

'There's another.' Lily points.

They watch the two silver ships speeding North.

'Sky ships,' Mara murmurs. 'Only the sky cities could have such things . . . what are they doing *here*?'

Lily's heart jolts. 'Scarwell said my father is in a sky city.'

'So *Scarwell* told you,' says Mara bitterly.

She faces her daughter and the guilt-clouds in her eyes all burn away.

'I don't know where he is now,' Mara says. 'The sky city of New Mungo was his home. When we broke out of the city he went down to the netherworld.'

Once again, as she did when she looked at Scarwell's beast, Lily remembers her people's stories about the drowned ruins they once fled and tries to picture the strange netherworld beneath the sky city where her unknown father might be.

'Why didn't he come here with you?' she wants to know.

'His world sickened him. He had to change it,' Mara answers. She takes a deep breath. 'Fox's grandfather,

Caledon – your great-grandfather – founded the empire of sky cities. Caledon was a pioneer of Natural Engineering and he dreamed up the giant cities that saved people from the floods all over the Earth.'

Mara's eyes shine as she watches the airships sail across the ocean of sky.

'Caledon was a genius,' she continues, 'but brutal, and his empire was too. It shut out the rest of the world. Fox felt he'd be living with blood on his hands if he didn't try to undo the wrongs of his own family. We were refugees,' she gestures towards the forest of Candlewood and its people, 'shut out of the cities with nowhere to live in the world. I found Fox when I was desperate – first through my cyberwizz, Granny Mary's old computer. Somehow I found him again in the sky city. It felt like a miracle. I fell in love too fast, too young – but Fox and I, we – we had different destinies.' Mara's voice is hoarse, breaking now. 'I *had* to leave him, Lily. I didn't want to. I didn't know until I crossed the ocean that I was pregnant with you.'

Lily is silent, numb.

'All this,' she says at last, 'you kept *all this* from me?'

Mara nods, her hands clenched in her lap, knuckles white.

'What else?' Lily demands as the airships fade into the northern skies. 'I want to know *everything*. You haven't even told me my own father's name. Fox who?'

'His real name is David Stone,' says Mara.

'And he doesn't even know I exist?'

Lily scrubs away angry tears.

'It was the last thing I told him,' says Mara softly. 'We lost all contact soon after.'

'When Tuck stole the globe,' Lily adds curtly. 'Wing told me. But who *was* Tuck?'

43

'A young gypsea pirate who landed up with us in Ilira, on the other side of the mountains. He was all alone in the world. I thought he was my friend. Ilira was a brutal place. We had to escape. He came through the mountains with us. There was a landslide. The mountain crashed down on Tuck and he had the globe . . .' Mara pauses. 'I – I'd caused a great wreckage in his life. I didn't mean to. So maybe we're quits.'

'What d'you mean?' Lily presses her. 'What did you do?'

Mara shakes her head, doesn't answer that.

'The globe,' says Lily slowly, frowning, 'is buried somewhere in the mountains.'

'It's *gone*, Lily.'

'How did it work?' Lily persists. 'What did the globe *do*?'

'It was my connection to the Weave – the virtual network of those old twenty-first-century computers.'

'The stories you told me about the Weave when I was little – that was all *real*?' Lily is amazed.

'When the great floods came,' Mara explains, 'life changed all across the Earth. People abandoned the old technology – they were fighting to survive. The Weave was left forgotten in the ether, but it's still there. The ruins of a cyber-universe . . . wrecked boulevards and Weave towers, crammed full of – oh, *everything* that ever existed in the drowned world. All sparking and glittering. So beautiful. I wish you could see it, Lily.'

'The Fox you met in the Weave,' Lily remembers. 'Was that . . . *him*?'

Mara's eyes grow darker, softer.

'See, I *did* tell you about him,' she says, 'in a way. The Weave was our special place. No one else went there any more,' Mara's face burns with the memory, 'except Fox.'

Lily feels shot with envy as she looks out at the emptiness

of Lake Longhope, at the vast enclosure of mountains, and thinks of her small, suffocating life in the summer tree huts and winter earth burrows of Candlewood. What incredible adventures her mother has had . . .

'So much happened, so fast,' says Mara, unconsciously echoing Lily's thoughts. 'Every day was a fight to survive. All Fox knows is that we reached the top of the world. He doesn't know if we survived.' Mara hesitates. 'I don't know if *he* did. I'm sorry, Lily.'

'You're *sorry*?'

Lily stands up. The whole world has turned on its head. Her father is not her real father. Ships are sailing across the sky.

Now, the sky ships seem like a signal from the world of her unknown father.

'What does he look like?' Lily asks, needing to know about him, hungry for more.

Mara meets her daughter's untamed eyes, a fiery dreamer's eyes, darkened now with hurt, in a soft, intense face amid a tousle of tawny hair.

'You,' says Mara simply.

Lily feels like one of the steaming hot geysers that burst up between the rocks by the lake. She can't contain the emotions boiling inside. She abandons Mara by the lakeside and races like a fury through Candlewood's trees. Everyone has lied to her about who she really is.

She will find her Fox father. Somehow she will.

And they'll all be sorry they've lied to her – once she's gone.

THE NETHERWORLD QUEEN

The lagoon shudders. The rumbling of engines fills the netherworld and shadows loom in the waters as huge vessels pass overhead.

For many days now, the tops of the sky towers have been busy with airships.

Fox and Pandora paddle their canoe from its anchorage in the flooded undercroft below the museum, through waterlogged archways, to the broken bridge. Wading though a seaweed swamp that throbs with saltwater salamanders, newts and frogs, they clamber over the rusted shell of an ancient land vessel called a bus and scramble up the steep limb that reaches up out of the netherworld sea.

At the top of the broken bridge Fox unhooks a telescope from his belt and focuses on the activity around an airship just landed on a tower above.

'Building materials, equipment, crew,' he murmurs.

'All heading North,' Pandora adds, squinting up as a slat of sun breaks through the sky tunnels and the tiara she wears on her tangled head bursts into diamond fire.

'The Arctic pirates were right,' says Fox.

Radio chatter on the soundwaves between the Arctic pirate

ships say that the empire's airships have begun to invade the Northlands.

'My Surgents were right too,' Pandora reminds him.

In virtual gatherings in the electronic wastes of the Weave, Pandora relays Fox's plans and readies the troops of secret Surgents – rebels within the sky cities, drawn to the revolution by lures planted all across the cyber-universe that draw in daredevil, questing minds. The secret Surgents have backed the Arctic pirates' radio reports. The sky empire plans to conquer the Northlands, say the rebel insiders, once the long darkness of winter is at an end. The fleets of airships now loading up and taking off from the sky towers are heading to the new continent to build empire settlements there.

Fox's face darkened when Pandora told him what the empire means to call the land once known as Greenland, though it was, in past times, a vast whiteness of polar ice.

Caledon.

It's the name of the grandfather who founded the world Fox has set his whole existence against.

The vast island that's emerged from the ice *is* now greening, with rich sweeps and plateaux of summer pastures, the Arctic pirates say; most of it undiscovered still by the small populations living in the North.

Green, fertile farmland is what the sky empire seeks, as the numbers in the sky cities soar and the ocean food farms struggle to feed so many. The vast mountain ranges are rich in the metals, minerals and fuels the empire needs to launch its Stellarka project, a long-abandoned venture to the stars.

With airships full of young empire builders and their guards headed for the new continent of Caledon, the sky cities of the northern hemisphere are now vulnerable to attack.

It's the moment of weakness the Surge has waited for.

So why, Pandora wonders, is Fox so grim? All day he's been avoiding her. Now he can't seem to look her in the eye. Something is wrong.

He glares up at the giant towers as if he'd like to tear them down with his bare hands. Yet he has always insisted that the cities will not be destroyed in the coming war. It's the one part of his grandfather's legacy that makes him proud. The empire must be broken but the towers will stand.

Miracles of natural engineering, each city is powered by sun, wind and waves. Over the years Fox has tracked the changes in his erstwhile home, as the sky imagineers seemed to bring their city to life. The once-gleaming towers are now crusted with bacteria that's fed dead matter and breathes in carbon and plankton to make the city a living, growing power source of lumenenergy.

In the old books in the tower Fox found pictures of ancient standing stones, built by the earliest peoples of the Earth; uncanny images of the cities that now stud the world's oceans. As daylight fades to night and the sky city glows with the same luminous phosphoresence as the underwater ruins, the great towers seem ever more like timeless monoliths of the Earth.

Pandora reaches up to touch Fox's face. He has shaved off the tawny beard that keeps him warm in winter. His bare face is much younger, though tiredness shadows his eyes. He was up all night again, checking out the radio links. He smiles absently at her touch, still avoiding her gaze.

'You need to rest. Look.' Pandora points to the draped fishing nets that hang from the edge of the bridge, down into the lagoon. 'The nets are *heaving* – I'll dive down and get us a feast!'

Fox takes Pandora's hand and strokes the membrane of webbing between her fingers with a look in his eyes so strange it sends a tremble through the girl.

'I'm sorry, Pan,' he murmurs.

'Sorry? What for?'

Fox has always touched her webbed fingers and feet and the delicate gills in the back of her neck with a gentle reverence and wonder. He's envious of her water skills and of her sleek, downy skin that keeps her warm in winter. Now, there is something quite different in his face. Pity? Shame?

Pandora draws her hand away.

'There's something I need to tell you. Something I've suspected for a while,' says Fox. 'Now I've found out for sure.'

'What is it? What's *wrong*?'

He scratches at an infected insect bite on his neck, nervy and grim.

'The sky people made you,' he says reluctantly. 'The people of my grandfather's time.'

'*Made* me? What do you mean?'

'The empire made you what you are.'

At last he faces her and Pandora tries to read the strange darkness in his eyes. She has never understood what she is. She has raked through the books in the tower, peered into all the aged biological freaks and experiments that float like ghouls in glass bottles in one of the museum halls, yet nowhere has she found a hint of another human like herself.

'What am I?' she asks blankly.

'You're beautiful,' says Fox.

Pandora looks down at her hands and spans her fingers wide. The membrane of webbing is like the waxy wings of a moonmoth. Her skin is velvety in the netherlight, the gills on the back of her neck soft as feathers.

'Am I the only one?'

But there *were* others; of course there were. The netherworld urchins who escaped North in the ships had the same seaworthy skin, the same webbed fingers and feet.

Fox turns away with a murmur she can't catch but Pandora glimpsed his shamed expression, saw in it the awful truth he is trying to hide: what was once beautiful to him is now tainted, forever changed.

Pandora grabs Fox's hand, feels it warm and clammy in her cool-blooded fingers. All of a sudden she is acutely aware of all the amphibian life at their feet; it makes a moving carpet of the seaweedy bridge.

'Tell me what I am,' she pleads.

Fox looks into her distraught green eyes. Deliberately, gently, as if to erase his shameful feelings, he raises her hand to his mouth and kisses it.

'You are a wonder. A new kind of human made to survive in a flooded world. But the world didn't like what the scientists created.'

The sun slips behind a sky tower and the netherworld plunges into gloom.

'Go on,' whispers Pandora.

'So the empire decided to erase its Amphibian Experiment.'

Pandora absorbs the brutal meaning of it all.

'I am an experiment they didn't like. What do you mean, *erase* . . . ? Kill us all?'

Fox nods.

'But there were renegade scientists,' he continues, 'who couldn't bring themselves to destroy the life they'd made. Your parents must have been among the ones those rebel scientists set free. But the outside world drove them away too.

They were hunted down, but they hid their children wherever they could. Under the bridges, in the netherworld . . .'

'Then they *didn't* abandon me?'

Fox squeezes her hand. 'Somehow, they saved you. They did all they could to make sure you lived. There's no greater love than that, Pan.'

Pandora's world seems to turn inside out.

'So the boat people,' she sees, 'are *not* my people? They – they *hunted* my parents? Killed them.'

'Some of the older ones did. The world was full of fear, Pan. The great floods had struck and people were trying to survive. Desperate people can do terrible things.'

Devastated, Pandora clings to Fox's hand. And yet, he has gifted her two things she has always longed for: to know who she is and to be truly beloved.

'All this is true? How do you know?'

'I trust the outlaw pockets of the Noos,' says Fox. 'The truth of things is hidden there, as it is in the Weave. And this truth came from the renegade scientists, that older generation who never forgot and joined our Surge.'

Pandora's mind reels as she tries to take it all in. The Noos – the virtual universe of the empire – is the sizzling energy of millions of computers and human brains. As mysterious to Pandora as the inside of a sky city, the Noos is where the citizens of the empire work and play and dream. She can only try to imagine the wonders of the cities and their stunning cyber-universe from what Fox has told. The twenty-first-century cyber-Weave is hers to roam but he won't let her near the Noos. Far too much is at stake, he insists, to risk her discovery there.

The trusty old computer godgem of his youth still connects Fox to his beloved Noos. He slips through its wild undergrowth, teeming virtual jungles of frenetic brilliance, sneaking into renegade pockets where rebels uncover the truths he has set free in the cyber-universe; shameful truths the empire has tried to erase.

But now she, Pandora, is one of those ugly truths.

'The empire wants to experiment again.' Fox's voice is leaden. 'It wants to engineer humans designed for life in the Far North, for colonizing space – humans who are better engineered for life in the sky cities too.'

All-powerful the empire might be, but the rebels have said that its people are weakening. Lack of sunlight over generations is causing new deformities and diseases that the ingenuity of the sky scientists cannot seem to solve.

'Some older citizens know what happened with the Amphibian Experiment,' says Fox, 'and there's a spreading horror that it could happen again – and this time the experiment might be with their own descendants, their own flesh and blood.'

'If the empire doesn't like what the scientists make this time, they'll kill them too?' Pandora feels sick.

'And maybe they won't stop there,' adds Fox. 'Maybe they'll get rid of the sun-sick ones. Or the old ones. Who knows? Those are the seeds of doubt I've sown in the Noos and there's a – a *surge* of distrust,' Fox's troubled eyes lighten, 'against the Guardians of the empire. I've never known it before. Their defences are weak and so is the trust of their people. This is our time. We have to break them, Pan.' He glances at the city above. 'And my father has to be broken – he's behind so much of this.'

Fox has tracked the activities of his estranged father through the Noos. Mungo Stone, Caledon's son, has lost the influence he thought was his birthright now that power in the empire has swung East and to younger cities in the southern hemisphere. The City Fathers who ruled the New World under Caledon's leadership have been replaced by a new generation of Guardians ruthless in their rivalry for power in their sky empire. An early stake in the riches of the North would rekindle Mungo's fire in his world. *My father*, says Fox, *is a desperate and dangerous man*.

But there are good people in the sky cities too, thinks Pandora. People who didn't want her kind killed and who don't want anything like that to happen again.

Another whale-like darkness moves across the dusky netherworld and engulfs them in its shadow. Pandora shivers, reeling from all that Fox has told her, and he pulls her close.

'It doesn't change anything, Pan,' he says, through the thunder of the airship. 'You're still you.'

But *everything* has changed. Now Pan thinks of the boat people with a wrench inside. Is she to risk her life and fight for people who would see her as a freak to be hunted down? People who drove away her desperate parents or did nothing as they were killed?

And now she begins to understand why she can never seem to break through Fox's fond, brotherly affection. She used to think it was the coming war that worried him. Once their battles are all over, she thought, *then* she would be his true queen in a far greater realm.

But it wasn't the risks of war or the netherworld, she now realizes. It was her own self that repelled him and the kind of child she might produce. How long has Fox suspected what she is? When he looks at her now, what does he really see? An alien creature? A freakish mistake? So he might be tender and close and tell her she is beautiful, but he will never love her as she wants.

Not now, not ever.

Pandora can no longer bear the hopping and slithering creatures on the bridge. Is that what she is? More amphibian than human? She pulls away from Fox so fiercely the tiara jolts from her head. The diamonds once worn by a queen of the drowned world sparkle in the gloom as they fall from the broken bridge and splash into the lagoon. Pandora could easily dive from the bridge and rescue it from the depths of the murky waters but, heartbroken, she lets go her crown.

What Fox once loved as her strange netherworld beauty is now a deformity, inflicted on her by the empire he hates. When he looks at her now all he sees, she is sure, are the sins of the past he yearns to escape.

A SCAR FROM OLD TIMES

Harpoon on her back, knife between her teeth, Mara climbs Wolf Mountain, filled with a murderous rage. Shadows chase her as the sun falls behind the western peaks and she moves fast to outpace them. Darkness is the realm of the wolves.

Lily hasn't been seen all day, not since she ran off from the lakeside at dawn. She will have gone tracking with the hunters to cool her head, Mara told herself, trying to keep calm. But as the brief day dimmed and the hunters returned with a trussed deer and a clutch of wild rabbits, there was still no sign of Lily. Mara left the little ones with Rowan, saying she'd search once more around the lake, but knowing in her heart that hurt, headstrong Lily must be with Wing.

The thin moon is a sharpening blade as Mara climbs towards Scarwell's cave. None of this would have happened if Scarwell had kept her mouth shut, thinks Mara, tucking herself into a rocky crevice to light the resin-soaked torch she has brought – and just in time too as a growl, almost too low for human ears, menaces the dusk.

Suddenly Scarwell appears above her, on a ledge.

Mara steadies her nerve. The eyes of the young wolfwoman watch her every move as she hauls herself up on to the ledge, sweating and breathless. Mara raises the torch and sees the wolves perched, still as statues, on the rocks all around.

'What's our fight this time, Scarwell?' Mara demands. 'What is it you want? Why hit out at Lily just to get at me? I know you did. Scar, if it wasn't for me, you'd still be in the netherworld – maybe dead by now. Why such hate?'

Scarwell was a child still when Mara, barely older than Lily, found her in the netherworld – a ferocious urchin, abandoned by the world, fighting to survive among the rooftops and land scraps in the drowned city. Mara touches her cheek in an unconscious gesture, remembering the long-faded wound that Scarwell once gave her that, in turn, gave the wolfwoman her name.

Scarwell stares, the memory sparking in her eyes too.

'Always you *take*,' Scarwell spits out. 'Once, my urchins all mine. Wing all *mine*. Then *you* come to netherworld, take us all away on ships. Take *my* urchins to Candlewood.' Scarwell bares her blackened teeth. 'World is *not* all Mara's. Wolf Mountain *mine*.' Scarwell stamps her foot on the ground. 'Girl is like you,' she mutters. 'She *takes*.'

'Lily? Takes what?'

But the instant she asks, Mara knows. Lily takes Wing. She takes him whenever she can. All summer long, Wing comes down to live by the lake close to Lily. Now that Lily is no longer a child but a striking, fiery young woman, she threatens Scarwell's bond with Wing.

'Is Lily here, Scar? Is she with Wing?'

Desolation flits across the wild beauty of Scarwell's dirty, battle-scarred face.

'Gone.'

'Gone?' Mara repeats.

'Gone away. *Gone*.'

The lake and its mountains seem to swoon out around them in a vast emptiness. In that moment Mara feels the world as Scarwell must, as a place of constant loss.

'Help me, Scar,' she pleads. 'You want Wing back. I want Lily. Tell me where they've gone.'

The dread Mara has been keeping at arm's length wraps around her now, cold as a ghost.

'To find Fox,' Scarwell hisses. 'Gone to sea!'

PHANTOMS AND LEGENDS

Mara gusts cold air into the burrow as she bounds down the steps. Rowan stares as she grabs her old backpack from the bottom of a large store cupboard dug deep into the curving wall of the burrow.

'Didn't you find her? Mara, where have you been? It's been dark for hours. The kids have been wanting you . . . wait, what are you doing?'

Rowan prises the backpack from Mara's freezing fingers and holds her close until he feels her shuddering panic soothe.

'Pollock and I will search Wolf Mountain the second it's light,' he says.

'I've already been.'

'To Wolf Mountain? Alone?' Rowan breaks his embrace, exasperated. 'Mara—'

'I *had* to. But she's not there.'

Mara sees the scrap of wood-pulp parchment on the table covered in Lily's angry charcoal scrawl and seizes it.

'I found it on her bed,' says Rowan. 'Can't make much sense of it, but at least she's with Wing.' Yet his doubts about the wolf boy are clear on his face. 'There's nothing we can do tonight.'

'Wing is wild and she's still a child and—'

'I know, Mara, but think of what you did at Lily's age.'

'That's exactly what I'm thinking of! Lily's just as headstrong as I was.'

'Still are,' Rowan retorts, as Mara takes up her backpack once again and begins to stuff it with provisions: a leather water flask, a pack of dried fish, a chunk of nut loaf.

'Some pine spirit for wounds,' she murmurs. 'She could be lost in the mountains, injured . . .'

'Stop *panicking*.'

Mara isn't listening. She digs deep into the bag, unzipping its inner compartment. Rowan watches her rummaging, his face darkening.

'What is it you're looking for? That cyber-whatsit?'

'It's gone,' Mara cries. 'Granny Mary's wooden box – it's where I keep the halo from the cyberwizz. They're both gone. Lily must have taken them. But the halo is useless without the globe.'

'What does it matter?' Rowan slumps down in a chair.

The cyberwizz always annoyed him when they were young because it took Mara to a place he couldn't follow: into the Weave, a mysterious virtual world she never let him see. There were too many secrets to do with the wizz that she always kept to herself. Mara knows Rowan was secretly relieved once the globe was lost.

'Wait a while,' Rowan urges in a gentler tone. 'Give her time.' He pulls Mara towards him. 'Let her have her own adventure, Mara. Let her *be*. We don't know where she is, anyway. She'll come back.'

'Her *own* adventure?' Mara's smooth brow crinkles in bewilderment.

'Have you never thought,' Rowan challenges her, 'what

it's like for her, growing up surrounded by tales of the legendary Mara? It's bad enough for me.' He breaks into a grin that softens his face into the boy Mara grew up with on their drowned island. 'Maybe she just needs to escape your shadow for a while.'

'She's not in my shadow. She's far too bright for that.' Mara pauses. 'Though I remember Mum felt like that about Granny Mary.' She rakes her long, dark hair back from her face in a fretful gesture of old. 'But that's not why she's gone.' She falters, swallows hard, 'Scarwell told Lily about . . . about . . .'

Mara stops, the name freezing on her lips. She has barely spoken it in all the years Lily has been alive. She's not quite sure why, although she knows something in Rowan flinches from the very thought of that other presence, the one who is part of Lily and flutters like a tree-ghost at the edges of their lives.

'The legendary Fox.'

Rowan finishes the hanging sentence in a flat voice.

Mara wants to escape his piercing blue eyes but they pin her to the moment, as always.

'You've had all the time in the world to tell her. *Years*, Mara. She should have heard it from you. You should have told her the truth in the beginning.'

'I tried . . . I . . .'

'Once. You tried *once*.'

'She wanted *you* to be her dad. You love each other. I couldn't bear to spoil that.'

'Maybe what you couldn't bear is to talk about *him*. You can't even speak his name.'

Silence falls between them.

'Scarwell says,' Mara tries to steady her shaking voice,

'that Lily has gone with Wing to find him.'

'To find *him*? Fox?'

Rowan, stunned, reaches out to stop Mara as she pulls on her parka and slings her backpack over her shoulder.

'I'll go,' he grabs her arm. '*I'll* find her. The children need you here, Mara. *Our* children, fast asleep in their beds, who will wake up wanting their mother.'

'*Our* children have their father.'

'So has Lily.' Rowan's ice-blue eyes burn into hers. 'Right here.'

'I'm sorry,' she whispers, but turns away.

The thought of leaving the little ones is unbearable. She hesitates for an anguished moment then stumbles up the wooden steps and pushes open the burrow door.

The wind wrenches the door from her fingers. Mara climbs up out of the burrow and the wind bangs the door shut again at her feet. She stands alone in the forest. The wind sobs through the pines and swooping owls hoot like lost souls. Everyone else in Candlewood is below ground, like all the other forest creatures. Only the lamps among the trees puncture the dense black night. Even the glittering map of the stars is blanked by cloud.

Dread grips Mara as the warmth of the burrow seeps from her.

The bang of the door has woken little Coll. Rowan will try to soothe him but the toddler's cries of *Mummy* penetrate the floor of earth between them, tugging at Mara's insides as if he is bonded to her with invisible strings. It's *her* arms he wants, her scent, her hair twirled around one thumb as he sucks noisily on the other. Mara's body aches; she feels torn in two.

Rowan is right. She can't leave.

61

Mara tries not to think of all the calamities that might befall Lily in this abyss of night. An owl screeches like a terrified girl and the wind-frittered tree lamps play tricks with her tear-blurred eyes, as Mara seems to see a flame of hair streaming through the forest like the fiery phantom of a fox.

WHERE THE SUN FELL TO EARTH

Her deerskin boots are a splattered mess. She's been sick all over her own feet.

Trembling, Lily pulls a water pouch from her pocket and takes a sip only for her stomach to heave again and again, until she fears she'll turn inside out. Head thumping, she slumps back against a rock and tries to make sense of the unfamiliar shapes of the mountains.

Where *is* she?

'Wing,' she whimpers.

He was with her, wasn't he?

It's all such a blur.

A shadow looms over her and Lily yells with fright. But it's only Wing, looking down at her, perched on the rock above.

Lily stands up, unsteadily. The world spins.

'Lil!'

Wing's shout breaks into endless echoes. Lily slumps back against the rock with a gasp as she sees the plunging abyss, a few steps away.

An immense gorge lies between the mountains. Ice sparkles in its depths. Chunks as big as icebergs sit marooned like stranded ships waiting to set sail in the spring meltwater that pelts down from the mountains.

The sun balances on a peak at the faraway end of the gorge and it seems to Lily that once, in a time out of mind, the sun must have toppled from that mountain and crashed down to Earth, gouging out the wide gorge before bouncing back up into the sky, leaving this brutal wound in its wake.

'Where are we?' she croaks. 'How did we get here?

Wing gives her a dry look and chucks an empty leather flask at her. Lily catches the aroma of pine resin as the flask lands in her hands and feels her stomach heave again.

Groggily, she begins to remember.

The flask of pine wine, stolen from the winter store.

The lovely, dizzy, soaring feeling as she hid deep in the trees, ignoring all the worried voices calling *Lily, where are you? Lily, come home!*

She'd gulped the oily, aromatic wine until everything felt woozy. Nothing hurt, nothing mattered. Anything was possible. She might jump off Candlewood spire and land on a star, or sail to the furthest shores of Lake Longhope and explore the distant, unknown Northern reaches with the reindeer – or run away to the world's ocean to find her real father and make everyone suffer for lying to her all her life.

The moon hung like a lamp in the sky and she'd followed it past Candlewood Spire into a landscape of giant, bleached rocks that looked as if they'd dropped from the moon. Now, here she is, among the ferocious peaks of the southern mountains, with a head like a thunderstorm.

Wing must have tracked her every staggering step.

Lily shrieks as he smashes an ice-bomb over her head. Wing jumps down beside her and scrubs her face with ice until she's gasping, then mushes a handful down her neck for good measure. It does the trick. Her face stings but her head is clearer. Now Wing hands her his drink pouch. Lily's stomach heaves at the scent of pine mixed with the musky wolfskin pouch. But tree bark tea is not pine wine. She sips the cold, bitter drink and feels her queasy stomach settle.

'Come on,' says Wing.

He hauls her to her feet then continues a precarious journey along the ridge of the gorge, deeper into the mountains, instead of heading home.

Lily's heart bangs.

One little word. That's all it would take. All she needs to do is cry *home* and Wing will snap out of his wolf-trance. But the word sticks in her throat and she begins to follow. And the further they go, the harder it becomes to swallow her pride and head back.

The sun falls behind the mountain as the short day ends, and the gorge deepens as it fills up with night.

There is no moon-lamp tonight, or stars. One stumble and she will hurl down into the darkness. Lily grows ever more nervous, less and less sure that Wing *would* turn back now because he's hot on the trail of his own small self when he came through these mountains before; re-tracking with animal instinct, tasting the wind, reading rock lichen patterns as if they are signposts, becoming ever more wolfish as he retraces the steps of his old journey.

She bangs into Wing as he comes to a sudden halt. A great rubble of rocks blocks their way. With a rush of relief Lily sees that they must turn back now. Above is the sheer back of the mountain, below is the abyss. To clamber over the precarious rubble would surely risk it collapsing into the abyss, taking her and Wing down too.

There is no way to get beyond the giant landslide. They've

65

reached a dead end.

'Tuck here,' says Wing softly. 'Or there,' he adds, pointing down at the dark void.

The stolen globe, then, is under the landslide or down in the abyss too. Either way, Lily sees, it is truly lost. Devastated, she kicks the rubble of rocks.

It shifts. An ominous rumble comes from the landslide and she jumps back as rocks tumble down into the darkness. Lily counts to six before she hears them crash-land in the gorge. If the rock rubble is so unstable, then the landslide must be new.

Was *this* the Earth thunder Wing heard from Candlewood Spire? The roar of rocks hurtling down into the gorge, here, as they did when they killed Tuck?

Lily shivers.

'Let's go home.'

At last she's said it.

There's no answer. Lily whirls around. She scans the rocky rubble, checks the rough path behind her.

Where's Wing?

The faintest echo of the rocks crashing into the abyss still hangs in the night. Panic seizes Lily and she closes her mind to the horror that Wing has hurtled down with them.

But he is nowhere to be seen. Lily is alone in the dark in the place where the Earth smashed down on Tuck and the globe.

THE DOOR INTO THE MOUNTAIN

'Lil!'

Never has Lily been so glad to hear her own name. Wing's shout comes from the landslide. Is he under the rubble?

'Where are you?' she panics.

'Here!'

Lily edges towards his voice and sees a dark gap in the rubble – a narrow doorway between the landslide and the mountain.

The vivid firestone eyes of Wing's wolf head glisten in the darkness. The cool fire of Wing's own eyes burn beneath.

'Are you hurt?' she cries.

In answer, Wing grasps her hand and pulls her into the dark mountain doorway.

'Taste the wind,' he urges.

Lily opens her mouth and draws in a breath, as Wing has taught her, then licks her lips.

Salt! The wind carries a taste like the air of the salt caves of Mooncrumble Mountain on the far side of their lake, yet stronger and tangier with strange, lively scents.

'Sea!' says Wing.

'I can't see *anything*!'

Then Lily understands. Blowing through the mountain is

a sea wind. The wind of the world's ocean.

Wing disappears into the darkness of the mountain. Lily must turn for home now, alone, or follow him.

She steps through the mountain doorway into darkness deeper than night. She stumbles over rubble, picks herself up and walks bang into a rock wall.

'Wing?'

The musky scent of wolfskin cuts through her panic. She feels Wing's cool, rough hand grasping hers.

'We can't walk blind into a mountain,' she tells him. 'I didn't pack a torch or a tinderbox . . . nothing.'

And how stupid was that? But there *is* something: deep in the pocket of her parka and not much bigger than her hand. Lily's fingers trace the soothingly familiar carvings of the little wooden box that once belonged to Granny Mary. It's Mara's precious heirloom from her drowned island home.

Storming from the burrow in a furious haze, glugging the flask of pine wine, Lily had given no thought to what she might need for a journey into the mountains – but she'd grabbed the box, with Granny Mary's other heirloom inside; the halo that belongs to the lost globe. Her wild hopes of digging up the globe are dead now, but the halo has its own power. Lily opens the wooden box and takes out the sleek silver crescent. The heat of her hands will make it glow.

And so it does.

Lily holds up the brightening crescent and the wall of darkness retreats. She gasps as the light reveals what lies beyond the pile of rubble: a maze of tunnels, endless branchings into the mountain, where aeons of ice and meltwater once wormed their way through.

Lily turns around in circles. They'd be crazy to walk into those dark tunnels. They might be lost forever.

A fiery eye winks from a small crevice. Lily freezes with fright. What unknown creatures lurk deep inside the mountains? The halo reveals another, past the rubble, deep in one of the tunnels. And there's another, and yet more, all glinting at her from the rocks. Ah, but she knows what it is! It's a firestone trail, just like the one that marks pathways through Candlewood's trees.

Lily feels a surge of emotion as she sees the evidence of a petrifying journey that until now, for her, has only been a story, a cosy fireside tale. *This* was the way her people once came from the world beyond, marking their steps as they went. When they came through this mountain Mara was barely older than she, Lily, is now – fleeing into the unknown with a baby growing inside her.

For the first time in her life Lily imagines her mother as a girl of her own age – one with no father or mother, no family or home; all of it lost to the ocean. She must have been terrified, and so brave.

Lily's nerve steadies – and her resolve. She *will* have this adventure. She will do something brave and grand, something that will gleam down the years and be told as a fireside tale one day. Something worthy of a girl descended from the likes of Caledon and Fox and Granny Mary and Mara.

The globe Tuck stole might be well and truly lost, buried deep in the gorge, but it can't be the only wizz in the world! If there are others, if she can find just one in the world at the other side of the mountain . . . well, she has a halo. She *might* still find a way to connect with her Fox father. So she must get through this mountain. It's her only chance. She will never know her real father if she turns back now.

The halo's crescent glows in the dark like a brave smile as Lily steps into the unknown as her ancestors once did.

THE WORLD'S OCEAN

Amazed, Lily clings to a rock. She gapes at the astounding night they have plunged into on the other side of the mountain.

The world's ocean is terrifying! It roars and tears at the land like a ravenous black bear. Endless hills and valleys of silvered waves stretch as far as she can see, like a landscape of living rock. None of the stories, not even the worst storm on Lake Longhope, has prepared Lily for this.

How did her people ever cross such a fearsome thing?

Wing stares out into the ocean blast.

'You know where we are?' Lily yells.

Her courage shreds in the wind when he shakes his head.

Inside the mountain, as the scent of the ocean became strong, Wing rushed on, ignoring the firestone trailblazers, tracking the salt wind instead. Lily feared they'd be lost forever as they stumbled through a neverending maze of dark tunnels for what seemed like long nights and days. But Wing led them at last to the ocean. Yet they emerged from the blunt darkness of the mountain into this billowing black night in a place he did not seem to know.

Lost and confused, Wing searches for bearings and scents. They clamber over rocks, Lily keeping close as he turns away from the open ocean, following the waterline as it cuts sharply inland around the heel of the mountain to form a wide inlet of sea.

Wing stops with a sharp cry. Lily follows his gaze down the great sea fjord.

'Great Skua!' she gasps.

Moonlit pathways criss-cross the winding black channel of sea.

'What is it?' Lily clutches Wing's hand.

'Bridges,' he whispers.

The only bridge Lily has ever seen is a coarse wooden one across a stream. These are brilliant, silvery, dreamlike creations, weaving this way and that across the sea fjord that snakes between the mountains.

Wing studies the jagged peaks around them and gives a satisfied grunt.

'You know this place?'

'Ilira,' he says.

'Ilira?' Lily shakes her head, recalling her people's stories of the mountain city with its tumbling waterfalls; a bleak, brutal place. 'Ilira doesn't have bridges.'

But Wing nods, wonderstruck.

'Ilira,' he insists.

As they move deeper inland, the air fills with a strange rumbling and the moonlight reveals the shoulder of a great mountain at the far end of the winding fjord, studded with lantern lights. Now Lily sees that Wing is right. This *is* Ilira! The moon glistens on the doors to the cave-dwellings of the mountain people and silvers the waterfalls that thunder into the sea from great heights. The ghostly billows of masts loom out of the dark from what must be a ships' harbour near the neck of the fjord.

Ships that cross the great oceans! Lily's heart beats hard at that thought.

Wing has climbed down to the edge of the sea and throws his wolfskin and the rest of his ragged clothing on to the rocks. He dives smoothly into the water. Moments later, Lily sees him leap like a fish among the heaving waves and hears his yell of joy. She reaches out a hand to feel the froth of a wave and gasps. Her heart might stop in sea as cold and wild as that! But Wing's tough, sleek-haired skin, webbed hands and feet and fish-like gills give him powers beyond ordinary humans.

When he drips back across the rocks he has a bundle of dark pebbles in his hands, strung together with seaweed. He splits a pebble open on a rock and shows Lily the nugget of meat inside, then slurps it in a gulp. A blissful grin spreads across his face.

'My food when I lived in sea,' he says.

Lily's stomach groans. She's hungrier than she has ever been in her life. She breaks open the sea pebbles and gulps mouthful after mouthful of tangy ocean meat. Thirsty, she climbs down to the waterline and scoops up a handful of ocean to drink. Wing bursts out laughing as she splutters and retches. It's vile! Nothing like the pure, clear water of the lake.

No fire, Wing warns. He closes his eyes and his face softens as he falls, like a wolf, into instant sleep. Deep shivers run through Lily. She's gripped by cold now they're no longer on the move. Who is there to spy a tiny blaze? The mountain city of Ilira is away at the head of the fjord.

Lily scrabbles around in the dark and finds a small miracle – a gnarled limb of dry wood wedged between two rocks. Now she is grateful for those long evenings Ibrox spent so patiently teaching her the one thing, he said, every child of the Earth should know – how to make fire. As always, it takes her ages, but Lily coaxes a tiny fire from wood and stone and snuggles under Wing's wolfskin. Her eyes grow heavy as the flame blurs into a half-dream of the summer sun, hot and red above Lake Longhope.

A jolt startles Lily awake. Wing has sprung to his feet, his animal senses always on alert, even in sleep.

'What's up?'

He stamps out the fire, growling under his breath at some threat. Lily scans the fjord but all she sees are moonbeams and reflections of the bridges, wriggling upon the black sea. Then a sleek shadow slides across a ribbon of moonlight. Then another and still more.

'Boats,' whispers Wing.

The scrape of a boat on the rocks below sends them scrambling away from the darting shadows that are suddenly moving all across the rocks.

A shout close behind makes Lily stumble with fright. She falls sideways and lands hard, wedged between two rocks. Wing yells her name, but she's too winded by the fall to shout back. A cold wet weight falls over her. A net! Someone breathes, hot and hard, in her face as he binds her in the net. Lily kicks and struggles but she's trapped, can't break free, can't see Wing, and the hunters' shadows are closing in all around.

SUNDER

Driven by the forces of love, the fragments
of the world
seek each other, so that the world may come
into being.

Pierre Teilhard de Chardin

DRAGONS' TEETH

Squeezed knees to chin in her cup-shaped coracle, Pandora paddles across the netherworld sea. She keeps a wary distance from the huge trunks of the sky towers. The security sensors will set off shrieking sirens if she gets too close.

A sign with a **P** for Pandora marks the place she wants. The old sign lies deep in the water by the broken bridge, where the rest of the bridge was lost to the sea long ago.

The tide is low, the dusk glooms, and the underwater city glows with phosphorescence.

Pandora dives into the lagoon, deep down into ghostly drowned streets. The soft gills on her neck flutter open as she swims through dense algae bloom where the sea is so green and murky she can barely see.

But there it is! Pandora lunges towards the mysterious **P**.

Crops of seaweed shiver as she swims through phos-furred heaps of wrecked vehicles until she finds the lorry that hoards the treasure she wants. She dives into the blind-dark body of the lorry where the only light is a silver ray of fish and rummages in slimy seaweed until she feels the cold roundness of a tin.

Pandora breaks back through the surface of the lagoon.

Clambering back into the coracle she wipes the slime from the tin with the ends of her hair and looks to see what she's got.

Classic Pie, says the rusted lettering. Pandora's empty stomach rumbles approval.

A long, strangled shriek in the swamp grass at the foot of a sky tower almost makes her drop the pie tin. Pandora scans the netherworld. She looks up at the giant towers of New Mungo, at the web of sky tunnels that connect them, a network of streets in the sky.

No sea police or sky patrols. The shriek wasn't human. It was the sound, Pandora reckons, of a creature being eaten alive.

Her quick, green eyes scan the steamy surface of the netherworld sea.

Could it be . . . ? Dragons? So soon?

She begins to paddle back across the lagoon, dread prickling her scalp. The hot, swampy heat sneaked up on them suddenly this year, hard on the tails of the winter storms. It's still too early, surely, for *them* . . .

But the planet has lost its old patterns. Summer stampedes across the world with barely a lull between the North Wind's winter storms and the tides of heat that sweep up from the wide swelter of tropics around the middle of the Earth. There, the sun is a deadly fireball that no human, even in a sky city, can bear.

The dragons follow the sun, swarming North the summer seas, and swim into the netherworld through underwater tide shafts in the city wall. Night after swampy night, they prey on the boat refugees then swim back in through the wall, haunting the gloomy lagoon with a reptilian gleam as they digest their suppers on the mudbanks and

80

seaweedy roofs that emerge at low tide.

Only now does Pandora see that the fishing nets that hang from the broken bridge are in shreds.

Dragons' teeth!

A ripple disturbs the water. Pandora sees it out of the corner of her eye but there's no time even to aim her spear.

The swamp dragon lunges towards her. Pandora screams, slamming her paddle into the water and the coracle hurls across the lagoon.

THE WRONG WAR

Fox hears the scream and rushes to a tower window. He sees the flash of Pandora's blue silk dress as her coracle skims across the water like a leaf in a storm. Horrified, he sees the thing that looks as harmless as a log, close behind. But no log moves at that speed.

Swamp dragons.

And there's another, camouflaged on the slippery mudbank at the foot of his tower. The beast raises its long snout, scenting the approach of fresh meat.

Fox gallops down the twisting stairway. Grabbing a sword and an axe from the weapons rack at the foot of the stairs, he hauls open the huge oak door.

The coracle spins from the water, up on to the mudbank.

'Pan!' roars Fox, and he jabs his sword towards the dragon she has not yet seen.

Pandora spills from her coracle and sprawls in the mud, finally spotting the swamp dragon that awaits her. The first dragon, having chased her across the lagoon, now lunges from the water. Pandora gives an agonized cry, and seizes up the coracle as a shield, seeing herself trapped between the two beasts.

He won't reach her in time! Fox skids on the slippery mud as the squat beasts use their legs like paddles to slide on their bellies at amazing speed. He hears the creak of a dragon jaw as the jagged teeth open wide in expectation.

This is not the war they are meant to fight! They won't lose their lives here, Fox vows, as inglorious suppers for the swamp dragons.

Pandora stands still, as if in thrall to the beasts. She turns a heartbroken face to Fox.

'They can have me. I don't care. I see your eyes when you look at me now. I'm not me any more, I'm just one of the empire's mistakes and you hate me!'

'Would I be out here saving you if I hated you?' With seconds to spare Fox must break the death-spell that grips her. 'Come on, Pan – move!'

She drinks in his words for one lethal moment, green eyes glittering with tears. Then as the dragons lunge she hurls the coracle at one and spins around to fire the round pie tin she clutches hard into the wide-open mouth of the other. That beast gurgles and slithers to a halt, the pie tin stuck fast in its throat.

But the other dragon shunts aside the light coracle and slithers up from the water's edge. Fox slides down the mudbank, feet first, and kicks the dragon's tail. The beast flicks the huge armoured tail – a swipe could kill him – but Fox is on his feet, and ready. Sweat pours down his face as he taunts the dragon with his sword, poking it, dancing around it, risking another flick of the tail, one that will swipe the legs from under him – and then he'll be gone in a snap.

A shadow moves across them and the netherworld vibrates with the rumble of an airship. It unnerves the dragon. The beast raises its snout and swivels up its tiny eyes. Fox takes his chance and plunges the sword deep into the unarmoured flesh of the dragon's throat.

He reclaims his sword and clambers up the mud towards the other beast, still choking on the pie tin, and slaughters it too. Then he stands gasping for breath as Pandora flings her arm around him, sleek and cold against his hot human body.

'You saved me,' she whispers. 'When you love someone, you save them. There's no greater love than that, you said.'

'So no more silly talk,' he says gently, and peels her off him.

'Can we save my pie too?' she asks.

'Your *pie*?'

He bursts out laughing and the tense moment breaks. He wipes the sweat from his eyes and scans the mudbank and the lagoon.

'I can do better than a stinking old pie. We'll have dragon for supper.' He raises his axe and begins hacking at the nearest one. 'Keep watch, Pan. There's sure to be more.'

THE SURGE RISES

Fox bolts the door of the tower and climbs the winding stairs with two huge dragon steaks, dripping hot blood, skewered on his sword. Pan has the fire ready and he flame-roasts the steaks on the tip of the sword. Once he's eaten his fill of the rich, tangy meat Fox finds his godgem and in the guise of his old fox avatar he connects to the Noos . . .

. . . and leaps into a virtual universe of brilliance and chaos: a frenzy of imagineering, ideas-wheeling and dealing, cyber-trading, news and data. Fox travels through maelstroms of energy, ever-changing cyberpatterns and links, as the global Supermind of the Noos endlessly expands and re-creates the miracle of itself.

It's as if the sky people, so close to the heavens, peered into the mind of the universe and captured its neverending spirit of creation in their Noos.

Spellbound by their own magic, the sky citizens have no need to wonder about the world outside, as Fox knows all too well: he too was caught in the trance of the Noos, once upon a time. It's that global trance he has worked so hard to break.

Deep in the rumpus of Noospace are doorways to secret clubs. It's here that young Noosworkers flock after long shifts of cybertrading and imagineering the endless products and technologies – galaxies of invention – that are the engine of the empire and create lives of sizzling luxury for the sky citizens.

In the rowdy gatherings of the clandestine cyberclubs a raw, rebellious energy beats hard and fast. The police rooks ban them if they find them – but the Noos has grown so vast and complex it's impossible to police it all. No sooner is a cyberclub shut down than it springs up again in another shady corner of the Noos, and the boisterous brilliance beats on.

These restless young spirits weave a chaotic dark energy all through their beloved Noos. Forever adding new links and patterns, endlessly spinning ideas – just to see what happens – each bestows their own random gifts to the virtual universe.

It's here that Fox found rebels who ask the same hard questions about the world that he once did. They have become his Surgent allies, working up a revolutionary spirit in the dense jungles of Noospace. It's a gift of pure rebel energy from the Noosweavers who want to see what happens when all systems crash and everything is rebooted in the real world. The best of human nature, Fox has realized, exists deep within an empire built on the worst.

We are creeping along a ledge of history, Fox tells the young rebels in the Noos. Are you ready to jump with me into the unknown?

Fox zips through the beautiful tangle of energy, the hairs tingling on the back of his neck. At last he finds the outlaw den he seeks, deep in the undergrowth of a simmering electronic jungle.

'Kitsune?' he hisses.

The eyes of an old friend shine through the thick cyber-foliage. 'About time. What happened to you?'

'Unexpected rescue mission,' says Fox. 'Early invasion of swamp dragons. I thought we'd be gone by the time they came, but the heat – it's so early this year.'

'Hottest spring ever known,' Kitsune responds. 'About the *other* invasion,' he reminds Fox. A turquoise fractal of data spins by, ruffling the electronic foliage. Its mutating patterns glint in Kitsune's warm, excited eyes. 'I was updating you before we were so rudely interrupted by your dragons.'

Fox checks the shimmering cyberjungle for snooping presences, then burrows deeper into the foliage beside his greatest ally and friend. Kitsune is his most trusted Surgent, a secret rebel at the heart of the empire in the powerful sky city of the Eastern oceans, New Jing. Noosrunner rivals in their youth, he and Fox are bonded in friendship and name. In old Eastern legends, Kitsune is the sly trickster fox.

So well hidden is the trickster fox that only his cyber-eyes can be seen.

'Sky fleets have been landing at various places in the Northlands,' Kitsune reports. 'At Coldheaven in the Far North, inland of Narwhal Sword Bay in the west, and now at Fort Aurora in the east. The Arctic pirates are scouting their activities. But that's just the start,' he warns. 'You know what's to follow – fortresses all over the North, slave camps to mine for resources, domed cities for the empire-builders . . .'

'My father is making a huge stake in the Northlands,' Fox agrees. 'But he's so desperate to grab power from the eastern cities, sent away so much guardpower and weaponry in the airships, he's left New Mungo weak.'

'Other cities have rushed to follow,' Kitsune continues. 'They all want their stake. All the cities of the northern hemisphere have left themselves open to attack. But what we do here will shake the whole empire. The global Surge is ready to fight for high lands all across the planet. The empire is too overstretched to cope with attacks on so many fronts. You're right, Fox. This is our best chance. It's now or never.'

Fox's jaw unclenches. The line between his brows smoothes out. Tension seeps from his muscles.

At last.

The frozen years of waiting and planning are almost over. The moment he has been moving towards for so long, like the captain of a ship in blank fog, rises up before him like a brand new continent.

He takes a smooth, deep breath. He feels sharp and clear and sure.

'Alert all Surgents within the empire to begin the attack on the Noos.' His voice catches in his throat. 'Let's begin.'

Kitsune's eyes sparkle with reflections of Nooswonders unfurling all around. He winks at Fox, then disappears.

Back in realworld, Fox feels Pandora's arms enclose him. Her tangled head is cool and soft on his shoulder but Fox seems to feel the weight of a planetful of desperate hopes and dreams.

HISTORY WHISPERS,
HISTORY JUMPS

All across the Earth, the Surgency waits in tense readiness as the comrades in the sky cities launch the biggest robbery in history upon the Noos.

Fox leans from a window of the old steepled tower to look at one of the last netherworld nights he will ever see. The sky city is draped in a luminous glamour of phosphorescence. Beads of starlight glitter on the interlinking sky tunnels. He breathes in welcome dregs of coolness from the air.

It's hard to believe, this peaceful night, that every sky city on the planet is under the most audacious cyber-attack there has ever been. If all goes to plan, the trade systems that are the lifeblood of the empire will soon begin to collapse, as if a slow bomb has detonated in the Noos.

It's just the beginning. With so many cities vulnerable and their Guardians' attention fixed on the North, the vanishing of trillions of Noo$dollars will send the masters of the empire into spasms of shock. And all across the world's oceans, as the sky cities are left reeling and exposed, the Surge will break through walls.

Strike only when the enemy can be taken by surprise.

The mildewed pages of an old book, his touchstone, hoard

these dangerous gems of rebel warfare: *Seven Pillars of Wisdom* by Lawrence of Arabia, a freedom fighter of another age. Fox knows his diamond words by heart.

He should grab some sleep and food while he can. Fox scours the nooks and crannies at the top of the tower until he has gathered a pocketful of birds' eggs, then makes his way back down the tight-winding stairway to the tower room where Pandora is sprawled on a great heap of silk gowns, snoring softly, after a long session updating Surgents in the virtual wreckage of the Weave. She must have raided the museum's *Ancient and Lost Civilization* wing too because she has gathered around her a small armoury of luck-infested jewellery – a red scarab-beetle brooch, a small jade frog as green as her eyes, Norse amulets, magic square rings, pendants with crosses and mandalas and stars.

We'll need all of it, thinks Fox as he stirs the embers of the evening fire and places the eggs on to roast.

Nerves gnaw at him. He's dizzy with exhaustion but he'll never sleep. So he connects up his godgem and heads for the safe haven in cyberspace where Kitsune and fellow Surgent leaders have arranged to meet: the electric blue haze of the Nowhere that lies like a vast ocean between the virtual universe of the Noos and its long-defunct predecessor, the Weave.

Fox plunges through cyberspace towards that virtual hinterland.

Presences all across the Nowhere are buzzing excitedly. It's difficult to see amid its blinding blue brilliance but Fox recognizes the accents and avatars of the Argent Surgents, rebel leaders from the southern hemisphere of the world.

'Fox!' shouts a voice amid the waves of crackling static. 'We pulled all the fake Noofuel companies from the trade networks – all the scam core metal industries to vanish next.'

Fox watches the eruption of the vivid universe in the far distant ether: an electronic storm of panic as the vast wealth of the Trade Lords vanishes into mysterious black holes.

Kitsune's trickster fox materializes from a nearby starburst of static with a soft, satisfied laugh. 'All gone bust. Go get some rest now, Surgent Fox. You're going to need it.'

Fox disconnects with a wry smile for his cyberfox twin and a last glance at the combusting Noos. His years of exile have lead to this moment. He might not come out of the Surge into the city alive, but what does that matter when a whole world is at stake?

Back in realworld, he peels the hot shells off the roasted eggs and eats ravenously as he moves restlessly through the book-strewn rooms of the old university tower. He stops for a second beside the frantic industry of the genius who inspired his catastrophic attack on the Noos: an aged, fat spider whose web is so vast it drapes all across toppled bookstacks of Stone Age history, past tomes on medieval plagues and exploration, spanning age upon age of war, peace, evolution and revolution, past the shelf where he discovered the mould-ridden *Seven Pillars of Wisdom*, all the way to the twenty-first-century Oil Wars.

The spiderweb is a masterpiece. Whether the weather tears it or the rats rip through it, the spider keeps weaving with a ferocity of purpose that only makes the web more deadly still.

Fox has watched the web grow, measuring the spider's progress against his own. Day by day, night by night, he has woven his own vast web through the intricate business networks of the Trade Lords in the Noos. The Guardians of the sky cities depend on the backing of their leagues of wealthy trade kings to provide the funds for projects that win power within the empire – like the invasion of the Northlands.

Volcanfuels, MagmaWelth, Dynamantle were among a small galaxy of fake companies launched by Fox and his rebels among the real new businesses that were springing up to grab their stake in the rich resources of metals, minerals and fuels in the land grab of the North. The Surgents spread trade rumours of all kinds of wondrous new industries that would explode the possibilities of what the empire could do. The lie of Weathergeneering – satellite-controlled weather patterning to make the Arctic winters more temperate for the invaders – stirred up a rampage for shares in that fairytale company. A phantom Stellarka project was resurrected, with the Trade Lords convinced that the new industries of the Northlands would provide the materials needed for the empire to conquer the stars at last.

It was easier to create the fairy tales than Fox ever expected. The Trade Lords *wanted* to believe.

The tycoons of the sky empire have gambled their vast wealth on companies that do not exist. Now no one knows what is happening, what to believe in, what is real any more . . .

Shockwaves are radiating across the oceans – from the western sky cities of New Tex and New Tucky to the eastern ones of New Bai and New Hai, across the uninhabitable oceans around the Earth's middle, to New Zim, New Zeal and New Zil in the southern hemisphere of the planet. Imaginary towers of wealth built on electronic Noo$dollars are vanishing into the ether as the rebels within the empire surge like a swirling hurricane through the Noos, blasting away the cyber-lie of a trade network that was never real, leaving the Trade Lords caught like flies in Fox's vast and sticky web.

92

THE SCAVENGED GIRL

The goddess of the oceans has woken in a temper. The sound of shipwrecks haunts the shrieking winds.

Clay rows the walrus-skin umiak through seething waves, his eyes narrowed against needles of rain. Shipwrecks are his mother's nightmare, but they're a scavenger's dream.

He glances back at his night's scavenge: a girl wrapped in a fishing net, behind him in the boat. Her soft face, crumpled with fear, has only known fifteen or sixteen winters, he reckons; just one or two less than himself. She stares at him through the netting with terror in her wide eyes. Clay feels a pang of pity. He shakes his head and shrugs his shoulders to get rid of the feeling. A young human scavenge is the best of all finds. Sea-battered junk is all Clay usually nets. Kronk, his Scutmaster, will sell the girl for a good price at market and Clay intends to make sure that he gets the credit for spotting her fire in the dark then capturing her in his net.

She must be from a shipwreck and washed up on the rocks. Wrecks mean all kinds of new scavenges on the tides and the seabed. Clay and his scavenge team searched for other live humans and found none. How many ships, Clay wonders, are sunk on the ocean floor of the world? What leagues of treasure lie there, as unreachable as the stars?

He digs his oar deep in the water as the sea goddess tosses the umiak sideways into a wave.

The girl screams in his ear. Wrapped tight in the net, she has no way of holding on. He can't risk losing her. Clay grips his oar between his knees and signals to his fellow scavengers to go ahead in their boats, while he turns to free the girl from the net.

'Hold on!' he yells, placing her hands on his waist, in case his language is unknown to her. The ships that sail into Ilira bring people from all over the Arctic and far beyond, who speak with many different tongues.

A silken flame of hair blows across his face. The girl's hair, her wide eyes, delicate features and milky skin tell him she is from some distant place, as he is – the true Arctic people have the look of those who have faced the blast of the North Wind for time out of mind. But Clay must keep his focus on the boat now in this stretch of the fjord where the giant waterfalls thunder from the mountains and churn up the sea.

His scavenge grips him tight and he hears her gasp as they pass the tiny island where the glass palace of the Pontifix, the Great Sea Lord of Ilira, glistens in the early morning light.

'*Great Skua!*' she murmurs, as they pass under the magnificent network of bridges that link the mountains on each side of the fjord.

Clay looks over his shoulder, puzzled at hearing this gentle curse of the Ilirans, an exclamation borrowed from the name of the Pontifix's magnificent ship.

'You're not from Ilira?' says Clay, suddenly uneasy. If he has captured a wandering Iliran girl he's in big trouble.

But his scavenge is staring up open-mouthed at the Culpy

Bridge as they pass underneath. She is a stranger, Clay is certain. All incomers look at the wonders of Ilira in such a way. The deep moan of a horn makes her jump and once again Clay has to focus on his oars, plunging the umiak through the spray of a waterfall to swerve out of the path of a ship with billowing sails, its decks full of the Pontifix's guards.

They emerge from the waterfall gasping, soaked with ice-cold spray.

'Where's my friend?' the girl asks, once they are in calm waters near the harbour. 'What happened to him?'

'Your friend?' says Clay. *The wolfman is her friend?* 'I don't know. Where do you come from?'

'Candlewood,' says the girl into Clay's ear. The word is spoken so sadly that Clay only just hears her over the crashing waterfalls.

'Where did your ship sink?'

'Huh?'

Clay glances back over his shoulder. The girl looks blank. No shipwreck then.

'Where's Candlewood?' he asks, wondering where a pretty girl and a wolfman could have come from.

'Over the mountains,' she replies, hesitantly then panicking. 'But *where's* my friend? I can't see him in the other boats.'

Clay ignores her and squints through a blast of sea spray to look at the wall of mountains that enclose the fjord and its bay.

There is nothing beyond the mountains, the Arctic legends say. It's where the sun rests at the end of a day and where it sleeps through the long night of winter. The mountains stop the oceans pouring off the end of the world. The Pontifix's maps and star charts and ships have proved there is a vast world beyond Ilira's seas, as do the raggedy boats and ships that venture into his new harbour laden with goods from faraway ports. But Clay has barely thought about what lies inland, behind Ilira's mountains. They're just *there*.

He's given plenty of thought to the ocean though. If he could, he'd jump on the next ship and sail out to see the world. But slaves never leave Ilira. They're bound for life to the Sea Lords and their scavenger Scuts. And if he did escape and go he'd break his mother's heart.

During Clay's short life, the Pontifix has sent ship after ship out on to the world's ocean and each has returned with tales of the tiny settlements that are sprouting across the Northlands. In recent summers Clay has watched the boats from those budding ports begin to venture up the great fjord into the bay of Ilira – if the Pontifix gave them safe passage through his lethal sea traps. Clay has mingled in the harbour bars with the visiting seafarers who came to see with their own eyes the magnificent new mountain metropolis of Ilira. They'd heard rumours on the Arctic trade winds of its glass palace and the steam gondolas that puff through the fjord's glistening bridges, of the thundering waterfalls that will soon power the city and the little cable trains that rattle up and down the mountainsides.

Clay steers his umiak past Ilira's new port and heads for the rocky harbour at the head of the bay. Kronk, his Scutmaster, is there, stamping his boots, impatient to see if his night scavenge team has found any goods. Clay lets out a laugh as he sees that Kronk is in full sea armour. But his heart sinks when he remembers why – it's for the wedding, of course.

He only has a moment left with the scavenged girl before his Scutmaster hauls her out of the boat. Then she'll be gone to market and he might never see her again.

'What's over the mountains?' Clay whispers to the girl. 'Tell me.'

She is staring in horror at the bulky monstrosity that is Kronk, in his helmet and vest armoured with the spiky shells of sea anemones.

'Tell me what's there and I'll help you,' Clay lies.

The girl gives him such a desperate look that Clay wishes he wore a helmet too and could pull it down over his lying eyes. He throws the boat rope to Kronk.

'Lake Longhope,' the girl whispers back. 'A lake so big you can't see the end of it. Forests. Wolves and bears and eagles live in the mountains. The wind doesn't stink of sea or nip your eyes with salt. Our wind is the breath of the pine trees.'

The Scutmaster pulls Clay's umiak into place at the harbour. A sob escapes the girl and she puts a shaking hand over her mouth.

'*Please let me go!*'

The sob gets to him. Suddenly she is no longer just scavenged goods; she is a girl in a trap. A girl with a soft face that he likes. But it's too late. Kronk is beaming at the sight of her. There's nothing Clay can do.

'Why did you come here?' Clay hisses.

'To find my father. But my friend,' she pleads, 'where is he?'

The Scutmaster yanks the girl out of the boat by the fur hood of her parka. He looks her up and down then gives a satisfied grin, revealing black stumps of teeth. The girl tries to run but Kronk gives her a slap on the head that stuns her while he expertly lassoes her with a rope that binds the girl's arms tight to her sides. Clay gets out of the boat, feeling sick and odd.

97

'Good find!' The Scutmaster claps Clay on the back and rewards him with a black-stumped grin. 'Best scavenge in a long time.' He scowls at the others. 'You lot get nothin' again?'

Clay is unable to look at the girl. The Scutmaster's rare praise means not a thing. Does he want to be the best scavenger in Ilira? Is this what he's meant to be? He looks at the girl's tragic face and knows it is not.

'Wing, where are you?' she mutters, staring at the mountains that line the fjord. 'I'm sorry, I'm so sorry.'

Clay can't bear to add to her misery. He saw what happened to the wolfman.

'Where's your father?' he asks the girl, wondering why any father would leave such a soft-faced daughter at the mercy of the world. Then Clay remembers the Sea Lord who owns him and bosses Kronk. What a brutal father he is to his daughter.

The Scut is jumping on the back of his deer, arguing loudly with one of the marketeers. He'll be back any moment. There isn't much time.

The girl flicks him a wretched glance. 'My father's across the ocean, in a city as tall as the sky.'

Clay's eyes widen. A vision of towers fills his head; a vision he remembers from the stories told to him as a child by his mother.

'Market's closed,' the Scut shouts in disgust. 'One man gets married and the whole world's got to stop. *Urth*,' he curses. 'Lock her up in storage for today, dirt-boy.'

'The name's *Clay*, crab-face,' Clay mutters under his breath. Kronk's good mood didn't last long. But he knows better than to be heard; a Scut will cut off a slave's hand for less. At least he's got more time to find out about the scavenged girl.

Clay hauls his terrified prisoner along the harbour, across the rocky shore to the warren of sea caves at the foot of the mountain where goods and scavenges are stored. He pulls back the bolts on a rusted door and pushes the girl into a dank darkness – then checks that no one is looking and follows her into the cave.

THE GIRL AND THE PONTIFIX

'Clay?' whispers the girl.

'That's my name,' he replies, as he takes the long end of the rope that binds her arms and knots it around a rock. 'What's yours?'

Her name is Lily Longhope, she says. He studies the trembling girl in the dim light that filters through gaps in the battered door. The plea in her amber-brown eyes tugs at his heart.

Look away, Clay tells himself. *Tomorrow she'll be someone's kitchen slave and you'll never see her again.*

'The wolfman,' he begins, because if he doesn't tell her she'll never know what happened. He can give her that, at least. 'He – he was killed. The ocean currents took him.'

Lily blinks. The milky skin of her face grows paler still. She shakes her head slowly.

'Wing's not *dead*,' she scorns, as if that's something he would never do. 'I don't believe you. He wouldn't drown.'

Clay makes himself tell her. 'He got hit in the head with an arrow.'

She sits in disbelieving silence, shaking from head to toe. Clay takes a step closer and reaches out a hand to stroke her hair but she lunges at him, sinking her teeth into his hand. Clay raises his other hand to retaliate, but his mother's horrified face flashes up in his mind and he stops.

Grunting with pain, he retrieves his bitten hand when she opens her mouth to let out a wail.

He must leave yet there's so much he wants to know about this wretched, feisty girl with the temper of a wildcat and the soft eyes of a doe.

'Your father –' he begins, then remembers the other scavenge, one he hid from Kronk – a mysterious object he snatched from the girl's pocket after he netted her on the rocks. Clay pulls the carved wooden box from the pocket of his hide jacket. Opening the box, he stares at the strange silver crescent inside. When he takes it out, it begins to glow in his hand like a thin young moon.

The girl's heartbroken sobbing instantly stops.

'What's this?' he asks, mystified.

'Give it back!' Lily gasps, tears scattering from her face. 'I *need* it.'

'Why?' Clay holds up the crescent and its gentle glow falls upon the piles of crates and sacking that fill the dank cave. 'What's it for?'

'You've never seen one before?' Lily asks, suddenly curious. 'Don't you have these in your world?'

Clay shrugs. 'I see most things. I'm a good scavenger, the best. I've found all kinds of sea treasure from the drowned world,' he boasts, wanting her to know he is not just an ordinary slave. 'But I've never seen this.'

He looks up to find Lily's eyes fixed on his own so intently that something flips in his stomach, as if he has swallowed a tiny, excitable fish.

'Did you never,' she asks urgently, 'find a globe?'

101

Clay shakes his head. 'The Pontifix has a globe. But I've never seen it.'

'Ponty-fix?' Lily stumbles over the strange word.

'The man who rules Ilira. He's Bridge-Master, Overlord of the Sea Lords, Ocean Commander, Keeper of the Globe. Tuck Culpy's just about everything round here.'

'Tuck!' Lily's tear-streamed mouth falls open. '*Our* Tuck?'

Clay stares. 'There's only one Tuck Culpy.'

'But he's supposed to be dead,' says Lily wonderingly. 'My people made his name a curse.'

'My people have made him a god.'

Clay is unnerved. The Pontifix's magic globe is a subject he usually avoids – especially in front of his mother. It's guaranteed to get her weepy about the past.

'If it *is* him, if – if somehow he didn't die in the landslide,' Lily is muttering to herself, 'then – then the globe *must* be . . . I must see this Tuck!' she declares.

Clay bursts out laughing. 'I don't think so. The Pontifix is too busy to meet scavenged slaves today. He's getting married. To my almost-sister,' he adds, with a sigh.

He moves towards the cave door, avoiding the girl's scared, bewildered eyes.

'I'm no slave. Don't leave me here,' she cries. 'Please let me go.'

Clay lights a small oil lamp so she won't be left in darkness. He takes his own leather water pouch and a sliver of smoke-blackened seal meat from his pocket and chucks them in her lap. On an impulse he also tosses her the carved wooden box, now empty, telling himself she hardly deserves his kindness after that vicious bite to his still-throbbing hand.

'Help me!' she shouts as he leaves. 'I *must* see Tuck

Culpy. I need the halo and the globe to find my father!'

Clay's heart is heavy as he bolts the cave door against her desperate cries. He stuffs the crescent deep in his pocket and runs to hitch a ride on the back of the little cable train that *click-clacks* up the mountainside. His mind is buzzing. What does it all mean?

Nothing, he tells himself. She's just a scared girl trying to talk herself free.

Gripping on to the back rail of the train, Clay sticks his free hand in his parka pocket and fingers the crescent. A halo, she called it. A thought strikes him. The Pontifix is mad for strange treasures like these. If this halo is something to do with the globe then he, Clay, holds a powerful gift in his hand.

It's only after he has jumped off the cable train and is clambering up to the mountain cave where his mother is in the thick of wedding preparations that something jars in his mind. He stops, balanced precariously on a thin ledge of rock.

Clayslaps. Was that what the girl called him as he was running away from the cave? She couldn't have. Only his mother ever calls him that.

He looks down the steep mountainside to the harbour where Lily Longhope is locked in the cave, then stares across the ruffled waters of the fjord where the Pontifix's glass palace is raincloud dull in the dreary light.

How could a scavenged girl from beyond the mountains know that was his proper name? And how could she have anything to do with a man as powerful as the Pontifix?

THE BRIDGE BRIDE

'And once the babies arrive,' says Broom, wiping the tears from the blotchy face of her young mistress, 'that will make everything better. Having Clayslaps made all my hardships easier to bear – and you too, Candle, once I had you to look after. The Pontifix is a great man and you should be proud he chose you out of all the young women in Ilira.'

'But why? I'm not pretty. I'm nothing, not to him.' Tears spout once again from the girl's small dark eyes, splashing down the sides of her snub nose. 'You know why he's marrying me, Broom – because my father has ships and trade links. And he has enticed the Pontifix with all your ideas about sun- and waterpower. What would the Pontifix do if he found out my father steals *your* dreams and pretends they're all his own?'

'Even the dreams of a slave belong to her master,' Broom says drily, though she has told Candle often enough how her inventions began among the ruins of a netherworld, far across the ocean, long before she was an Iliran slave. 'The Pontifix won't care – as long as he gets what he wants. And don't you tell him, Candle. The young bride of such a powerful man must tread carefully.'

'I'm not a bride,' says the girl sullenly. She wipes her eyes and nose on the fur-trimmed sleeve of her wedding dress. 'I am a bridge between two men. My father and the Pontifix are marrying their businesses. It's their wedding, not mine.'

'You'll find your own power one day,' Broom tells her, patting the arrangement of shining coils she has styled out of Candle's heavy, straight hair. 'Just you wait.'

The girl's downcast face brightens at a scampering sound beyond the roughly hewn window in the mountain cave.

'There are worse things than this, believe me,' Broom tells the girl. 'You are not losing all the people you love. I'll still be with you, and Clay won't be far. You must make the best you can from the life you're landed with, Candle. It's the same for all of us. And no,' Broom casts a withering glance at her son who has just clambered in through the window, 'that doesn't mean *you* can go to sea. Slaves do not go to sea.'

Clay and Candle exchange grins as Broom takes a snow-goose feather and dips it into a scallop shell full of powdered pearls then dusts the girl's tear-stained face.

'But we're not slaves, Mother,' mocks Clay. '*We* are Treenesters – people of the wide world who ended up here by mistake.' He snatches the feather brush from his mother's hand and tickles her nose. 'Treenesters *do* go to sea – you did.'

Broom sneezes and grabs back the feather. 'And look how that ended up! Stop wasting the pearl-dust, Clay. It costs the Earth. Go and do something useful, you pest.'

'I just did.' Clay's teasing stops. 'I scavenged a girl.'

'A girl?' Candle's dark eyes narrow to slits. 'Where?'

'Out on the rocks. And a wolfman, almost, but he's dead.'

'Was there a wreck?' asks Candle excitedly. Ship and boat wrecks mean all kind of goodies. Not that she gets many, but she likes to hear about all the strange sea junk from Clay.

Footsteps echo through the winding mountain corridors and they fall silent, recognizing the heavy *clop* of metal-soled boots.

'Rodenglaw!' Broom hisses at her son.

Rodenglaw must not find a scavenger slave in his daughter's bedroom on the morning of her wedding. It doesn't take much for him to erupt. Clay may be like a brother to Candle, but to Rodenglaw he's just another slave.

Clay kisses Candle hard on the cheek, leaving the mark of his mouth on the pearl dust. 'Remember you are Candle. *Not* Tartoq. No one owns you – or me. *Ever*.'

Candle touches her tingling cheek. How will she bear it when she can't see Clay every day? He can't come clambering into a guarded palace the way he does the mountain home of an absent Sea Lord. The Pontifix rarely leaves his palace these days, not since his eyes grew so weak. There are no windows in the palace anyway.

How desolate Candle was when Clay was sent away to the harbour hovels to work for the scavenger Scuts. He was still a boy then, barely as tall as Broom. Now Clay is taller than most men in Ilira. Where Candle has the wind-planed cheeks, cave-dark eyes and sturdy body of her mountain people, Clay has his mother's gentle face and large eyes, but the strong body of his hunter father who went down with all the others in the shipwreck that Broom and her tiny son survived, years ago.

'Hide!' Candle tells him.

Clay jumps back out of the cave window as the door of the room bursts open and Sea Lord Rodenglaw stomps in.

'Father,' Candle murmurs, struggling not to flinch at his fierce eyes.

Fear annoys him. If she is going to act scared she may as

well have cause, he will say, adding that the mark of his hand can only add interest to such a plain face. But any boldness earns Candle an even harder blow. Candle has learned to grow an invisible shell and close herself up like a clam when her father is around.

'Wedding gift,' he tells her gruffly, pulling a bright red bundle from the fur-lined windwrap he has taken to wearing over his sea armour, in the style of the Pontifix. 'Belonged to your mother.'

Candle can't remember her father ever giving her a gift. There are never any on her birthday, a day of mourning for Rodenglaw.

On that day, fifteen Winter Darknesses ago, a fleet of gypsea pirates surged up the fjord and firebombed the city, ravaging Ilira's harbour of boats and ships. Rodenglaw's wife, heavily pregnant, was caught up in the sudden attack and so badly wounded in the firestorm that the baby had to be cut from her burned and blasted body.

The mother died, but the baby lived. Rodenglaw's small son perished too.

Broom was found that same day, washed up in the bay clinging to the lifebelt of her sunken ship with her own tiny child, and was taken by Rodenglaw as a slave to nurse his motherless baby. The unwanted scrap of life was named Tartoq, the Iliran word for the darkness the wailing baby seemed to embody for Rodenglaw now he had lost his fleet of boats, along with his beloved son and wife.

Broom and Clay became a mother and brother to Tartoq. But her new mother refused to call her by the bleak name given by her father. Instead Broom called her Candle, in memory of the old Treenester woman who had been like a mother to her because, she said, Candle's birth should be seen as a tiny bright miracle that happened on a dark day.

Her own story is almost as strange to Candle as Broom's tale of her shipwreck and slavery, after escaping the netherworld at the foot of a city of great towers.

Now Candle breaks into a delighted smile and clasps the red leather shoes her father has gifted her. It's the only heirloom of her mother the girl has ever owned.

'Look, Broom! They're beautiful.'

Broom's large, shocked eyes stare at the red shoes as if Candle holds a ghost in her hands.

Rodenglaw grips his daughter's shoulders and she stiffens as he turns her around so that he can appraise the black coils of hair, the weighty cloak made from the aged white fur of the last polar bear ever seen in Ilira, and the pearl-seeded silks underneath.

'What this dress cost me!' he says, his lips pressed thin in his weathered face. 'Siberian silk! This dress, the wedding dowry I gave to the Pontifix – I could have built a whole new ship for less!'

Rodenglaw takes a box from under his arm and hands it to his daughter. Candle is astonished. Another gift?

'From the Pontifix.'

Candle takes the dented metal box. Ancient writing is still visible on its rusted surface but Candle cannot read. She studies the faint image of the exotic delicacies that must be inside. Her mouth watering, she opens the box – and blinks as she pulls out a handful of what seem to be tiny, blazing suns.

It's a necklace made of a hundred amber gems.

Rodenglaw grunts in appreciation. The gems trickle through Candle's fingers and she sees that each amber droplet has a tiny dead insect trapped inside. Broom's quick hands are already draping the jewels around her neck and shoulders in a glittering cloak. Candle moves towards the window and each gem becomes a tiny sun-catcher. The girl spins around, delighted, in a dazzle of amber.

'I am not Tartoq any more,' she laughs, and her small, dark eyes sparkle. 'I am all light!'

Rodenglaw raises his arm so casually he might be going to caress the girl's face, but he brings his hand down on her with a blow that sends Candle sprawling against the rock wall. The amber necklace splashes up over her face and the red shoes fly from her hand.

'You will always be Tartoq,' Rodenglaw mutters darkly. 'The girl who was the death of her mother. You have no reason to be pleased with yourself.'

He stumbles over the red shoes and his face darkens. He kicks them away but a brief, strange flush of shame remains, as if the boots are a flash of reproach. If her mother were alive, Candle thinks for the thousandth time, rubbing her throbbing elbow, she would never let Rodenglaw be so brutal.

Scrambling outside the window makes Candle jump. Broom's face turns ashen.

'Lord of the Sea, she's just a stupid girl,' Broom murmurs hastily. 'Please don't bother with her. I'll see that everything is as you want it.'

She ushers Rodenglaw towards the door, just as Clay's head appears at the cave window behind him.

Rodenglaw stops by the door, pulling his furred windwrap around his burly body.

'I need your sunpower plans to be ready,' he tells Broom, 'as soon as the wedding is done. The Pontifix likes the idea.'

'Yes, Lord Rodenglaw,' gasps Broom, and almost shoves him out of the door as Clay clambers back over the window ledge, a dagger in his fist.

TODAY OF ALL DAYS

'I'll kill that brute!'

Clay strides across the room to the metal door that Rodenglaw has clanged shut. Broom gets there first and stands with her back against the cave door.

'Don't, Clay!' pleads Candle. 'Not on my wedding day.'

The echo of Rodenglaw's clopping feet recedes in the mountain corridor.

Clay throws down the dagger and helps Candle to her feet. The girl's eyes are dry but the rock wall has scraped her cheek and a trickle of blood runs like a scarlet tear towards her mouth. He stares at the necklace, at the tiny insect trapped in each amber gem, and remembers Lily Longhope's fire-flecked eyes.

'I'll get him another time,' grunts Clay. 'Like tomorrow.'

'How could he do this today of all days?' Broom's gentle face is flushed and furious as she dabs at Candle's cheek with seaweed balm. 'But this is the last you'll ever have to suffer him. The Pontifix is a good man. He must be. Look at what he's done for this city.'

The clang of a bell sounds deep in the bowels of the mountain, echoing through all the tunnels and caves.

Broom rushes to the window and looks down the mountainside to the bay. 'So many people! The whole of Ilira is coming out for you, Candle. And the sun too – see, it's chasing the clouds from your wedding day.'

Candle goes to the window and looks beyond the glistening bridges to the glass palace on an islet deep in the fjord. The morning sun blazes upon the palace that will be her home after today. What will it be like to live without the shelter of the mountain, in the blast of the sea and sun and the dark and the storms – with the Pontifix?

Broom gives Candle a tender shake. 'Your father won't dare mistreat you once you are the first lady of Ilira. No one will.'

Candle kicks off her embroidered sealskin boots.

'I will wear my mother's shoes,' she says, exerting the only power she has now.

Broom watches with a grim look as Candle tries to squash her feet in, and can't.

'I *will* wear them,' Candle insists.

'Clay, give me your knife,' says Broom with a sigh, and kneels to cut the leather upper of each shoe, almost to the toe, then stuffs Candle's feet in. They must still hurt but the look on Candle's face says that she'll wear them if it means breaking her toes.

Broom wipes her eyes and stands up, her hand shaking as she gives the knife back to Clay.

'These shoes were not your mother's,' she tells Candle. 'Candleriggs, the old Treenester I named you for, gave them to Mara. I could never forget them.' Broom stares down at the red shoes, distraught. 'But how could Rodenglaw own them?'

Clay and Candle exchange glances. They know all the

stories about Mara and the Treenesters of the netherworld and how emotional those old memories always make Broom.

'It's just a scavenge, Mum,' says Clay. 'Washed up on the shore – like us. They only look the same.'

'They were my *mother's*,' Candle insists, her face crumpling again.

Broom pulls herself together. 'Well, now they're yours. Ready?'

Candle shoots a last, nervous glance out of the window to the palace where she will meet her groom today, on her wedding day, for the first time. 'What should I call him?'

'Lord of the Sea Lords, Keeper of the Globe, Pontifix of the Bridges . . . take your pick.' Clay's voice is as dry as a bone.

'Can't I call him Tuck?'

'Just do what he says,' says Broom. 'At least, let him think you do.'

Clay's face has darkened again. He fumbles in his parka pocket, chewing his lip. Then pulls out the glowing crescent.

'Give this to your new husband.'

Red-faced, he pushes his wedding gift into Candle's hands – then thrusts his own hands back in his pockets before he changes his mind. But what else can he do for her? And Lily Longhope will have no use for it, not now, no matter what she says.

'It's a scavenge,' he tells her. 'Old world stuff that he likes. It might make him kind towards you. He'd *better* be.'

'What is it?' Candle's narrow eyes widen as the crescent begins to glow in her hands.

Clay shrugs. 'Dunno. But watch and see what the Pontifix does with it.'

'Mara's halo!' Broom clutches at her heart. 'From the

magic wizz. First the shoes, now this. Today of all days. What's happening? Where did you find it, Clay?'

'The girl had them.' Clay shoots his mother a troubled glance. The girl, he remembers, called it a halo too.

'Girl?' Broom demands. 'What girl?'

With trembling fingers she reaches out and touches the halo as if it's a sacred relic.

'The girl I scavenged from the rocks. I *told* you.' Clay's mind is buzzing again, as he remembers Lily's words. 'Mum, the Pontifix's globe . . .'

Another clang of the mountain bell drowns out his words. The march of feet resounds in the rock tunnels: the Pontifix's guards coming to collect his bride. Candle slips the halo into her goose-feather bridal bag before he can say any more. There is panic in her eyes. Clay hugs his almost-sister, feeling wretched because there is nothing that he, a powerless slave, can do to save Candle from a marriage she never wanted and cannot escape. At least his mother will be with her, as her palace slave.

Broom gathers herself together and raises Candle's chin with her workworn hand. 'Hold your head up and remember – now you are the most important woman in Ilira.'

Candle bites her lip and nods, then walks to the door where the Pontifix's guards wait to escort her to her new life.

Clay faces his mother as the stomp of marching feet recedes.

'No, I haven't lost my mind,' Broom whispers, as if the rock walls might have ears. 'Those red shoes *were* Mara's and that halo . . .' She shakes her head and gives her son a wobbly smile. 'Oh, I suppose you're right, Clay. Mara couldn't have the only red shoes and globe and halo in the world.'

But Clay's heart has quickened. 'It's strange though. Lily said—'

'Lily?'

'My scavenge. Mum, it's weird but she called me Clayslaps. No one else ever has, only you. How could a stranger know my Treenester name?' His buzzing thoughts are propelling him towards an answer that surely cannot be. 'She comes from the forest of Candlewood in the mountains and her name is Lily Longhope.'

Mother and son stare at each other with wide, wondering eyes.

'*Lily. Longhope.*' Broom savours each name. No longer upset, she is fiercely concentrated now. 'From Candlewood, you say? In the mountains? Is it possible?' she asks herself, fastening a long windwrap around her. 'There's a wedding gondola waiting to take me to the palace but – but . . . quick, Clay, take me to this Lily Longhope. I *must* see her first.'

SCUTS AND SKY FLEETS

The citizens of Ilira are pouring out of their mountain caves. It's easy for Broom and Clay to slip through the crowds that cram the rockways to see the procession of the Pontifix's bride. No one questions the trusted slave of Rodenglaw, rushing towards the harbour after her young mistress. But Clay is supposed to be sorting through piles of scavenge for tomorrow's market. He pulls up his parka hood, keeps his face down.

Mother and son rush under the pelting waterfalls, down past the rusted doors of the mountain dwellers and the labyrinth of market caverns where the air is thick with the smell of dried fish and seal meat, across the steep tracks of the cable trains, past the entrances to the factories of the deep mines.

As they reach the foot of the mountain, Candle is stepping on to her wedding gondola.

'Let me catch my breath,' Broom gasps, stopping to drink in the spectacle of the bridal gondola and the crowds. 'Look, Clay. The people love her, she's one of their own. How can her father not?'

Clay lifts his head to risk a quick glance. There's no sign

of a Scut. All eyes are on the wedding – then suddenly they are not. The cheering dies. People lift their faces to look at the sky. Clay expects a celebration kite but sees instead a silver fleet of vessels moving northward, straight and fast. That is not, Clay judges, the sinuous movement of birds.

But what is the strange silver flock?

Panic rumbles in the crowd. Then the fleet disappears over the peaks of the mountains.

Clay tears his eyes from the sky. No time to wonder right now. He hurries his mother on, pulling her into Ale Alley, a worming rockway punctured with stinking caverns. It's always crammed with revellers gulping down bitter seaweed ale. Today, there's even more of a crush. Broom screws up her face at the stale reek and steps over frothy ale puddles, trying to squeeze past a man so large and solid he might be a boulder. Clay's heart sinks to his boots as he sees it's Pavord, a particularly brutal Scutmaster, and his even more vicious wife.

'Hurry, boy!' Broom shouts at Clay, spotting the danger. 'A gondola is waiting for us and Rodenglaw is not a patient man. That barrel of smoked oysters should be at the palace already – I want to see it loaded up now!'

She throws a hurried, imperious smile at the Scut and he rolls aside. His wife gives Clay a thuggish kick in the shin as he hurries past.

Clay limps through the winding alley until they reach the warren of harbour caves.

'Brute of a woman!' Broom bursts out, once they're safely sheltered by a crop of rocks.

'Used to it,' says Clay, through gritted teeth. 'Right, keep a lookout and put your scary face on if anyone comes.'

He unbolts the metal door of the cave where he left the scavenged girl.

116

LOST FATHERS, LOST GIRLS

The girl's head droops on her chest like a wilted flower. She looks fast asleep but the moment Clay leans over her she becomes a wild, spiky creature – shrieking, snapping at him with her teeth, thrashing about until her hair is in his eyes and mouth. Clay grabs a thick handful of it and yanks the girl's head back.

'Bite me again,' he warns, 'and I'll leave you here for Kronk.'

'Won't bite,' she whispers, her fiery eyes full of fear.

'Lily?' says Broom. 'Lily Longhope?'

She brings the oil lantern over to peer at the scavenged girl and gasps, almost dropping the lamp, looking just as she did when she saw the red shoes – as if she's seen a ghost.

'Mara,' she whispers, and sinks to her knees in shock.

'I'm *Lily*,' says the girl, hoarsely. She blinks in the light. 'You know my mother?'

Broom brings the lantern closer to the girl's face.

'Mara's name was Longhope. Her hair was dark as midnight, yours is sunset,' says Broom. 'Her eyes were dark too where yours are fire. But you are hers all right.'

Lily studies the older woman, her amber-brown eyes

brilliant and curious in the lantern glow.

'Are – are you Broomielaw?' she croaks.

'I am Broomielaw the Treenester and this is Clayslaps my son,' cries Broom, her eyes full. 'Quick, untie her, Clay.'

Clay takes his dagger from his belt and cuts through the ropes he bound around the girl. Freed, Lily clambers to her feet, rubbing her arms. She turns to Clay and he steps back.

'No biting!'

'Pollock!' the girl exclaims. 'That's who you look like! Our hunter, Pollock.'

Broom's hands fly to her mouth.

'I wasn't sure at first,' Lily continues, her eyes flicking from one to the other. 'I couldn't see how. But I've been sitting here in the dark, working it all out, hoping and hoping you'd come back.' Her eyes settle on Clay's astonished face and her dirty, tear-streaked one breaks into a tentative smile.

All Clay can do is absorb Lily Longhope and her words. The strange thrill inside redoubles and more. His father is alive? And this fiery girl is one of his own people?

'Everyone thinks you both drowned when the *Arkiel* sunk,' says Lily. 'Another story that's wrong,' she adds.

'They are alive?' Broom asks incredulously. 'Mara and Pollock?' She pauses. 'Gorbals? And they live in the mountains?'

Lily nods at each question and Broom grasps the girl in a great hug, as if she embodies all the beloved friends she thought she'd lost. Then as Lily lists the names of everyone in Candlewood, Broom's soft eyes spill long-held tears.

'I thought *they* all drowned when our ship sank,' Broom explains. 'I thought we were the only ones who survived.'

'Some died,' Lily adds gently. 'But more have been born.'

'Who has been born?' asks Broom. The look on her face tells Lily that she can't yet bear to hear who died.

'Lots,' Lily smiles. 'Mol called her girl after you. I've got pests round my ankles all day.' The words catch in her throat as she realizes she'd love to have those little pests climbing over her, pulling her hair and squabbling right now.

'Mum,' Clay interrupts, 'there isn't time for this. We need to get out of here before a Scut comes.'

'Yes. And I need to be with my people again,' says Broom, her eyes yearning. 'You'll take us to Candlewood, Lily, won't you?'

Clay shifts from one foot to another. 'Us?'

'It's where we belong.' Broom is decided. 'It's where your father is, Clay.'

Lily hesitates. 'But – but I need your help first.'

'Of course we'll help you. You're one of us.' Broom frowns. 'But why *are* you here, Lily, all by yourself?'

'I came with Wing, but he – *he*,' Lily stabs a finger towards Clay, her eyes filling, face darkening, '*killed* him.'

Broom turns to her son, aghast. 'You killed *Wing*?'

'Not me,' Clay panics. 'Vollony. He killed a two-headed wolfman, with a wolf's head growing next to his own.'

'It was only Wing in his wolfskin coat!' Lily cries. She turns to Broom. 'Mum lied. They *all* lied to me. I thought Rowan was my dad, but he's not. It's someone called Fox in a city across the ocean. And I'm going to find him,' she finishes.

Broom's eyes grow soft. 'Now who does this hotheaded girl remind me of? Lily, Mara left the sky city so that she could save all of us. It was terrible for her because she'd found Fox after losing almost everyone else she loved. But she wouldn't desert us when we needed her most.'

'But she *lied*,' Lily persists. 'All my life she lied. She could have told me the truth. The least you can do for somebody is tell them who they are.'

Broom pulls the girl towards her.

'So you've run away and Mara doesn't know where you are? She'll be out of her mind!'

'And I've lost Wing.' Grief makes Lily shudder from head to toe.

Broom shoots an anguished glance at Clay. 'Mara loved that rat-child.'

'No one likes me being with him because he's wild. Not even Mum. Well, he's gone now.' Lily's lips tremble but she shakes her head stubbornly. 'I won't go back until I find my Fox father. Or else Wing died for nothing.'

'Fox is an ocean away,' Broom says gently. 'Mara should have told you, of course she should, but she was so young, like you, and she'd been through so much.'

'I know,' says Lily quietly.

'How can *we* help you find your father? Right now,' Broom remembers, flustered, 'I'm supposed to be at the palace.'

'Thought you were just about to run off to Candlewood?' Clay reminds her. He's been sitting on a pile of nets, frowning.

'I can't abandon Candle without a goodbye,' Broom retorts uneasily. 'Not just yet.'

'Candle won't let you go, Mum,' says Clay. 'Think about it. You're her *slave*. She'll be lost without you, especially now. If you really want to go, you have to just *go* – now.'

Broom shakes damp sand fretfully from the hem of her windwrap. 'I can't just go. Candle's like a daughter to me. We'll steal her away with us – she doesn't want to be married to the Pontifix. She's scared. Oh, I don't know.' She wrings

120

her hands together. 'I need to think!'

'The globe,' Lily reminds them. She glares at Clay. 'I want my halo back. All I need to do is get the globe from Tuck Culpy, then I can use the cyberwizz to find my father.'

'The Pontifix,' Broom is bewildered, 'has Mara's globe? But—'

'Mother!' Clay bursts out. 'If I'm caught in here by a Scut I'll get my hands chopped off – that's if I'm lucky. There's no time to tell everything. We need to get out of here, *fast*.'

And best he doesn't tell Lily what he's done with her precious halo, thinks Clay; not just yet anyway.

'I'll take you to Candlewood,' Lily bargains, 'if you help me. You'll never find your way through the mountains without me. Help me find my father,' Lily's pleading eyes meet Clay's, 'and I'll take you to yours. Deal?'

'Maybe,' says Clay, feeling odd.

The idea that Pollock the Hunter, the father he always thought was dead, is living on the other side of the mountains is a thought too strange for him to deal with right away. The excitement he feels now is to do with Lily, not for the father he was too tiny to remember. And how can he make a deal to leave Ilira for a new life in the mountains when his dream is to become a seafarer and explore the world?

He jumps at the scuffle of boots outside. The metal door rattles as someone starts to pull it open.

Clay draws out his dagger; Broom slaps his hand down.

'I'll sort this,' she says.

'He carries a *gun*!' Clay hisses at her, but his mother is already at the cave door.

He and Lily hold their breaths as Broom stalls the Scut.

'Listen to her!' Clay makes a retching sound. 'He stinks like a festering fish and she's—'

'Shh!' Lily puts her hand over his mouth.

'I'll take the girl as a kitchen slave for the palace – Clay knew I was looking for one – and the Pontifix won't forget your kindness,' Broom is saying, in a voice like warmed oil. 'I will see to that.'

'This wedding's already cost me a day's trade,' growls the Scut, but there's a sly smile in his voice.

'Well worth it,' coaxes Broom, 'if you end up on good terms with a man like Tuck Culpy.'

The cave door gives a rusty squeal. There's a rough laugh and some scuffling. Clay reaches for his dagger again but before he can act Broom bursts back through the door, looking flustered.

'Quick,' she gasps.

'What're we doing, Mum? Huh? Did you *kiss* fish-breath out there?' Clay makes the vomiting noise again.

'Never mind that,' snaps Broom. 'Just do as you're told.'

THE LIGHT OF ILIRA

Candle's wedding day spins around her in a dazzle.

The Pontifix's guards escorted her down the mountain under the new spring sun as the whirling songs of the windpipers rang out from the cavernous market halls of the mountain. The steep rockways were crammed with cheering citizens, their faces lit with smiles as she passed by. And lit up by *her*, Candle saw, as the necklace caught the weak sunbeams and burned them into fiery sparkles that made the eyes of other girls narrow with envy as her wedding procession swept past.

Now Candle steps into the steam gondola that waits in the harbour. The boat is decorated with bright billowing silks from distant Siberian ports. She takes her place in the cushioned seat across from her father who sits bolt upright, looking pained. He is furious, Candle notes with pleasure, that such a fuss is being made over her.

She bursts out laughing. The gondola's small funnel is behind Rodenglaw and it seems as though he's hissing steam from the top of his head. Her father glares at her as a long ribbon of silk slaps across his face. Candle giggles again. After all, what can he do to her now?

The crowd falls quiet. Candle stifles her laughter and looks around to see why, wondering at all the faces suddenly turned towards the sky. Steam from the gondola clouds her view but she senses the ripple of panic in the crowds. Her father frowns, glancing upward, and orders the gondolier to set off.

Candle forgets the strange panic as the wedding gondola *puff-puffs* towards the glass palace on the rocky islet deep in the great fjord. Her old, ordinary self has been left behind in her father's caves. The wedding has magicked her into someone new.

Light of Ilira! the people shout from the bridges, waving at the colourful spectacle of the gondola and its bride. Candle's brilliant necklace surrounds her with an aura of longed-for sunlight after the long darkness of winter. In that moment the girl has a fleeting sense of what Ilira wants from her as the Pontifix's bride, what she could *be* in her new life . . . some bright lodestar for her people that might bring Candle her own power in the world.

The gondola rounds an islet so cragged its rocks look as if they've been uprooted violently from an unwilling Earth. The graceful masts of the *Great Skua*, the Pontifix's ship, loom in front. Panic fills Candle as the gondola slides into the roughest of harbours and she sees the tall figure of the Pontifix with the vivid silks of his windwrap gusting around him – the man who rules Ilira and who will now rule her young life.

THE MAGIC GLOBE

The ceremony is a short, cold shock of words that fly over Candle's head.

She stands on the landing rock of the harbour, clutching her polar-bear cloak around her, swallowing angry tears. She had expected a grand wedding in the palace in front of the important families of Ilira. Why be dressed up in furs and gems for a trade deal between two men on a wind-blasted rock?

Her send-off from Ilira was only a spectacle for the people. Even the painted shaman – whose body charms of bones, walrus teeth and seashells make him rattle in the wind – chants the marriage spell as fast as he can then blows a blessing of air, ash, seawater, rain and earth over them, looking mightily bored.

Now Rodenglaw pushes her towards the tall man with sunlit hair. The light is behind him and Candle can't see his face. He leans forward and gives her a cold kiss on the cheek. Candle feels numb. Is that it? Is it done? Is she married now?

The shaman is already striding up the rocky steps to the palace. She must be.

'There was a fleet in the sky, Pontifix – did you see?' blurts her father. As soon as he has spoken Rodenglaw looks as if he'd like to bite off his own tongue. The Pontifix is said to be proud and unpredictable. Drawing attention to the weakness of his eyes is rash. 'I – I mean, your lookouts, did they spy them? Maybe you saw through your eyebox . . .'

Rodenglaw glances nervously at the slim silver box that hangs on a chain from the Pontifix's belt and helps him see the world. The old seafarers say people once captured pictures of the world in such boxes, though Candle can't imagine how.

'Not the first fleets we've seen,' her new husband cuts in, his voice as cold as his kiss.

'Ah,' nods Rodenglaw. 'But these planes – where do they go?'

'Ships,' the Pontifix corrects him. 'Sky ships. Planes have wings, like birds. These look like whales in the sky. They fly northward from the South.'

His demeanour is calm but Candle senses he is deeply rattled, as is Rodenglaw, by these alien presences in their skies.

She looks towards the chink of open sea. Beyond the last bend of the fjord are the armed ships that guard Ilira. Unarmed boats from other ports are given safe passage once they've been searched by the Pontifix's guards. Armed ships are made to surrender or are wrecked by lethal rocks and man-made traps in the sea. The Pontifix is revered for his power to keep their fjord safe from the pirates the city so greatly fears but even he, thinks Candle, cannot rule Ilira's skies as he does its seas.

Rodenglaw gives a gruff goodbye, anxious to leave now that he's traded his daughter, insulted the Pontifix's one weakness and shown his ignorance over sky ships. A father should surely embrace his newly married daughter at such a moment, thinks Candle, but Rodenglaw is already in the gondola. Yet as it puffs away he glances over his shoulder and the strange, shamed expression Candle saw after his earlier brutality flits across his weathered face. She raises a hand, expecting nothing in return for her bare little wave. But slowly her father lifts his own hand and dips his head in the slightest of bows. Candle could not have been more amazed if he'd blown her a kiss.

Rodenglaw's gondola disappears behind a ridge of rock, leaving a ghostly drift of steam.

The tall man beside her speaks and she jumps. *What did he say?* The wind has snatched his words away.

Her stomach feels like a basketful of needles as she follows her new husband up the rocky pathway to his palace. Candle panics as she realizes she can't see the city from here. The fat rump of Bear Mountain blocks it out. The doorway of her new home faces away from Ilira, towards the open sea.

The glass palace seems to sizzle. Steam rises from its domed roof. Sunlight sparkles on curving, mottled walls made of cemented fragments of bottle glass. It's said that a million broken bottles were scavenged from seabed and shore to build the Pontifix's dream. Candle shades her eyes against the glare to snatch glances at her new husband.

His long hair is the colour of a winter moon and his beard barely frosts his face. The crinkles around his eyes are not caused by age, Candle realizes with huge relief, because he's not old at all. It's because he peers at the world with piercing eyes that don't, she thinks, look weak to her.

Until now, Tuck Culpy has been a godlike presence on a bridge or sailing the fjord in a gondola, his hair and bright windwrap streaming in the wind. No ordinary man could create wonders like a palace made of glass and such majestic

127

bridges, or could scare away the marauding pirates that ransack the rest of the North.

Candle feels dazed. Is it really possible that she is married to this man?

The silks of his windwrap ripple around him as he walks, the colours as vivid as the aurora storm Candle watched cascade across the sky last night, too nervous to sleep. She limps to keep up, feet blistered by the red shoes, as he leads her into the palace through a whalebone arch. Once inside, the Pontifix stumbles slightly, his movements suddenly uncertain as if his natural element is under the wide sky riven by the wind.

A guard leads the way through a maze of corridors. Now Candle sees why the palace seems to sizzle. Hot geysers hiss within alcoves of rock. Like steamy fireplaces, they warm the air. The mottled walls fill the palace with a dappled, watery light. Mysterious objects – sea scavenges, she guesses – are shelved in the glass.

When they reach what must be the heart of the palace, the Pontifix gestures for her to enter a curtained doorway. Through the sealskin curtain is a large, round room with a wide stone table in the centre. More sea junk clutters the rocks that are scattered like small tables across the fur-carpeted floor. A geyser gurgles lazily at the far end of the room. A rack of cutlasses hang on the wall, the curving blades like the talons of a giant bird.

'Tartoq.'

She jumps. Only her father calls her Tartoq, if he calls her anything at all.

'Don't be scared,' says the Pontifix. 'Sit down.'

Candle looks around and sees she must sit beside him on a huge bed of furs. He blinks as she moves and her necklace

128

catches the light. How much can he see? His eyes seem to follow the bright glitter of the necklace. Maybe that's why she was to wear it, so that he knows where she is.

'You have your own room and your slave,' he says in the kindly voice of an adult to a child. 'Everything you need. It *is* Tartoq, eh?'

He's not even sure of her name. Candle hesitates. Broom has urged her to be careful, but also to begin as a human being.

'My *own* name is Candle,' she says. 'I have a wedding gift for you.'

She takes the crescent-shaped halo from the goose-feather bag. The Pontifix frowns as she places it in his hand.

'My eye,' he mutters, lifting the small silver box that hangs from his belt. A snout shoots out as the Pontifix puts the box to his eyes. He seems to use the silver snout to see, like an eye on a stalk, pointing it at the gift as he peers through the box.

'*Urth*,' he exclaims. 'Where did you get this?'

'I – I found it.'

She hopes he can't hear the lie in her voice. Slaves are not supposed to keep scavenges so she can't risk saying it was Clay.

'You *found* it? Where?'

Candle casts around for an answer she should have prepared. Gulls shriek and she sees a flock of fluttering shadows in the spangled dome above her head.

'A bird,' she lies again. 'An eagle! It flew into my cave and dropped it.'

'An eagle?' The Pontifix weighs the halo in his hand like a marketeer on the bridges with a handful of pearls.

'A golden eagle from the mountains. They steal things.'

129

Candle dares a question. 'Do you know what it is?'

But the Pontifix has forgotten her. He strides to the stone table in the centre of the room and opens up a jewelled casket. A gasp escapes Candle as he takes out something that looks like a small moon. The moon-like object begins to glow in his hand.

The globe! It must be.

People say he sees visions in his magic globe. Tuck Culpy arrived one day out of nowhere, it's said, with the magic globe in his hands. He was the Pontifix, he claimed, and his globe held visions of the future. He would build magnificent bridges and fleets of ships and make the pirate-ravaged bay strong again.

In the time it took Candle to grow from a squalling baby to a young woman, Tuck Culpy had stirred up the people of Ilira to transform their bleak, frightened city into a hub of trade and industry, famed all over the North.

Open-mouthed, Candle watches as colours swirl around the globe like a tiny aurora storm.

The Pontifix holds the globe in one hand, the halo in his other. He presses the globe with his thumb and a finger. It opens up, as if an invisible knife has sliced it down the middle into two smooth round halves.

'Take her away,' he orders, and a guard appears.

Candle dares not argue. Prickling with hurt at his curt dismissal, she is also relieved that her ordeal with her strange new husband is over, at least for today. She follows the guard through the palace where the scavenged mysteries shelved in the walls remind her of the insects trapped forever in her amber necklace.

All imprisoned in glass, she thinks. *Just like me.*

THE EAGLE, THE SLAVE
AND THE STORYBOX

Darkness drizzles through the palace walls. From her bed, Candle watches miserably as a hundred shades of evening drown the last lights of day.

A slave arrives with food. Feigning sleep, Candle watches through half-closed eyes as the woman rolls down the sealskin wall blinds, shutting out the dark and the cold. Heat builds in the room now from the gurgling steam geyser in the alcove.

The aroma of smoked seafood turns her stomach though she *should* be hungry, she's barely eaten all day.

'Go away,' she mutters, and pulls the bear-fur quilt over her head.

'Suit yourself,' says the slave.

'Broom!' Candle flings off the quilt and rushes over to bury herself in the familiar hug of her beloved slave. 'Where have you been? He's horrible. I hate him. I can't stay here forever!'

There's a strange, excited light in Broom's eyes. Years seem to have dropped from the slave's soft face.

Broom pulls her close and whispers in her ear. 'Candle, what if you could escape from this place?'

'Escape? On a ship? With Clay?'

'Shh!'

Broom nods towards the doorway where there must be a palace guard. She begins tidying Candle, tucking away unruly strands of hair and fixing her face, her voice as dry as the pearl dust she dabs on to the girl's blotchy face, but Candle hears Broom's quickened breath and wonders at her glowing cheeks.

'The Pontifix has *much* more important things on his mind than some silly girl he just married,' Broom says loudly, for the benefit of the guard outside. 'Eat up your supper!' Then in a murmur: 'We'll speak later.'

Candle imagines a lifetime of unhappiness in this palace. Can Broom help her escape? But how? Her imagination spins and Candle pulls the plate of smoked seafood towards her, suddenly hungry, and begins stuffing delicacies into her mouth.

'I saw the globe,' she whispers, through a mouthful of seafood. 'But he sent me away.'

'Well, he wants to see you again now you're fed,' says Broom, as Candle clears her plate.

The seafood churns in Candle's stomach as if the creatures have slithered back to life. Broom pulls her to her feet.

'Be brave,' she tells the girl, and gently pushes her to the curtained doorway, but Broom's words and her strange excitement have given Candle heart.

She follows the waiting guard back through the palace. In his room her new husband lounges on a bed of furs. Candle empties herself of all feeling, as she has learned to do many times. Nothing and no one can be worse than her father's brutal temper, she tells herself.

The Pontifix looks up as she creeps into the room. His hearing, Candle notes, is sharp as a bird's.

132

'Your gift was a shock,' he says bluntly.

Candle wonders what to say. 'Sorry,' she murmurs.

He gets up from the bed and makes his way to the wide stone table in the centre of the room, motioning her to follow.

'But the best of gifts!' He breaks into a smile and Candle loses some of her nervousness as the face of her peculiar new husband is suddenly young, bright and handsome.

'Do I,' she dares, 'call you Pontifix? Or can I call you Tuck?'

There is a pause, then he smiles again.

'Tuck's my name.'

If you call something by its real name, Broom always says, you draw the fear from it.

'Tuck,' she says firmly.

Amusement flickers in his eyes and once again Candle feels unnerved at not knowing how much he can see. He is far from blind, she has decided, but without his silver eyebox he would be lost.

Now Tuck takes another silver box, squat and bashed, from a rock shelf and sets it on the table. This one is bigger than his eyebox, with a face full of buttons and a stem sticking from its top.

'All this strangeness will pass,' he tells Candle, and she hears the lilt of the ocean in his voice. 'I found a new life here when I was young.' He pauses. 'No one will harm you now – not unless you deserve it.'

Candle absorbs the warning.

'You are kind,' she murmurs. And maybe he is, she hopes.

'The wedding gift you brought me,' he sits down beside her, 'is a treasure I've searched for all across the Arctic ports. I picked a good wife.' He smiles again and taps the box. 'So this is a gift for you.'

133

'What is it?' asks Candle, watching him pull on the box's stem until it's almost as long as his arm.

'A storybox.' Tuck begins to wind a small handle on the side of the box. 'One of my Sea Lords found it in a new port on the north-west coast.'

His fingers fiddle with the buttons on the box. He twitches the long stem. Candle jumps with fright as the buzz of angry insects bursts out. Tuck seems unworried and carries on tending to the buttons and stem, listening closely, waiting patiently until a voice, so crackly and buzzy it might be a giant honey bee, cuts through the noisy swarm.

'This is the Midnight Storyteller,' says the voice in the box.

Candle has gripped Tuck's arm in fright. She draws back.

'The storyteller,' she gasps, 'is trapped in the box?'

'His voice sails in on the winds,' says Tuck, 'and then harbours in the storybox.'

'I send this story out to you,' continues the voice, 'wherever you are in the world. In all the forgotten corners of the Earth and its oceans . . .'

'Where is he?' Candle whispers. 'Who is he?'

Tuck's brow furrows. He hates not knowing things, Candle sees, yet he has surrounded himself with a palace full of mysteries.

'He tells tales to the world,' says Tuck. 'That's all I know.'

'Over the years I've read you all so many stories from the books of the drowned world. My next is the most extraordinary of all. It's a tale of the sea-broken people,' says the storyteller, and Candle hears a tremble in his voice. 'A story called *Exodus*. And it begins with *The Old Woman Who Lived in a Tree* . . .'

'I know that one!' Candle exclaims.

She sinks into the deep pile of furs and feels all the tension of this strange day easing from her as she listens to the heart-rending tale.

Now the voice is so clear and strong that the storyteller might be right there in the room. Husky and warm, his voice wraps around her and she sinks into the story of the old woman who was thrown out of a tower in the sky to live in a tree in a flooded world. There is a crackly pause at the end of the tale. The sound of a hissing sea seeps from the storybox.

'Tomorrow night,' says the storyteller, 'in the next part of the tale, I'll tell how the old woman in the tree meets a girl from a drowned island.'

'Mara!' says Candle. 'That's when she finds the Treenesters in the netherworld.'

Candle is suddenly wide awake, her small eyes almost as round as the buttons on the storybox. *The storyteller knows about Mara?*

The storybox is silenced with a click.

'*Mara?*'

Tuck's voice is incredulous. The look on his face makes Candle want to run.

'How do *you*,' he demands, 'know about *Mara*?'

'I – I don't remember.' The back of Candle's neck feels icy even though the room is snug.

Tuck pulls her upright on the bed. 'I want you to remember.'

'My old slave,' says Candle, slowly, so that she can think fast. 'She told me lots of stories. She – she once came across the oceans on a ship with a girl called Mara. But – but that slave died years ago,' she adds hastily.

'Not the slave you brought with you?' he asks, all suspicion now.

'Oh no.' Candle is adamant. 'Broom was old, like the woman in the tree. She's long dead.'

135

Candle has no idea what is wrong, what the truth might mean for Broom with such an unpredictable man. It's safer to lie. Too late, she realizes she should have used another name, just in case, but a great man like the Pontifix will surely not seek out a lowly slave?

Tuck has cocked his head to the side, listening hard. She meets his cold blue stare with her arrow-sharp one.

'But how do *you* know about Mara?' she asks.

What can Broom's Mara mean to Tuck?

He seems overwhelmed by some memory or emotion. A chink appears in the aura he wears like an invisible windwrap. Candle peers through the chink and glimpses a man much younger and less certain of the world than he pretends to be. He is as unnerved by the mention of Mara as if he were standing on one of his great bridges and spied a lethal crack at his feet.

'And you said an *eagle* brought you the halo?' Tuck persists. 'Not this slave of yours? The one you say is dead?'

Candle recalls Broom's strange insistence earlier that the halo Clay scavenged was Mara's. Is that what Tuck thinks? Candle cannot work it all out but she feels the danger in the air. She must deflect Tuck somehow.

'It's all just as I told you!' she says, pretending to be piqued at his doubt. 'But never mind that. *This* is a much more curious mystery!'

She dares to pick up the storybox and peers into the regiment of tiny holes that perforate its silver front, half expecting to see a pair of eyes winking back at her. There is only darkness inside. She clicks the button and the storyteller has gone. All she hears is a storm of empty noise.

'The Midnight Storyteller,' urges Candle. 'Who is he? How does *he* know Mara's tale?'

OLD ZENITH

All day the sun beat down like a hammer. The sky tunnels hummed in the bludgeoning heat.

Even now, as the red gong of the sun falls behind the city wall, the heat-hum hangs in the steamy dusk. Fox leans out of the window of the old steepled tower, desperate for a breath of air, but there's none. The whooping coils that farm the winds high up on the sky towers are as stunned and still as the swamp dragons on the mudbanks below.

Fox slumps down on the cool stone floor and turns a dial on the old Zenith radio. A sudden whine and crackle fill the room, as if a star just zipped through the window. Pandora sits bolt upright in a rattle of jewels. Fox fiddles with the dials, searching the soundwaves, ear pressed to the carved mahogany box as if listening for the *click* that will unlock a safe full of gold. All he hears is a fuzz of white noise.

Old Zenith changed everything.

Fox almost smashed it up for firewood when he found it in a corner of the museum. But something stalled his axe. He scraped off layers of dirt then scrubbed with his sleeve until a patch of dark wood appeared, shiny as a new nut.

Beneath a century of grime Fox found a beautifully carved

cabinet with the legend **ZENITH RADIO** set like a spiky jag of lightning on the front.

Next to old Zenith, a bronze plaque on the museum wall listed all kinds of *Revolutionary Inventions*: telephones, cars, bicycles, photography, flushing toilets, electric light, steam-powered ships and trains, sewing machines, ice cream and Jelly Babies and many more mysteries – including radio.

Fox didn't know what any of it was. He'd lived the first seventeen years of his life in the sky empire where the outside world was hidden behind a great wall and history was locked in the past. He'd only ever snatched bewildering glimpses of life before the floods in the virtual news sites of the abandoned network of the Weave.

After finding old Zenith, he ransacked the university bookstacks. There, among the mouldy pages, Fox solved the mystery of the radio. He read about the era of discovery that changed human life on the planet forever and underpinned everything that happened afterwards – from the industries that revolutionized millions of lives to the towering New World sky cities built to withstand the floods that devastated the polluted planet.

Fox couldn't believe he'd grown up swamped in the techno-wizardry of the sky cities yet knew nothing about the soundwaves that once connected people all across the Earth – a whole century before the old computer network of the Weave and two hundred years before the vast cyber-universe of the Noos.

Radio waves.

Invisible and forgotten.

Tides of electromagnetic currents surging around the planet.

The soundwaves cross gulfs of storm and silence to the

survivors of the world's floods, and buzz once again with the voices of the planet's forgotten people. All of it unheard by the sky empire in its towers. The resurgence of radio has enabled Fox to reach out to the abandoned flood refugees of the Earth. He has stoked them up with stories that set alight their hopes and dreams, fired up a revolution to rescue them from wretched existences and amassed a global battle to win them new futures upon the remaining lands of the world – the precious high lands the sky empire wants to claim for itself.

Savaged by storms on a devastated Earth, the survivors of the great floods once had no way of knowing what land or who else might be left in the world – the global soundwave connection has changed all that.

Fox never forgot what Mara told him about her island in the Atlantic. *We thought we were alone in the world*, she said. *All the old communication systems were dead. We didn't know what existed on the rest of the Earth. I couldn't believe it when I found you and you told me about the sky cities . . .*

Fox was just as amazed. He'd grown up in New Mungo believing there was no land left in the world. That lie has been amended now that young empire builders are needed for the conquest of the Northlands and other fertile high lands in the east and the south of the world. But still the Guardians maintain the greatest lie of all:

We are the only ones. There is no one else in the world outside. All there is in the world belongs to us.

But as the sky fleets head North and the young empire builders see otherwise, that lie will surely unravel too. Or will they, as the Guardians of the empire must believe, be so consumed with the ambitions of their masters that the reality of the world will not matter to them?

If he had never discovered Mara, what would he, Fox wonders, be now? One of those empire builders headed North?

The lost girl from the drowned island touched his heart and became part of him, part of the man he is now – because everything changed for him, everything he was and everything he thought he knew, when he heard her desperate story and he discovered the brutal truth about the flooded world and its refugees. His home would still be a sky city and the bright, questing spirit of his youth would have dulled and hardened over the years until he was no longer Fox, but David Stone, doubtless in league now with Mungo, his father, carrying on the work of Caledon's dynasty; a vital cog in the machine of the empire, blocking his mind to the lies about the world . . .

If he'd never known Mara, is that what he would have become?

Is she still alive? Over fifteen years have passed since their connection died, yet Fox still hoards the hope that somehow, somewhere, in the home of the North Wind, she survived and gave birth to their child. A child who would be the same age now as Mara was when he knew her. Even if he survived the coming war and got himself there, how could he ever find them in that vast land mass of the North?

Too much time has passed anyway. She never came back to the Weave so either she is dead or she has broken with the past to make a new life. No, the best he can do for Mara and his child, if they are alive in the North, is fight to keep that land free from the empire's grasp. And if he must lose his life to keep theirs safe and free, so be it.

The radio crackles. A voice rises above the hissing soundwaves. Fox grabs the earphones and turns the dial but the voice drowns in an ocean of white noise.

It's the heat. Messages zip across the planet on cool nights. Heat makes them sluggish and weak.

A drop of sweat plops on to the radio's polished wood. Fox wipes his face. The timing couldn't be worse. Clogged-up communications is the last thing he needs at this crucial moment of the Surge. The solar winds of the night should clear the way for radio waves – but they also stir up the aurora storms. The vivid cascades of charged energy that stun the Northern skies at this time of year can wreck the radio signals too.

Fox snuffs out the image of a young woman with hair the colour of winter's midnight under a skyscape of brilliant aurora lights.

'Time!' Pandora jumps up from the bed of shredded books and grubby dresses that spills across the tower room and pins the tiny godbox to his collar, kisses his brow before she affixes his mindgem there, then pushes her lucky jade frog into his palm. 'For good luck.' Her voice thrills in his ear. 'For our future.'

The golden hands of the huge Chinese clock in the corner, a salvaged treasure from the museum, are about to entwine at the point of midnight. The radio waves are clearing at last. Now for the Noos. Fox connects up his godgem, gives a final tuning to the Zenith radio dials and grabs a thick pile of paper, the pages covered in his own handwriting.

Operate in depth, said Lawrence of Arabia, *rather than traditional battle lines*.

So now he's ready to do just that, in his last ever task in the netherworld before the Surge breaks into the sky cities of the world.

THE END BEGINS

Midnight is Fox time.

Time for him to do the impossible and exist in three dimensions at once: the netherworld, the Noos and the radio waves of the world.

Fox's voice travels the night, bounding across the Earth's soundwaves. A few scattered listeners soon became many as the fame of the Midnight Storyteller spread like a virus around the globe. Hundreds became thousands. Now millions listen in each night, huddled beside radios in boat camps and in the ruins of drowned cities, in gypsea pirate fleets and precarious mountain hamlets, in the floating caravans of nomads who fish the sea-logged plains of the Earth – and in the sky cities too. For Fox has become a phenomenon in an empire where books and stories belong to the distant past, broadcasting from secret, ever-changing hubs deep in the cyberjungles of the rebel Noosweavers.

Strive above all, urged Lawrence of Arabia, *to win hearts and minds*.

And he does.

When he and Mara broke out of New Mungo and escaped to their separate destinies, Fox discovered that it wasn't enough to cast people into crisis if you wanted to change their world. You had to ignite their spirits and give them dreams to reach for. His youthful attempt to stir up rebellion was extinguished almost as soon as it began, but this time the wildfire revolution he has sparked burns so deep and far it will not be stamped out.

To this end, Fox tells the forgotten stories that are preserved in the old books of the netherworld, as fossils are in rock. Once upon a time, says the Midnight Storyteller, this is who we were. These were our battles and breakthroughs, our best and worst of times. These were our passions and terrors. This is how we loved and fought and laughed and wept, all on the same Earth, under the same sun, moon and stars. This is who we are.

Fox's listeners in the flooded world cling to the tales that crackle from their radios as if to lifebelts in a storm, but his genius in the Noos has been to make Midnight an exotic harbour where frenzied Nooworlders come to anchor in one of the great stories of the lost world.

Fox has bound them together in a spell of imagineering, a wondering about the world that was, but has he also roused the sky people's curiosity about what might exist, now, beyond their towers and walls? Has the fear and apathy about the outside world, so carefully nurtured by their Guardians, finally been shattered by the Midnight Storyteller's husky *Once upon a time*?

As the sky empire descends into crisis and panic steams in the Noos, will its citizens – the ones who *must* hear this story – still dare to gather amid the storm to hear Fox's final tale?

They will come, Fox believes, because that's what people have done for time out of mind. From the distant ages when the first humans shivered in caves with wind and wolves howling outside to the boat refugees on the wild oceans beyond the wall, people have gathered for a story to fire up their spirits in a stormy world.

The story Fox will read now has never been told before. It is Mara's story, the tragedy of the Earth's sea-broken people. The most powerful part of this story, Fox will tell his army of listeners, is the ending. It has no ending, not yet. The end is still to be.

You, he will tell the people of the world, are the storytellers now. You must decide what happens to the sea-broken people. How the story ends all depends on you.

CANDLE, ALONE

'Broom!' Candle hugs her beloved slave as she enters the room. 'You'll never believe—'

Broom shakes her head and puts her finger to her lips. Candle hears the footsteps that have followed Broom's and falls silent.

'The Pontifix wants to see you right away,' says Broom.

Candle lets out a wail. 'He treats me like a slave, sending me away, fetching me . . .'

'Something's happened to upset him. Be careful,' Broom warns, as she pushes her out of the door.

Candle stomps through the palace after the guard. All day long she has waited to talk to Broom, who has been busy in the palace kitchen. Endless empty hours alone in her room have passed with only meals to punctuate the wretched boredom that is now Candle's life. And now, just as Broom arrives and Candle is itching to find out what Broom meant earlier about escaping, bursting to tell her that Tuck knows about Mara, she must run to her strange, cold husband.

Her father's constant seafaring gave Candle precious freedom when he was away; she cannot bear this shut-in life. She *will* escape.

But she must hide her feelings and calm herself now, as she enters his room.

Tuck stands by the wide slab of rock he uses as a desk.

'Bad news,' he says gruffly, before she even has a chance to sit down. 'It's your father.'

Candle stares at her husband, wondering what her father has done. It might be anything. His temper is as unpredictable as the moods of the sea goddess herself.

'Rodenglaw's boat didn't return to Ilira,' says Tuck.

He pauses and Candle hears the wind moan around the palace.

She shrugs, puzzled. Her father is always off somewhere or other – but where would he go in a wedding gondola?

Tuck hesitates. 'He is drowned,' he says, quick and tense.

Candle hears the words but they seem to bounce off her senselessly. She turns her head and looks through the layers of glass to the oceanic darkness outside.

'But – but the sea was calm.'

What is Tuck saying? He must be mistaken. How could a seafarer like her father, who has sailed on the ocean since he was a boy and knows the waters around Ilira better than his own face, drown in a calm fjord?

'The gondola hit wreckage, I'm told.' Tuck's glance flickers.

'A sea trap?' Candle bursts out before she can stop herself. The Pontifix's traps are meant to sink intruders and it was his own gondolier who took her father back down the fjord, so how could that be? The gondoliers know where the traps lie.

Tuck frowns and mutters something about rival Sea Lords.

'Another Sea Lord had him drowned?' Candle thinks of all the rivals her father has fought and feuded with over the years.

'The palace lookout found the wreckage of the boat on our shore,' says Tuck, ignoring her question. 'My guards have searched the waters and shores of the fjord. I'll have them search again.'

The reality of her father's death is sinking in. Candle begins to tremble with shock. What could have hapened? Was it an accident? Or was it by another's hand? Did some rival have him drowned?

I didn't hate him, she realizes. *I didn't want him dead. I only wanted him to love me and be kind.*

She remembers his final, unexpected wave and a sadness wells up in her that is beyond tears. Now she is all alone in the world, at the mercy of this strange man.

The steamy gurgle of the geyser in the alcove sounds like a drowning man. Candle covers her ears with her hands.

'I want to go my room,' she pleads.

'This is your home,' says Tuck, his voice suddenly gentle and lilting as a calm sea. 'You are free to do as you please. The guards and slaves are here to look after you.'

Free? thinks Candle, bitterly.

He moves towards her but she has already turned away so an awkward kiss lands cold upon her ear.

'I'm sorry,' he says. 'But he was a cruel father,' he adds unexpectedly. 'I could tell.'

It's a relief to escape. In the corridor Candle waves the guard away, wanting to be alone. Only the hiss and gurgle of the geysers break the stillness of the palace. The ocean booms on the rocks outside. Last night, it was full of dark whispers, a hushed sea. Not a sea to drown in.

A sudden thought filters through Candle's shock.

What if it wasn't a rival Sea Lord but *Tuck* who made sure her father never made it back to Ilira? With Rodenglaw dead, it's Tuck who will inherit all his ships and trade and wealth. Did her new husband have her father killed on her wedding day?

147

Candle stops, lost. Wandering aimlessly, she has come to a dead end in the maze of glass.

'I will!' a voice hisses.

Candle jumps with fright. The voice came from the ground at her feet. She looks down and sees she has almost hurtled into a dark hole where the rocky floor gives way to a flight of steps. The steps lead to an underground cavern. Deep in the cavern is a brightness. Candle crouches and peers down into the cavern and sees a long table lit by an oil lamp. The glow of the lamp reflects dully on the metal table as the moon does on a fogged sea.

A girl's face leans close to the lamp, towards two figures who sit with their backs to Candle.

'You can't stop me!' the girl bursts out.

'You'll do as you're told,' says a familiar voice. 'It's too dangerous.'

'Broom!' Candle cries. She clambers down the rocky steps.

'Candle! What are you doing here?' Broom turns around and rushes over. 'It's lucky the kitchen workers are all in bed. What would the Pontifix's people think of you coming down here?'

'But – my father – Broom, haven't you heard?'

Broom takes in her stricken face. She leads Candle to the table and sits her down.

'What's he done now?' says one of the others at the table.

Candle's eyes have blurred with tears so it's only when she hears the voice that she knows who it is.

'Clay!' Candle clings on to him as he grabs her in a hug. 'You're here?'

She glances at the young kitchen girl at the table. 'Send her away, Broom. I must talk.'

'She's a friend. She can be trusted,' Broom assures her. 'What's happened, Candle? The guards know something but they wouldn't tell.'

Candle blurts out the story of Rodenglaw's drowning and her suspicions about Tuck.

'You can see why he'd do it,' Clay agrees. 'Now he gets everything, doesn't he? Rodenglaw's share in the cable trains, his ships, all his wealth and power in Ilira. And control over the new waterfall and sun energy industries. Rodenglaw promised him the plans, Mum.'

'*My* plans,' says Broom, 'and he won't be getting them now. But to do this so brazenly, on the very day he married Candle . . . ?'

'A very convenient accident,' says Clay. 'But that's what Tuck Culpy does. His fleets wreck trade boats and ships all the time. Why d'you think there's so much work for scavengers? Piracy's what made the Pontifix so powerful. Bridges are just his hobby, Mum. Piracy's his real work. It's what keeps other pirates away from Ilira. There are old seafarers who swear he was a gypsea pirate before he was the Pontifix.'

Broom and Candle stare at Clay, aghast.

'Why did you never tell me all this before?' cries Broom.

149

Clay shrugs. 'You prefer the fairy story.'

'Why did you never tell *me*,' erupts Candle, 'that I was marrying a *pirate*!'

Clay looks guilty at that.

'There's something else,' Candle remembers. 'He knows about Mara – and there's a storyteller in a box and he does too. And—'

The kitchen girl who has been sitting in rapt silence gives a gasp. When she leans across the table into the glow of the lamp Candle sees she has soft, rounded features like Clay and Broom. Her eyes are beautiful in the lamplight and they meet Candle's boldly. The new wife of the Pontifix straightens her back and glares at the girl. No kitchen slave should dare to look at her like that.

'Tuck stole the globe from my mother,' the girl declares. 'I want it back. And the halo. He's just told me,' she shoots Clay a furious look, 'Tuck's got *that* now too!'

Candle tries to stare down the impertinent girl with the too-bold, too-beautiful eyes.

'This is Mara's daughter,' says Clay, sounding as if he needs to take a great gulp of air. 'Lily Longhope from Candlewood in the mountains.'

Candle keeps her eyes on the girl. She doesn't want to look at Clay. She has heard all she wants to know about Lily Longhope in Clay's breathless voice.

'The globe and the halo belong to my mother,' Lily is insisting. 'I want them back.'

'Candle will help us,' says Clay, still sounding as if he is holding his breath. 'She'll get them back for you and we'll get out of here, all of us, and escape to the mountains.'

Candle turns to him in amazement. 'The *mountains*? What about all your ocean dreams?'

Now Clay looks torn.

'We must go home to our own people,' says Broom, her face flushed with the thought. 'Come with us, Candle. You can't stay with a pirate who killed your father.'

Candle stands up, feeling uncertain and lost. 'And leave Tuck with everything that belonged to my father? Everything that should be mine! You want what Tuck stole from your mother, don't you?' she challenges Lily. 'Well, I want what he's taken from my father.'

Lily appraises Candle, then nods.

'Then maybe we can help each other,' she suggests, but the other girl has already turned to leave. 'Wait, Candle – the storyteller? In a box, you said? He knew Mara? But who is this storyteller? I don't understand.'

'Neither do I,' says Candle wearily. 'And I don't care any more. I need to sleep. My head's thumping.'

'I must go home, Candle,' Broom quietly persists. 'Lily's people are mine. Clay's father is one of them. I thought they were all dead but they're alive, in the mountains. Can't you—'

'Can't you all stop yapping and hounding me?' Candle bursts out. 'I can't *think*. You're still my slave, Broom, and you won't go *anywhere* unless I let you.'

Clay frowns at his almost-sister, his eyes turning hostile and hard.

'Gone to your head, has it? Marrying Tuck Culpy, living in a palace. You're sounding like Rodenglaw's daughter *now*, aren't you, Candle – desperate for money and power. You'd really stop my mum from being with her own people? After everything she's done for you? You know how unhappy she's been all these years.'

What about me? Candle wants to shout back. *Haven't I*

been unhappy too? Don't turn against me now – all because of that girl! But if she speaks she'll cry, and she will not cry in front of Lily Longhope.

She has been stupid. The globe has some secret power that Tuck and Lily seek. Yet she held that power – the halo, the very thing that would unlock the globe's magic – in her hands. And she gave it away to her husband like a silly, unthinking girl. Well, she will never give away her power so easily to anyone ever again.

Lily whispers to her but Candle pretends not to hear and runs up the steps, anxious to escape with all her churning feelings and be alone in her bed with the furs drawn over her head.

She can get rid of Lily Longhope any time she likes, she tells herself. The guards would deal with a palace intruder, intent on stealing the Pontifix's treasures, in the blink of an eye.

But Candle's heart is heavy. Is Clay right? Has she inherited her father's brutal greed? If the palace guards tossed that girl into the sea, would she care? But Clay would. She can't bear to lose him and Broom. How could she stand this life without them if they were to run away to some faraway place in the mountains that Broom has never known but calls home – and she never sees them again?

She has a chance to escape this glass prison and she should grab it, Candle tells herself – but Ilira is *her* home and the injustice of Tuck getting away with murder, looting what is hers by right, fills Candle with an injured fury that all her father's cruelty never did.

Am I Candle or Tartoq Rodenglaw? Do I belong with Broom and Clay or is my destiny here in Ilira? What is my life to be?

She has only been alive for fifteen Great Darknesses; she might live another fifty or more. What will she do in this barren, empty palace on a rock? Candle sees the years like relentless tides of the ocean, rolling over her, wave after wave.

As she runs through the palace the words of Lily Longhope's last, brazen whisper seem to hiss from the steam geysers in the rocks.

'Don't you want to be free?'

THE LETHAL NECKLACE
AND THE LOST SPELL

Lily lifts her sleepy head from the kitchen table. She yawns and rubs her eyes. Snoring softly on the floor under the table is Clay. Broom has gone to her bed and the rest of the palace is quiet.

This is her chance, Lily tells herself. All the talk about Clay's lost and found father has intensified her desire to find her own – and make at least some good of the horrendous mess she's landed herself in.

She grabs a plate of oysters from a kitchen shelf and creeps up the stairway cut into the rock.

At the top of the steps Lily finds herself in a maze of glassy corridors. *Which way?* She hurries along dim-lit winding passages, until she almost trips over a group of palace guards sprawled out on the floor. She feels a blush spread all over as they eye her languidly from the legs upward.

'So who's this out wandering in the dead of night?' drawls a young guard.

'I'm lost,' says Lily breathlessly. 'I'm the new kitchen maid and I've to take the Pontifix some oysters and I – I got lost.'

'The Pontifix sleeps in his ship,' yawns a second guard.

'Uhuh,' says Lily, thinking fast, 'but he wants an early breakfast set out in his room. All I know is that I've to take him oysters then get back to the kitchen and do three washings before sunrise.'

'Work you day and night, do they?' an older guard shakes his head.

Lily nods wearily. The fatherly guard takes pity on her. He gets up and steers her past the others, around a bend in the corridor, then points to a flaming torch on a wall beside a doorway.

'In there.'

'You supposed to be guarding it?' Lily asks, with a smile. She raises the plate of oysters to the helpful guard.

'What the Pont don't see, he don't know,' laughs the guard.

He winks at her and steals the largest oyster. Lily walks up to the doorway. If Tuck sleeps in his ship then she is safe. For now. She slips through the sealskin curtain that hangs across the doorway and steps into a large, dim, circular room and looks around at the strange objects set in the thick glass walls and upon the rocks that are the furniture of the room.

In the centre of the room is a large stone table. Lily peers through the dim light of a sputtering oil lamp and sees a jewelled casket there. And beside the casket – she can barely believe her eyes – lies the crescent of her halo and a small, moon-like globe.

Her mother's stolen globe!

Six quick steps is all it takes. Lily runs soundlessly across the furs that carpet the floor, stuffs the globe and halo into her pocket.

Just as she is about to make her escape her eye is caught

by another object on the table. A book! There is only one book in Candlewood. Lily has never seen another in her life, except the stack of tough, wood-pulp paper on which Gorbals writes stories and poems.

She picks up the book and reads the title.

NATURAL ENGINEERING by C. D. STONE

She flicks through the fine, soft pages full of pictures and diagrams.

Something flashes in front of her face. Lily drops the book, too shocked to scream, as a cutlass blade curves like a lethal necklace around her throat.

'Don't make a sound,' her captor hisses in her ear. 'Or you're dead.'

The blade presses on the side of Lily's head, nicking off a glossy coil of hair.

The cutlass slips from her neck but she can feel the point of it digging in her back as she is prodded towards the door. Around the bend in the corridor, the guards are yawning and telling raucous jokes.

The cutlass point in her back nudges her in the opposite direction. Lily walks through the palace corridors, her heart jumping with fear. She tries to turn her head to see who her captor is – it can't be Tuck; he'd surely have called the guards – but is shoved into a room.

'Candle!'

Lily lets out a shuddering breath.

Candle points the tip of the curved cutlass at Lily's nose.

'Give them to me.'

Lily sighs and pulls from her pocket the halo and globe – but just as Candle is about to grab them, Lily snatches them away.

Candle jabs the cutlass at her stomach.

'You'll kill me?' Lily challenges. 'Really? Go on then. It's not just Broom and Clay who'll never forgive you if you do. You'll never forgive yourself.'

'No?' Candle's sharp little eyes shine like splinters of jet.

'No! You need me alive or Broom will never get home to her people. Clay will never meet his father – and you'll never know what the wizz does because I won't be here to show you. And if you knew what it could do you'd have power over Tuck – because I doubt he knows.'

Candle draws a breath between her teeth.

'He's the Pontifix – of course he knows,' she jeers at Lily. 'Tuck sees magic in it – look!'

Candle points at the vivid storms that swirl around the globe in Lily's hand.

'That's all it does without the halo,' says Lily.

'The globe gave him visions of Ilira's bridges!'

'Oh, really? Not that book on his table?' says Lily drily. 'Tuck *can't* work the wizz even with the halo if he doesn't know its secret spell. And I doubt he does. Only my mother knows it – and me. I didn't even remember it,' she adds, 'until now.'

She learned the spell, Lily remembers, along with the letters of the alphabet when she was small. It was an old language, Mara told her, a lost language. Her Granny Mary had passed down the Weave code that unlocked the cyberwizz and Lily *should* know it, said Mara, because if it hadn't been for the wizz and its secrets Lily would not exist; she would never have been born.

Mara had been trying to tell her, Lily sees now, about Fox. But when her mother came to the next part of the story Lily didn't want to hear and ran away.

Yet the spell became part of her. Lily carved it into the

earth burrow walls in winter, on to her favourite trees and rocks when the sun came back. She'd scribbled the old code all over Candlewood like a secret signature and imprinted it in her heart, as if it had some mysterious power to keep her safe.

And maybe it does, after all.

'Do the spell then,' orders Candle, jabbing the cutlass at her nose again.

Lily is suddenly scared, remembering the tales of Mara's strange adventures in the Weave. Can a whole world really exist in a globe that fits in her hand? What if she gets stuck in the Weave and can't get back? But of course she won't, she reminds herself. It's not real. It's only the strange computer magic of the old world and she must use it now. Besides, what choice does she have?

Lily steps back from the glinting cutlass and slips the halo on to her head – then looks uncertainly at the globe.

'So you *don't* know! Ha!' Candle grabs the globe and copies what she saw Tuck do with a finger and thumb. The globe springs open.

Lily sees the round screenpad and small wand inside, and smiles.

The little wand slips in her nervous fingers as she begins to write on the screen. The patterns of the Weave spell flow through her and she tingles with excitement. Is this really happening? Can she find the amazing world of the Weave where her mother once met Fox?

'*Self or avatar?*'

A smooth voice from the globe makes both girls jump.

'Avatar?' Candle screws up her face.

'What's an avatar?' Lily shrugs. 'Self?'

'*Body scanning in progress,*' says the voice of the globe.

158

The round screen blinks at her like an eye. Nothing else happens. Then Lily remembers she must pull the halo over *her* eyes.

Candle and the palace vanish as Lily is sucked by a wave of pure energy through a vast, flickering force. The wizz is wholly in control, as if it knows exactly where it's taking her, hurling her now towards a wasteland of glittering ruins with such incredible speed it's impossible to –

'*STOP!*'

Lily crashes to a painless halt among the ruins of tumbledown towers that stretch as far as she can see.

SNAKES AND RUINS

The wrecked towers flicker as if they are the keepers of the last embers of a great fire.

Lily stands near an intersection of the ruins. BOULEVARD OF BREAKING NEWS says a sign that buzzes high in the darkness above her. She looks down the dark boulevard and cannot see its end. The strangest creature, made of a motley assortment of legs, is scuttling across the intersection. It screeches to a halt when it spots her. Lily draws back into the shadows and the bizarre creature scuttles away into BOULEVARD HABERDASH. Lily follows nervously and sees crooked towers, propped up by the squat Hostel for Pedlars of Quantum Mysteries. The scuttling creature has vanished into a fizzling heap of junk that spills from the doorless entrance to the hostel.

Lily wanders into BOULEVARD OF NOTIONS, past the Clandestine Cafe, Club Paradox and Inklings Inn. OPEN LATE FOR NIGHTHAWKS says a sign at her feet. She looks up and sees it must have crashed all the way down from – she strains to read the flickering sign high on the tower – the OVERNIGHT LODGE FOR INSPIRATIONS.

Is this what a city was in the old world? Lily tries to

imagine the vast Weavescape as it might have been before it crumbled to smouldering ruins. Yet nothing here is real. It's all make-believe magic of the wizz. A computer weave of all the stuff of the old world made by the Earth's people before the great floods. Lily knows it from the stories of her childhood, as if she has visited it all before in a dream. This is where Mara was stalked by the fox.

'I said stop! Can't you read?'

Lily looks around nervously. Someone did, she realizes, shout 'stop'.

The cross voice comes from the ruins but all Lily can see is a snaky presence, like a trail of green smoke. The snakiness wraps itself around a flashing red sign sticking out from a pile of rubble.

'What does THIS say?' the voice demands, as if talking to a stupid child.

'STOP,' Lily reads. 'Well, I have.'

'Now you have,' says the voice, which, Lily is now sure, belongs to the green snakiness. 'But you were starting to wander. This is private territory. No Weave-ghosts, lost trolls or anyone else allowed here without permission.'

The thing comes closer and Lily sees intelligence in its green eyes. She edges backwards through the rubble.

'Who do I get permission from?' asks Lily.

'Me,' says the snake. The voice is that of a girl; a bossy, bad-tempered girl. Lily has had more than enough of bossy, bad-tempered girls, including the one breathing down her neck in realworld. 'So? Weave-ghost? Troll? What are you?'

'I'm just a girl,' she replies, trying to step through the snakiness that has coiled around her legs. 'I'll move on and get out of your way.'

161

Lily reminds herself that all she has to do is yank off the halo to get out of this weird world, so what is there to fear? She is desperate to explore the vast forest of towers that buzz and spark as if there's a small lightning storm in each one.

She ventures a question before she goes.

'You, um, haven't seen a fox?'

The green snake grows intensely still.

'Fox?'

The word is a venomous hiss.

Lily tenses, scared. But what can a wispy green snake do to her in a place that's not real? She spies the scuttling creature emerge from the sizzling junk heap and hurry towards them on its jumble of legs, reels of broken numbers frothing from its mouth. With a flick of her tail the snake zaps the creature, which flies apart. A smouldering stump of leg lands with a clang nearby but immediately the limb scuttles back towards the junk heap in search, Lily supposes, of its other missing parts.

So that's what a wispy green snake can do.

'What,' demands the snake presence, 'do you want with Fox?'

'It's private,' Lily retorts. She's not going to confide her deepest secrets to a bossy snake-stranger. Except she's desperate, and there's no one else to help. 'I'm looking for my father,' she confesses. 'His name is Fox. He met my mother here, years ago.'

The snake rears up, dangerously. Lily jumps back as a forked tongue lashes towards her face.

It can't hurt you, she tells herself, closing her eyes. It's not real.

'Who are you? Where are you from?' hisses the snake.

Lily opens her eyes. The snake stares back.

162

'I'm Lily from C-Candlewood,' Lily stutters. 'Who are you?'

The snake draws so heart-stoppingly close that the ether flickers and for a moment Lily seems to glimpse a girl within the wispy presence. The snake-girl glances across to a flickering wasteland. Lily follows the glance and sees the broken arm of a bridge jutting out into nowhere.

'I am Pandora. Stay out of my world.' The luminous eyes are lethal. 'If you ever come here again I'll blast you into a million pieces. Go! And stay clear of my bridge. Do you hear? My bridge guard eats strangers and I'll tell him to look out for a girl with hair like a – a . . .' The green eyes flare as if the snake-girl finds something offensive in Lily's fox-flame of hair. 'Just go and don't ever come back here!'

The snake's tail shoots a spray of venom-fire. Lily takes the hit on the side of the head. Her hair sizzles. The snake-girl laughs as Lily screams . . .

'Shh! You'll have the guards in!'

The green snake, the ruined boulevards and towerstacks and the darkly sparking wasteland have all vanished. Lily is sprawled on a fur rug on a floor. Candle's face stares down at her crossly.

'What's happened? Who were you talking to? Let me see!'

Candle grabs the globe and the wand from her. She already has the halo.

Lily shakes out her hair but it's all there, not even singed.

She looks around the lamplit room. 'Was I here all the time? Did I disappear?'

'You were here all right. Why did you scream? What did you *see*? You were supposed to show me!'

Lily stares at Candle, trying to readjust to dim, ordinary

reality. 'I saw a green snake and a – a scuttling thing, all legs. Ruins and towers full of lightning. A broken bridge and . . .'

Candle looks nonplussed as Lily stops, lost for words.

'I saw a snake,' Lily repeats softly, 'who knows a fox.'

And not just any fox, Lily realizes. *What do you want with Fox?* That's what the snake-girl said. Fox. As if he belonged to her.

'I need to go back,' Lily tells Candle.

'Not now. You can't. Look.' Candle points to the drizzle of light spreading across the mottled glass of a wall. 'We need to get the globe and halo back because if Tuck finds them missing—'

'Too late,' says a voice behind them.

Lily and Candle gasp and spin round.

There, in the doorway, stands Tuck.

THE LETHAL NEED

Cold sea air clings to his windwrap. Starlight is caught in his light blond hair, or so Lily thinks as the tall man steps into the room; but it's only sand and salt grains, glistening in the lambent light.

'I rise with the birds,' Tuck says in a light voice, as if beginning a humorous tale, but his eyes are like cracked glass. 'I come from my night ship and find my globe and halo gone, one of my cutlasses too, and my guards dozing. They'll sleep forever now.'

Panic flashes between the two girls.

Candle's eyes spark with fright as Tuck holds out his hand. She surrenders the parts of the wizz.

'She knows the spell for it,' Candle bursts out. 'She knows how it works.'

Lily shakes her head at the other girl, then sees Candle is not betraying her; she's playing for time.

Tuck's eyes crinkle as he peers at Lily. 'Is this your slave? I know you lied. A woman called Broom *did* come with you. Never try to fool me. My eyes may be weak but my hearing is sharp. I can always hear a lie.'

'This is Lily,' Candle says, cursing herself for her earlier witlessness. Why did she ever mention Mara and name Broom? 'She's just a kitchen girl.'

Lily is thinking fast. She must not lose the wizz, not now.

'I do know the spell,' she says to Tuck. 'I can show you.'

'How could a *slave*,' demands Tuck, 'know the magic of the wizz?'

If she tells him she is Mara's daughter, Lily panics, would that save her or not?

'My grandmother knew it,' Lily replies. 'She had a wizz when she was young and I learned all about it from her.'

'That's the only reason we took it,' says Candle nervously. 'So we could show you – as a surprise.'

Tuck sighs and beckons to the guards by the door.

'I said no one would harm you here unless you deserved it,' he reminds Candle. 'But you have lied and stolen. That must stop.'

He mutters something to the guards and turns away. One guard pulls Candle over to the glass wall and places her hand flat upon it.

Lily can't believe what she is seeing. The second guard draws his cutlass and brings it down on the hand. The tips of Candle's plump fingers scatter like pebbles. She makes no sound, just stares at her hand then droops like a wilted flower on to the ground.

'Never take what belongs to me,' Tuck says quietly.

It doesn't belong to you, Lily wants to scream, but fear chokes her and she backs away from this dangerous man. The glass wall is behind her, the guards are at the door and Tuck is in front. There is no escape.

Lily stares at her own hands. Should she tell him who she is now? Or would she lose her life instead of her fingers because Tuck will guess that she must be here to steal back the wizz?

'Come with me.'

Lily looks up, terrified. Is it her turn now?

'You will show me the spell,' says Tuck, 'and all that the wizz can do.'

'What about Candle?' Lily bursts out. 'She needs help.'

Candle is slumped on the floor, staring at her maimed hand, too shocked to cry.

'Bring her woman to see to the wounds,' Tuck orders one of the guards. 'Take this girl to my ship,' he tells the other.

And he is gone.

'Let me bind her hand, please.' Lily looks into the eyes of the young guard and sees a fleck of sympathy there.

Lily looks around and finds Candle's nightshirt on the bed. As gently as she can, she binds the bleeding fingers with the soft cloth. The white cloth turns dark with blood. Lily pulls Candle over to the bed and lies the trembling girl down.

'Broom is coming,' she tells her. 'She'll know what to do.'

Lily goes with the guard. She'll do whatever Tuck Culpy wants. She'll show him everything she knows about the wizz. There's a chance for her now, if she's clever. He has said his eyes are weak, so if she can be Tuck's eyes for the wizz yet keep him blind to what she's really up to . . .

Because she *must* find her Fox father. She will find her way back into the Weave and search for him, if it kills her – and there's every chance that it will.

INSIDE EARTH AND OUT

This is the place of my nightmares, thinks Mara. She leans against the wall of the mountain and stares into the dark.

How many nights has she dreamed of this mountain collapsing on her, like it did on Tuck? Or woken in cold sweat having dreamed she'd lost one of the children in this deadly maze?

And now she has walked right into her nightmare, having run out on Rowan to search for Lily after days and nights of unbearable worry ending in a final, furious row.

Mara was a jumble of emotions as she retraced the desperate journey she once made into the mountains, past the very spot where Lily was born, back along the precarious gorge. When she reached the blockage of the landslide, she turned back, scared and at a loss – only to trip over a leather wine flask made by her own hands that told her Lily had indeed been this way. She searched and searched until she found the gap in the rubble: a doorway into the mountain. And at once Mara knew, with a sinking heart, that this was where Lily must have gone.

These mountains have been like the walls of a great fortress, secluding Mara and her people from the dangers of the world beyond. It's hard to believe that the same sun, moon and stars that wheel above Lake Longhope still shine down upon her drowned island in the Atlantic, on the ruins of the flooded cities, on the boat camps and pirate fleets and the sky towers; all that Mara once fled but cannot ever forget.

A world so vast and perilous that Lily might never make it home.

Mara lifts her torch flame. The firestone trailblazers were easy to find at first but now she sees only rock and darkness. Where is the moon cave with the hot springs and the story of the drowned world carved into the rock? She should have reached it a while ago. Mara swings her torch this way and that in a rising panic. As her thoughts wandered, so did her feet. She tries to retrack and find the previous firestone – but which way was that? Now she doesn't even know in which direction she is walking. Forward or back?

She is lost.

The mountain is vast, the tunnels endless. What if she can't find her way out? She might die here and never see any of her loved ones again.

Mara shouts Lily's name over and over until her throat aches. The only answer is the mountain's echo of her own voice. But she keeps moving, reigning in her fears. She will not let old terrors beat her. She will not give up.

A soft wind blows through the mountain and her torch shivers. The air is suddenly thicker, scented, tangy. It tastes of salt, of . . .

Ocean.

A tremor runs through Mara. The thought that she would never again see the ocean sometimes falls on her like a blow – even though it's the ocean that wrenched her apart from the people she loved. Maybe now it will save her. Just this once.

Mara breathes in the salty air and follows, step by step.

One moment she is blindly feeling her way around a twist in the tunnel . . . then the dark drains away and she is dazzled by light at the mouth of a cave. She draws in a sobbing breath of sea air. The last time she stood here Lily was a tiny mite of life inside her. Mara shades her eyes against the sun and looks out at the world on the other side of the mountain.

And wonders where on Earth she has landed up.

LAND GIRL IN ILIRA

Brilliant pathways cross the sunlit water, linking the mountains and islands of a great fjord.

Mara sits down on a rock, rubs her eyes, and looks again.

Bridges?

This is not the place she fled years ago – not the bleak mountain city of Ilira where she was once captured as a slave.

Yet beneath the magnificent bridges she recognizes the same snaking channel of sea. Across the mountains are the rockways and waterfalls and ranks of scavenged car doors, a riot of rusty colour, that front the cave homes of the mountain dwellers. There, stuck in a high cleft of rock, is the crashed plane.

But there are tracks in the rockways where dark machines creep up and down. Mara rummages in her memory for the forgotten word: she remembers seeing them in Granny's old books when she was young.

Trains.

Elegant long boats puff up and down the fjord, engulfing the bridges in steam. Beyond the bridges, a mysterious sphere on a small islet far out in the fjord glows like a firestone in the embers of the setting sun.

Mara can barely believe her eyes. Ilira is a city transformed.

Maybe Lily is safe here, she tells herself. *Maybe it's all different now.*

A ship sails up the sea fjord. The falling sun has turned its billowing sails into nuggets of gold. Mara gasps as bridge after bridge breaks in the middle. Each bridge separates into two arms that open and rise up towards the sky, one after the other, to let the tall ship pass through. The arms fall back into place. The ship heads towards the grandest bridge with its bustling market and just as Mara is wondering what will happen to all the shops and traders if that were to break open, the ship eases into a harbour and joins a cluster of tall masts, just beyond.

The wind carries the sound of the seafarers' excitement. Mara cannot stop herself. She hurries down the heel of the mountain and across the rocks towards the incoming ship.

Mara plunges into the crowd of traders and seafarers that pour off the ship. The jumble of scents and smells, strange words and accents stirs up a buried longing for the ocean world. Yet the back of her neck prickles with alarm as a word rumbles ominously through the harbour hubbub.

War.

A tall, young seafarer disembarks from the ship, so striking in appearance that he draws Mara's eye. The layers of his windwrap are the colour of storm clouds. His black hair is a regiment of long braids. His strong face is as smooth and brown as an acorn. There is something imperious in his stride. He seems very sure of his place in the world, thinks Mara, wondering who he might be.

He waves to a commanding figure at the bow of his ship, *Mirkwood*, as he strides alongside an older seafarer who is so wrapped in Arctic furs that his grey-flecked beard seems part of the animals he wears.

The word *war* is on their lips too. Mara follows as they walk along the harbour towards Ilira, drawn to the exotic young seafarer and his frenzied talk of the outside world.

'*Surgents on the move. War is coming, Greyfus, all across the Earth . . . sea against sky . . . pirate fleets . . . global attack . . .*'

Mara struggles to keep pace with the seafarers in the bustle of the harbour. When they reach the shore the crowd thins out and it becomes easier to hear what they say.

'Ever see one of those cities?' the grey-bearded man in furs is saying. 'I only travel the Arctic seas and I've never seen one here.'

'There are none this far north,' his young companion replies. 'I used to think they were only legends. But there are settlers on Hallow, on the west coast of this land, who know about the sky cities. I wintered with them during the storms and made good friends there.' His voice has a lilting rise and fall that Mara knows of old, the ocean voice of a gypsea. A soft smile relaxes the young seafarer's intense face. 'One day I'll go back,' he says, 'when this war has all blown over. Yes, there is a girl,' he laughs, answering the mischievous question on the older man's face. 'Her people were refugees. They fled a sky city when she was a child.'

'Fled a sky city?' The smile on the older man's face turns to amazement. 'Well, they'll have stories to fill a winter!'

The young seafarer lowers his voice and again Mara strains to hear. 'Their stories of the city of New Mungo turned this scholar into a warrior,' he tells his companion, who looks at him closely, now.

'Well, don't wait too long to return to your girl,' the older

173

man tells his young friend. 'Wars don't blow over as fast as storms. From what you have said, this one,' he shakes his head, 'could take a lifetime to burn out.'

The young seafarer nods. 'All around the planet the fuses are lit.'

The seafarers stride ahead as Mara slows to a halt. *Sky city refugees? On the west coast? Is it possible?*

A whole fleet of refugee ships escaped New Mungo, along with hers, but they lost each other out on the ocean. Mara has always held on to the hope that the others survived. She couldn't bear the thought that, as she did with her own islanders, she led all those desperate people out on to the ocean only to lose their lives there. But if refugees from New Mungo have settled on the western coast of this vast island then it's possible that other ships made it across the ocean and made new lives elsewhere too.

Mara's heart lifts. She can't help smiling. There *are* still miracles in the world.

'That pretty smile for me?'

A man who looks as if he has weathered a thousand hard sea voyages has stopped bang in front of Mara. He studies her with eyes so flinty they might have been chipped off the mountain. He leans in close. Mara draws back at the reek of beer and oysters on his breath, but he grabs her arm.

'Passed you by on the harbour and smelled you, girl. Smell of land, you do.' He pulls her towards him and pushes his face into her hair. 'Trees!' he exclaims. 'I never smelled trees on anyone since I was a boy.' Mara shakes him off, but the man shouts after her. 'Hey, land girl! Where you from?'

People are turning to look. Mara puts her head down and hurries along the shore towards the mountain city. Her heart is thudding. An old scar seems to ache: the slave-brand once scorched into her arm right here on the shores of Ilira. Mara scolds herself. It hasn't hurt in years. The ache is from the man's grip, that's all.

But Mara's hate of Ilira, a place she once journeyed through a mountain to escape, has returned. Her eyes search the bay and the bridges and the mountain rockways.

Where are you, Lily? Please, please be safe.

Ilira might look like a stunning new city but Mara can't shake off the dread that it's every bit as dangerous as it ever was.

War all across the Earth, the young seafarer said in his lilting voice. *Sea against sky.*

Mara thinks of the sky ships she and Lily saw flying north over the lake. But who are the Surgents? What did the young seafarer's cryptic words mean? What great changes have occurred while she has hidden away in Candlewood? Mara walks through the bustling sea traders on the shore, as if through the phantoms of another world.

An old feeling fires up inside her. Fox promised a revolution. A war against the sky cities.

Is it possible? Could this be his war?

Mara kills the thought. This is no time for wondering. War is on its way, that's all she knows. So she must find Lily, and fast. Dusk is deepening over Ilira. Mara glances up at the salmon-streaked sky. She'd better make a start before it's dark.

The islands and waterfalls on the far side of the fjord clang with industrial noise. Cargo wagons trundle across the bridges, pulled by teams of yelping dogs. Ilira is all business and brashness, a riot of voices and smells. After the intense peace of Candlewood, Mara's senses jangle and reel.

175

Only the tiny island with the palace near the neck of the fjord is solitary and still.

As the marketeers crammed upon the largest bridge shut up their shops for the night, people spill into the city's wide bay. Mara wills herself to find Lily's fox-flame hair among them but the only head she recognizes is the dark-braided one of the young seafarer with the rolling gypsea voice who knows so much of the world she has been exiled from for so long.

OREON

In Ale Alley Mara keeps to the shadows between the swinging lanterns above each drinking den. *Not here, Lily, please don't be here*, she prays, peering into noisy cave bars, avoiding eye contact with the drunks.

Someone speaks to her in a language she doesn't understand.

Mara flicks a nervous glance at the woman leaning against the entrance to a bar as if the rock wall depended on her for support; clearly, it's the opposite.

'Whassup, stranger?' Now the woman speaks in Mara's tongue.

'I've lost my daughter,' says Mara desperately.

'She pretty?' the woman slurs, closing one eye and tilting her head back to focus.

Mara nods.

'Bad place, this, for a pretty girl.' The woman slithers a bit down the wall then props herself up. 'Should keep a tighter grip, Mum.'

Thanks for that, thinks Mara. A torrent of guilt sweeps through her because it's true. Nothing in Candlewood has prepared Lily for this place. *I'm supposed to protect her*,

Mara chides herself, but hiding the truth about the past has led her daughter here, like a lamb among wolves.

'Watch out for the wolves,' the woman warns with a black-toothed grin.

Mara jumps and stares as the woman seems to read her thoughts. 'Wolves?'

'Lotsa wolves here to eat up a looker like you.' The woman cackles then grabs Mara's arm. 'An' there's a *real*—'

Mara pulls away from the drunk woman and barges through the revellers until she is out of the lantern-lit alley and into a darker rockway full of the secret scuttlings and furtive mutterings of nocturnal trades and business deals. She rushes on until she finds her way to the old fishing harbour.

Night pours down from the mountains. The sky and the sea are full of stars and the moon sails above the fjord like a galleon ship.

Mara slumps down on a rock.

Now what? Where would Lily go? Think!

In the big harbour at the other side of the bay the sailing ships are lit up by hosts of lanterns. Mara is now consumed by the fear that made her chase Lily through the mountains. What if she got on a ship? What if she is already crossing the ocean to try to find Fox? But surely she wouldn't cut loose from her own family like that?

I did, Mara reminds herself, with a plunging heart.

She found herself cut loose from her family in one desperate moment of rage – and never saw them again.

Mara puts her head in her hands and wills Lily to be safe in Ilira.

'What kind of man is your Pontifix? I've travelled far to meet him.'

The voice cuts through Mara's fear. *Pontifix?* The word is

strange, yet she has heard it before, somewhere.

Mara turns around, recognizing the soft rise and fall of the voice. The young seafarer from the *Mirkwood* sits at a long, lamplit table outside a harbour shack with a group of fisherfolk, all busily mending their nets. The *click-clack* of their knitting needles is suddenly a nervous sound. The fisherfolk look wary.

'He's setting himself up as some kind of Emperor of the Arctic, I've heard.'

Mara sees it's the older seafarer from the *Mirkwood*, Greyfus, with the heavy beard and furs. She slips from her rock and creeps closer, hiding behind a stack of kayaks to listen.

A sturdy fisherwoman brings a large jug to the table and fills tall tankards with frothy ale.

'He'll be challenged on that,' the young seafarer responds. He raises his tankard, takes a long drink of ale and wipes the froth from his mouth. 'He's not the only power in the Arctic. Though he likes to wipe out his rivals. I heard he had Rodenglaw drowned.'

Around the table, busy fingers grow still. A fisherman grunts but no one else speaks.

'It's the talk of the seas,' Greyfus confirms.

'Bad news grows wings,' agrees the young seafarer. 'Messenger hawks spread news of his death all over the North.'

'It was the thugs that guard the Pontifix's palace who killed Rodenglaw.' A fisherman breaks from his net-mending to give the young seafarer a challenging stare. 'That's what *I* heard.'

'But who told them to?' The young seafarer sets down his tankard with a clunk. 'Tuck Culpy always had a ruthless streak.'

Mara can't believe her ears.

Tuck? Tuck is alive? Gypsea Tuck?

Suddenly his lilting ocean voice is in her head. She can see Tuck's eyes in the firelight one night years ago, deep in the mountain behind her, as he tells her about his Da, Jack Culpy, the best gypsea bridge-maker there ever was – and yes, he told her too, didn't he, of his dream of being a pontifix. It was a special name, he said, for a bridger in ancient times. That's what he'd be one day, he said, trying to impress her – Tuck the Pontifix, the greatest bridge-builder in the world.

And she tried not to laugh at the scruffy gypsea pirate boy with his glittering eyes.

Mara looks through Tuck's magnificent bridges to his moonlit palace, amazed.

'My brother thought he was dead,' continues the young seafarer. 'But his fame spread across the oceans and it turned out that your Pontifix was *our* Tuck.' He laughs. 'So, two old gypsea friends are set to battle each other over who rules the Arctic seas – though a much bigger battle is brewing.'

'Who,' says Greyfus, taking up the prompt, 'is your brother?'

'Pendicle Prender,' says the young seafarer in his mild voice. 'No doubt you've heard of him.'

Knitting needles clatter on to the table. The fisherfolk exchange frightened glances and shift in their seats.

'Prender the *pirate*?'

'The Vulture of the North?'

'Well, well! All that time on the ship and you never said a word.' Greyfus sits back in his seat eyeing his young companion warily now.

'I'm not my brother,' the young seafarer assures them. 'I am Oreon. A scholar gypsea.' He looks out at the fjord. 'I am on a historic mission,' he offers enigmatically, 'to save the North.' He turns back to the fisherfolk. 'You must have seen the fleets in the sky?'

'We see 'em,' says a wizened man Mara recognizes as the one who grabbed her on the shore. 'You know what they are then, eh?'

'My brother keeps lookouts in the Northern oceans,' says Oreon. 'Since the spring sun rose, sky fleets have been landing in the Far North, others around Narwhal Sword Bay and at Aurora, north-east of here.'

'An invasion?' says Greyfus. 'From the sky?'

Oreon nods.

'What do the sky cities want with our land?' demands a young fisherwoman, clutching a sleeping baby close to her. 'They've all the world's oceans!'

'The tentacles of the sky empire are spreading far beyond the oceans,' says Oreon. 'Now they want all the lands of the world. Soon there will be invasions of the high lands all across the Earth.' Oreon leans towards the fisherfolk. 'The Vulture sent scouts inland on the trail of the first sky fleets,' he says. 'They have driven out the people of the Far North – Inuits who have lived there for time out of mind. They fled south, their villages razed. Some joined my brother's fleets on the seas. There are fuels and metals deep in your land that the empire wants. Teams have begun tunnelling and building settlements. New cities.'

'Sky cities?'

The faces in the lamplight are aghast at the idea of towering cities on their land.

'*Underground* cities.' Oreon's long fingers draw patterns upon the table. 'Burrowed cities protected by great domes that will stay warm and light all winter. So the scouts say.

181

There are rumours,' he leans forward, eyes alight, 'that the empire even plans to own the weather and the stars.'

'The weather belongs to the Earth!' the old fisherman scoffs. 'And the stars to the sky.'

But the others watch Oreon's restless fingers with stricken faces as they seem to glimpse the frightening future he draws upon their tabletop.

'The Pontifix will never share his sea power, no matter what,' the old fisherman grunts.

'We'll see,' Oreon responds. 'Your Pontifix is blind in more ways than one. His sights are fixed on his old rivalry with the Vulture but he'll soon be forced to put that aside. The Vulture aims to take conquest of the Arctic seas and battle the sky empire. He is the one with the vision and the power to do that.'

Oreon curls his fingers into a fist and thumps the table lightly, as if carefully bursting one of the bubble cities.

'If we don't have the right leader for this fight, the sky empire will take everything. Your city, these seas, this land. And you will all be its slaves – if you survive.'

THE VOICE IN THE WATCH

Oreon holds the startled gaze of his listeners. 'The only way is for the Arctic peoples to combine under a strong leader and join the Surge against the sky empire,' he tells them.

'The Surge?' a fisherman queries.

'A rebel force around the globe that wants to keep the Earth's high lands free. The Surgents are mostly flood refugees,' Oreon explains, 'and empire rebels.'

Mara's heart jumps. She creeps out from the stack of kayaks where she's been hiding, listening hard.

The large fisherwoman slams her tankard on the table, outraged. 'An' they all want to come here?'

'Not all. There are other high lands in the world. But you have a whole new continent here, sparsely populated. Don't you know how vast this island is?' Oreon demands. 'I have helped my brother map the south and west coasts – there are endless empty swathes of land, as far as you can see, all risen from the White Age of ice. As for the deepest North and the interior beyond the mountains, who knows what expanses of empty lands are there too?'

Around the table, the fisherfolk exchange uneasy glances.

The young scholar looks out impatiently at the dark sea

fjord. He shakes an arm from his windwrap and taps a disc strapped to his wrist. The glassy face of the disc flashes symbols that Mara is too far away to see.

'A watch!' exclaims the wizened fisherman. The lines of his face intensify as he peers at the disc and his eyes sink deeper among the creases. 'Haven't seen one of those since I was a boy.' He sweeps a glance across the sparkling arena of the sky. 'The stars say midnight,' he challenges. 'What time do *you* say?'

Oreon looks at the watch-face.

'Twenty-three minutes and thirty-two seconds past,' he replies with a laugh. 'The stars are on time.'

'Is that a radio watch?' Greyfus exclaims, staring at it. 'But we could have listened on the ship!'

'There was nothing to hear,' Oreon shrugs. 'The soundwaves were crackling like an aurora storm. In Hallow the winter was so wild we barely heard a whisper on the soundwaves. But last night I heard him again.'

'Who?' says Greyfus. The keen, sharp eyes that have been watching Oreon since he revealed who he is now light up.

'We might be too late but . . .'

Oreon fiddles with the watch and pulls out a small stem from the disc. The figures around the table look startled as a voice speaks out.

It seems to Mara that she doesn't hear the voice, she absorbs it as a bolt of shock, a live current, a kind of incandescence that sends her reeling out of the moment and down a tunnel of time to land back in her own past.

It's him.

Mara moves towards the voice as a tide rolls to shore, a moth to a flame.

But how can it be? How?

The voice wraps around her like a tingling spell. A man now, not a boy. The years have weighted his voice but it has the same hungry, husky tone and she feels the same elemental tug inside, as if by a fine hot wire, as she did when she first reached towards him in the ether wastes of the ruined Weave.

If she saw him, would she even know him now? Once the globe was gone and the connection between them cut dead, Mara learned that it was best not to remember. She pushed his face and memories of that fierce, fleeting time with Fox to the very hinterland of her heart. She had to. She couldn't step into the future while forever looking back. Yet she couldn't ever truly forget because he was always there, in Lily, who would look at her through a tumble of hair and the walls around her heart would crumble as Mara glimpsed him in their daughter's eyes.

Beyond will, beyond thought, somewhere far deeper than memory, some essence of Fox lodged in her, kept faith all this time, like the secret rings in the trunk of a tree.

And she knows, beyond doubt, that the voice in the watch is him.

'Land girl!'

Mara jumps. The spell shatters.

Faces stare, curious faces, all turned towards the stranger who has stepped out of the dark and into the edges of their lantern light.

'You can smell the land and trees on 'er,' says the wizened one who grabbed her on the shore.

The voice that is Fox breaks into crackles. Oreon taps his watch and the voice is silenced. His dark gaze is fixed on Mara.

'Let me hear him,' Mara bursts out. 'Please!'

'He'll be gone now,' says Oreon, studying her with

surprised interest. 'His story had finished.'

'He tells stories?' Mara stares in confusion at the shining watch-face. 'I don't understand.'

'He is the Midnight Storyteller,' says Oreon. 'But the spring auroras break up the radio waves.'

He nods to the fierce eruptions of colour in the sky above the mountains.

Mara doesn't look; she doesn't care about the sky.

Radio?

She remembers the word. Granny Mary had one. A small silver box covered in buttons and dials. She'd switch it on from time to time. *You just never know*, she'd say, but it was always full of empty noise. Radio communications had died out in the Great Floods, yet Granny kept hoping for a voice.

'Who is this storyteller?' Mara demands of Oreon. 'Tell me what you know about him.'

The gypsea scholar raises an eyebrow at the incomer's imperious tone.

'No one knows for sure,' he responds nonetheless. 'Some say he is a Siberian hermit in a mountain cave. Or a ghost in the airwaves telling the tales of what has been and what is to come. Others say he is a secret rebel in New Jing. Whoever he is, his midnight broadcasts have set the world alight.'

The sturdy fisherwoman jumps to her feet, pointing to a flotilla of gondolas that sweep like dark arrows up the moonlit fjord.

'The palace guards!'

'At last,' exclaims Oreon.

He drops a handful of pearls on the table with thanks and the grateful fisherfolk make a grab. Oreon shakes hands with Greyfus, gathers his windwrap around him and hurries towards the end of the harbour.

The fisherfolk watch nervously.

'There are claw emblems on their helmets,' one whispers. 'The palace guards should wear the moon crescents of the Pontifix!'

The claws adorning the helmets of the guard fleet are burnished gold in the moonlight. But Mara can only think of one thing.

Oreon cannot leave. She can't let him disappear with his watch, the watch with the voice, the only chance she will ever have to find –

What am I doing? Mara stops dead, heart pounding. *But it's not for me*, she tells herself. *It's for Lily.*

A scream rips through the rockways.

A creature scampers from the dark alleys out on to the harbour rocks.

Mara sees pointed ears, a long snout, amber eyes and sleek fur glistening in the moonlight.

The wolf pauses, lifts its nose in the air as if sniffing out an escape path, then darts from rock to rock as a rabble staggers out of Ale Alley on the hunt.

'Wolf!' the human pack yells. 'Kill the wolf!'

SEA WOLF

A crack of gunshot. A bullet clangs off a rock. Mara ducks behind the stack of kayaks.

Run! she wills the wolf as it bounds past. A sudden sense of kinship with this unwelcome intruder from the mountains makes her root for it. But now the wolf is stranded on the outermost rocks of the harbour.

The hunting crowd jeers. Weapons glint as the rabble move in for the kill – then halt as people spot the fleet of guards in the fjord.

Oreon turns. He looks at the wolf. Two bounds, Mara sees, and the wolf will be on his neck. But Oreon smiles. A surprised, amused smile. He raises his hand. A weapon like a silver dagger gleams in his fist.

A thin bolt of light shoots from the weapon.

The wolf gives a loud yelp then crashes into the harbour water among the crush of fishing boats and the incoming gondola fleet.

The lightning-bolt weapon silences the hunting pack. They draw back from the lethal stranger and creep away fearfully to the rockway bars, muttering amongst themselves. When Mara looks around the fisherfolk are gone too, their shacks shuttered up, the table dark, the lamp snuffed out.

Oreon leaps into a gondola. Only once the fleet have surged back up the fjord towards the palace, and the harbour is quite empty, does Mara emerge from her hiding place in the kayaks. She walks towards the spot where the wolf hit the water. She knows what she saw.

The light-bolt did not hit the wolf. Oreon deliberately misfired and hit the rock behind. The wolf *leaped*. And there's something else Mara is quite sure of . . .

She peers down at the dark water in between the harbour rocks and shifting fishing craft. Nothing. But she waits, holding her breath until . . . at last the surface of the water breaks. Mara lets out her breath in a great gasp as the head of the wolf appears, spluttering.

'You!' she cries.

The wolf clambers from the water, panting, seawater dripping from its coat. When it reaches Mara it lifts its snout to the moon as if about to howl again. But from under the wolf head, another pair of eyes sparkle.

'Me,' says the wolf.

Wing grins and lifts the dead wolf head from his own. He throws off the wolfskin and grabs Mara in a sodden hug. She holds him tight, then holds him at arms' length.

'Where is she, Wing? Is Lily safe?'

Wing points towards the sea.

Mara puts her head in her hands, distraught. 'She's gone to sea? How could you let her go? Why did you let her come here at all? You *know* this city – we were all lucky to get out alive before. I'll never find her now.' A great sob bursts from Mara. 'I can't bear it.'

'Not stop Lily,' says Wing, stroking Mara's hair. 'Lily is like Mara. Wing try keep her safe.' His head droops. 'My

189

wolf save me – see?'

He shows Mara the arrow lodged in the dead wolf's head and the small red wound on the hairline of his brow. Crashing into seawater has reopened the wound and blood is trickling through his hair and down his neck. Mara takes the cloth foodwrap from her bag to bandage him up.

'My wolf take arrow – bang!' Wing explains. He points to his head. 'I dizzy, fall in sea. I see hunters take Lily.'

'Oh no.' The fear that has swirled inside Mara ever since Lily disappeared now takes the shape of the vicious hunters who once captured her in Ilira. 'Is she – Wing, please tell me she's—'

'Wing watch.' He pulls his telescope from his belt. 'Wing see.' He points with it to the glimmering palace on its islet in the fjord. 'Lily *there*.' Now he touches his head. 'Head sick from arrow. Wing lie on rocks long time then swim for Lily – men chase me. We go find Lily now!' he finishes, shaking with emotion.

Relief sweeps through Mara.

Lily is alive. That's all that matters. She is not lost, far across the ocean.

'That's Tuck's palace,' she tells Wing. 'Yes,' she says to the astonished wolf boy, 'Tuck is alive. They call him the Pontifix. He changed this city and they talk as if he owns it – and half of the Arctic seas.' Her eyes harden. 'But he doesn't own my daughter.'

'Guards,' Wing warns. 'All round palace.'

Anything is possible, Mara tells herself. Tuck survived a mountain landslide. Fox found a way through to her, sending his voice across oceans and time. There is always a way.

Hurrying back to the kayaks, she begins to heave one of the narrow boats across the harbour rocks towards the sea.

WEAVE WEAPONS AND DREAMS

Lily clicks open the globe. Clumsy with tiredness, her trembling hands no longer feel as if they are her own. They belong to Tuck, who controls what used to be her life.

Here in her prison in the belly of Tuck's ship, the chain around her feet lets her walk no further than a water pot or slop bucket or the rough sealskin that is her bed. She is only unchained to work. She must sleep when Tuck says so, and she does; it's her only escape.

Still, his voice reaches into her dreams.

Go, search, find . . . Tell me . . . what do you see?

Tuck sits across from her at the long table where he has assembled a collection of sea-battered relics. Mysteries for her to solve. *What was this in the old world? What was its power? What did this do?* But rummaging for answers in the ruins of an unreal world is like searching for a single needle on a pine forest floor.

His breath is hot and hungry. His face is too close. Lily slips on the halo, avoiding his parched eyes.

Day and night he preys on her, peering as she scribbles in the globe. But her fingers are too fast and furtive for his weak eyes. The Weave spell is the only thing she still owns in the world, except her thoughts. She will not surrender either to Tuck.

Her head is heavy as a rock. She has no idea if it's day or night. Time has mulched into one long dimness here in the depths of the ship, as it did in her winter burrow, except there she belonged to herself.

Lily snatches at memories as her old life begins to feel distant, unreal.

Midsummer nights, when the sun moves like a halo around the top of the world, swimming far out on the lake with Wing.

Warm sleepy heaps of little Corey and Coll snuggled up beside her at the sundown fire.

The mournful bellow of reindeer at summer's end, the saddest sound in the world.

'Weapons,' Tuck reminds her.

He wants to know about the weapons of the old world. Weapons are harpoons, knives, spears, arrows, sometimes teeth and fists – but Tuck wants to know about bolts of light that will melt a man and shells full of death that raze cities to dust. Lily must ransack the Weave for lost knowledge of the drowned world that will give Tuck a deadly new power in *this* one.

'Go,' he orders her.

And once again she dives . . .

. . . into the Weave, hurtling down the boulevards, senses on alert, pretending to do Tuck's bidding – but intent on her own desperate quest.

She keeps a wary lookout for Pandora, but the venomous snake-girl has never appeared again. The only presences have been the weird scuttling creatures of the junk heaps. Lily begins her work, foraging among the sparking ruins, then halts, sensing movement deep within the boulevards. She slips into the shadows and spies a procession of whispering creatures pass between the crumbling Weave towers.

Whatever they are, whatever they're doing, they're her only hope.

The procession moves down through the boulevards between ranks of towerstacks at various stages of collapse. Lily follows at a wary distance and watches the creatures enter a dark alleyway. Once the boulevard is empty, she creeps up to the alleyway and sees a bolted door beside a pulsing blue sign. Is this where the whispering creatures went?

DREAM the pulsing sign commands.

An unlit S droops upside down at the end of the word. Lily turns the hanging curve of the S the right way up and it clicks satisfyingly into place.

The bolts slam back. The door springs open.

Lily stares in surprise. So that was the key to open the door?

She steps through the door into a dark passageway. It leads into a hidden wasteland fortressed by the walls of the crumbling towers. The whispers are now an industrious hum – like bees in summer, thinks Lily, clambering over fizzling heaps of rubble towards the huge crowd in the wasteland.

She creeps closer, heart thudding, unable to believe her eyes.

The Weave creatures are gathered around the snake-girl and – and –

A fox!

A fox with vivid eyes and a flame-bright coat.

Noise erupts overhead. Lily glances at the electronic sky. Does the Weave have storms? But the ether is dark and calm, apart from shooting stars of decay.

'Commander Tuck!' bellows a voice.

BY TURN OF THE TIDE

The bellow comes from Tuck's ship, a universe away from the Weave.

In realworld, someone pushes past Lily so roughly that the globe slips from her fingers and the halo jolts from her eyes. She clasps her head in confusion, lurching between worlds. The Weave connection flickers.

No!

Lily resettles the halo but the Weave world is fading. Her desperate scream flies across the cyberwastes. The heads of the Weave creatures turn, ether lights sparkling in their eyes. For an instant the fox's vivid gaze looks up as she whirls away, yanked across the ruined boulevards into seas of static, ripped out of the Weave.

The connection cuts dead.

Lily crashes back into Tuck's ship. Devastated, she pulls the halo from her eyes. She can't find the globe. The figure that is Tuck seems phantom-like in the dim lanterns of the ship's hold. The thunder is the pounding of feet on the deck overhead.

Tuck has the globe in his hand.

'I need it back,' Lily gasps. 'I was on to something. Please!'

'Shh!' Tuck hisses, the sound as harsh as a lash.

A crescent moon looms out of the cavernous dark of the ship's belly. Lily rubs her eyes, then sees it's the silver emblem on the helmet of the Pontifix's personal guard, Genk. Sweat drips from the brow of the lumbering man and splashes on the tabletop.

'Emergency, Commander Tuck,' gasps Genk. 'Alert by sea hawk from the west-coast lookouts. A Vulture fleet's gatherin' at Atlan Point.'

The globe drops from Tuck's hand. It rolls across the rough timber table and settles in a groove.

'The Vulture? At *Atlan*?' Tuck rakes a pale strand of hair from his stricken face. 'My tracker ship said he headed Far North with the first sun.' A wan smile creases his face. 'Aha. So he's fooled me. How many ships?' he demands, the smile dead on his lips.

'Twenty by sundown,' the guard replies. 'We can sort that, but – but –' The guard braces himself against the brittle expression on his master's face. 'There's more on the way.'

'*More?*'

Genk looks as if he is trying to spit out unsavoury words, but swallows them instead.

Tuck slams his fist on the table, so hard he dislodges the globe from its groove. It rolls slowly across the wood, stopping short of Lily's reach. Dare she grab it?

'Bring my Skua fleet in from the deep oceans,' says Tuck in a quiet, deadly tone. 'All my best war ships. Fix it, Genk.'

'The – the Skua fleet?'

Tuck draws his cutlass. The curved blade flashes in the lantern light.

Genk stares. 'Eh, the thing is, Commander Tuck, messenger hawks say the Skuas just joined the Vulture's fleets. Alongside Rodenglaw's.'

Tuck laughs. 'Rodenglaw's ships just joined *ours*.'

'Eh, they *did*. An' then they, eh, didn't. The Vulture made 'em think again.'

Tuck slices the blade of the cutlass into the tabletop. Whether by luck or design, he just misses cutting off the tip of Genk's large nose.

'I want,' says Tuck, in a murderous tone, 'an attack fleet at Atlan Point. By sunrise.'

'Sunrise?'

'Don't lose your head, Genk.' The cutlass is resheathed in the broad leather belt of Tuck's windwrap. 'Just get it done.'

Genk hurries away and thuds up the stairs to the deck.

'You,' Tuck turns to Lily, 'must do the impossible too. I need more from you. Now! The lives of your friends depend on it – your own too.'

'My friends?'

Lily turns cold inside.

'There's a cave under the palace kitchens where the sea takes away waste,' says Tuck. He puts his mouth so close to her ear that his voice seems to be inside her head. 'The morning tide will take the woman and her son. So race against the tide if you want to save them.'

Lily panics. 'It's all dead stuff – junk. I can't find what you want.'

'Somewhere in that junk are the secrets of weapons that no one in this world can match.'

'Surely the sky people will match anything,' Lily murmurs.

'The sky people are in their world, not in mine,' says Tuck.

'They are in your skies,' Lily dares.

'Just get me what I need,' Tuck commands, and Lily reads the chilling desperation in his handsome face. 'By sunrise.'

A man's scream on the deck overhead makes them both jump.

Tuck is on his feet. In seven measured strides he finds his way to the stairs that lead up to the deck. Then he is gone.

Leaving Lily unchained and . . . *alone*?

She looks around.

Where's the guard?

There's always a guard. Lily lifts the lantern and swings the light around the innards of the ship.

No guard. No chains.

It's her chance to escape.

But she must get straight back into the Weave or she might never find the fox again – the fox that might be *him*.

One chance to escape.

One chance to find her father.

One chance to save the lives of Broom and Clay.

Lily grasps the globe. The smooth sphere tingles at her touch. Something violent and ugly is happening on the deck overhead. The blood-curdling cries make her shudder. She looks at the stairs that lead up to – who knows what? Freedom? Death?

Whatever she chooses is a deadly risk.

Lily closes her eyes, decides, and takes her chance.

CRESCENT AND CLAW

The sea is full of urgent whispers. A green flare of aurora crackles in the sky. The moon is sharp as a cutlass: a Culpy crescent, Tuck's emblem, hanging above the palace as if by his command. Mara digs her paddle into a wave and the kayak cuts across the water, under the bridges.

Her thoughts speed with the boat. Oreon is on a deadly mission of the Vulture's, she is sure. Why else has he gone to the palace with the lethal lightning-bolt weapon she saw on the harbour?

Wing, crammed in close behind her, yells in her ear as a rock juts from the water like a shark fin. They steer frantically with the oars but all Mara can think of is Lily, in the very place that Oreon and his lightning gun have gone – and the watch that carries Fox's voice.

She will swim to the palace if she must.

Cleverly, Oreon cast his news among the fisherfolk – the gossiping hub of every port. His news would have been lost among the muddle-headed drunks in Ale Alley; by sunup, the threat of the sky invasion will have spread all through the boats and bridge market of Ilira. Why, people will whisper, has the Pontifix allowed another empire to sink its claws into the North? In a few, sly words Oreon has destabilized Tuck in his own city. And by sunrise, what else will Oreon have done?

Mara scans the darkness. No sign of the gondola fleet. They must have landed on the palace isle.

Wing pulls his wolf head over his eyes as they clear the last of the bridges. The round dome of the palace glows like a fallen chunk of moon set in a claw of rock. As they draw towards the small island, Mara sees the tall-masted sailing ship docked on the far side.

A bitter mist blows in, stinging her eyes, catching her throat. Over her shoulder, Wing's wolf snout seems to sniff the air and the beast's dead amber eyes flicker with an ominous glow.

'Fire!' says Wing. He points his paddle. 'Ship!'

Flames lick the lowest sails of Tuck's ship. The eye-stinging mist is smoke.

They push forward until the kayak bumps against rock. Mara clambers ashore, Wing at her heels.

Now Mara sees the gondola fleet, positioned all around the ship. Guards in the boats fling up ropes on spiked anchors that catch on the ship's rails. Spider-fast, they climb the ropes and invade the deck, whipping up fires in the rig-ropes and mast sails. Screams rip through the blaze.

'*Great Skua*!' she whispers, reading the flame-lit name of Tuck's ship; the name of the pirate bird of the Northern seas.

Bullet-shaped longboats have invaded the fjord, steering carefully around jutting rocks and ship-wrecking traps. In the time it takes Mara and Wing to scramble around the palace isle, the invaders have begun spilling from the longboats and on to the rough harbour.

Mara looks out to sea and her heart jolts. There, at the

199

mouth of the fjord, moonlight falls on what seems, to her startled eyes, to be a cluster of silver pines in the wind. She blinks and the swaying treetops become the tall masts of ships.

So Oreon did not come to Ilira alone.

But Tuck's fate is his own problem. Lily is all Mara can think of now.

Fire threads the masts of Tuck's ship and Mara is consumed by a panic so fierce she doesn't know which way to run. Where is Lily? The palace, surely? Not the ship?

Smoke stings her eyes. Mara scrubs them with her sleeve and sees Oreon standing imperiously on the rocks of the rough harbour, watching as a man is marched along the deck of the ship. The man's hair is like a dash of moonlight against his dark windwrap. Mara knows she is looking at Tuck.

She slips on seaweed and crashes to the ground. Pain shoots through her but she ignores it, barely able to believe that the man she thought long dead is still alive; the one who stole her connection to Fox.

Mara creeps across the rocks. She must tread carefully now. Too much is at stake. Thinking fast, she sees Tuck forced down the ship's ladder and into a gondola. By the time she has crept as close as she dares, he has been brought ashore to Oreon.

'Let him go,' he orders the guards. 'My brother is not your enemy, Tuck. Neither am I.'

'Your brother can't be trusted,' Tuck replies. 'Not by me.'

'He says the same of you,' Oreon retorts. 'But you're not bickering gypsea boys any more; you are both the powers of the North, and the North is under threat. War is coming. A great new enemy faces us all. We need to band together as gypsea brothers. You're still a gypsea, Tuck,' he urges, earnest now. 'We need to forget our differences, remember our bonds and fight the real war. We've made contact with the Surgents—'

'This,' Tuck interrupts, gesturing to his burning ship, 'is your idea of bonding?'

'It's our way of making sure you see the seriousness of the situation,' says Oreon. 'Your ship is burning, your guards have abandoned you.' He stoops and picks a guard's helmet from the ground and presents it to Tuck. 'See? Now your men wear the Vulture's claw.'

'I *see* that your brother hasn't changed,' says Tuck, brittle-eyed. 'I *see* plenty.'

Mara recalls the short-sighted gypsea boy with his eyebox and knows that beneath the fierce composure of the man is the same boy who grasped whatever he could of the world, trying to own and absorb what he struggled to see.

'Never trust a gypsea, eh?' Oreon gives Tuck a wry smile. 'My brother knew that, Tuck, so he made a secret pledge with Rodenglaw and his commanders that they would ally to our Vulture fleets if anything happened to him, once you married his daughter. Now they are all in the Vulture's grasp.'

'So your brother took Rodenglaw's pledge – then had him killed? To get his hands on his fleets?'

Oreon nods.

'Urth!' Tuck curses and gives a harsh laugh. 'Rodenglaw was a fool.'

'He was,' Oreon agrees. 'But his men are ours now and your fleets have scuttled to join us too, like rats from a sinking ship. The Vulture is ready to claim his place as Emperor of the North. He's ready to lead the fight against the sky empire alongside the Surgents. But he asks you to join him as a gypsea brother. You know things that we don't.

You have knowledge and talents that we need – look at the wonder you've made of Ilira. Join us, Tuck!' Oreon pauses. 'What choice do you have?'

Tuck responds like a true gypsea. He draws the cutlass from his belt and lunges towards Oreon. Guards surge forward as the young scholar pulls his lightning gun from his windwrap. Mara sees what she must stop.

'Tuck!' She rushes forward. 'It's me, Mara – Oreon, no!'

Tuck's head jerks towards her in the instant he falls hard to the ground. Oreon glances at Mara in confusion, then at the unfired weapon in his hand.

Tuck lies face down in an awkwardly crumpled heap on the harbour rocks.

'Get up,' says Oreon, unnerved at the sight of the Pontifix of Ilira sprawled at his feet. 'There's no need to beg – your life will be spared. My brother doesn't want you dead; but he won't allow you to steal his power. Work with us, Tuck. A great man like you shouldn't be my brother's prisoner but that's what will happen if we can't agree.' Oreon's warrior facade breaks again to reveal an awestruck and eager young scholar. 'I want to learn from you!'

Mara struggles in the grip of a guard.

'He's not begging you for his life,' she shouts at Oreon. 'Can't *you* see?'

With a shaking hand Mara points to the blade that has ripped through Tuck's windwrap and protrudes from his back like a silver fin.

'He fell on his cutlass!'

Mara tears free of the guard and runs over to Tuck.

He lies with his face twisted towards her. His wide-open eyes are glassy as watch-faces and the flickering reflections of the burning ship seem to flash the hour, the minute, the very last seconds of his life. Mara pushes away the moon-pale hair from Tuck's face, feels his neck for a pulse. She puts her mouth to his ear.

'Hey, gypsea,' she whispers.

'Mara,' Tuck murmurs. 'Getting dark now.'

And he is gone.

Mara cannot believe it. All these years she thought he was dead, she couldn't bear to think of him, though some nights he'd steal into her dreams and she'd wake full of desolation, plunged back into that searing moment of betrayal when he vanished into the mountain with her globe. Now, she lays her head against his, overcome once again by a furious sense of loss.

'He always took whatever he wanted.' Mara raises her head to look up at Oreon. 'He took his life from *you* so he could keep it as his own.'

Oreon's shocked silence shatters. He drops down on his knees beside Mara with an anguished cry, transfixed by the deathly silver fin in Tuck's back.

'My brother wants him alive. *I* want him alive! There are things only he knows. The secrets of the globe . . .'

He looks at Tuck in horror, as if he has let a precious relic slip through his fingers and smash on the ground.

Shaking, Mara seizes her chance.

'The globe is mine,' she tells Oreon. 'Tuck stole it from me years ago. I know all its secrets. I know who the Midnight Storyteller is. I know where he must be. I know about the sky cities too. I've been *inside* one.'

Oreon drags his eyes from Tuck's body to Mara.

'What?'

'I'll tell you everything,' Mara persists. 'Things a scholar of the world *should* know, secrets that can help your brother's

203

war – but only if you help me find my daughter. She's being held here somewhere . . .'

A hot wind blasts across the harbour as fire rips through the *Great Skua*'s masts. In the light of the blaze Mara finds what she seeks.

The solitary figure of a girl is running along the deck of the ship.

Mara screams. It's a scream to kill the moment, to stop it happening, as a flaming branch of the masts droops, breaks and slowly tumbles towards the girl with fox-fire hair.

SURGE

I loved you, so I drew these tides of men into my
     hands and wrote my will across the sky in stars
To earn you Freedom, the seven-pillared worthy
     house, that your eyes might be shining for me
                                   When we came.
          T. E. Lawrence (Lawrence of Arabia)

CREEP TO THE SKY

'*Pan!*'

Fox digs a paddle into the sludgy water of the netherworld sea and heads his canoe towards the broken bridge. The dark path left in his wake lasts a bare moment before the parted green slime slides back so seamlessly it might have lain undisturbed for a thousand years.

Phosphorescence glimmers on the sky towers, sending a magical glow across the netherworld. Somehow everything seems possible at twilight.

Pandora is skateboarding down the great severed arm of the bridge. She skids around a wrecked bus towards a rusted pile-up of traffic near the waterline where the bridge collapsed long ago. The ancient wreckage seems to come alive as she races towards it. A nest of baby swamp dragons, their coppery-green scales in camouflage with the slimy rust heaps, scuttle out. They raise snouts to the sky. Their jaws open. Hungry eyes gleam at Pandora's approach.

The tiniest wrong move, a mistimed twitch of a muscle or a moment's lapse of will and she is supper for a family of swamp dragons. Fox holds his breath, and his tongue.

Pan flips the skateboard with a slam of her heel and

somersaults over the heads of the reptiles to land neatly on her feet on the crushed shell of a car. She catches the skateboard deftly before slamming it down on a sly dragon snout that pokes from the car's empty windscreen.

'See *me*? See *that*!'

Her yell of delight ricochets off the trunks of the sky towers and echoes across the netherworld.

'Beautiful,' Fox shouts back.

And she *is* beautiful, standing on the wrecked car like a warrior queen on a battered chariot. Her armoured tunic, made from the bronze scales of an animal called a pangolin, belonged to a Japanese samurai of ages past. She is even wearing a golden crown. Pan has prepared for war as if it's a game, practising daredevil tricks and weapon skills, forever rummaging in the museum for the perfect battle costume and weapons belt.

'Kitsune says go,' shouts Fox. 'Right away. They're about to blast the walls!'

Pandora whoops and jumps back on to the skateboard, outwitting the swamp dragons again. At the edge of the broken bridge she skids to a halt to meet the canoe.

Fox stares at her.

'Where's all your hair?'

The soft crown on her head is a cluster of curls. The long, tangled mass is gone.

'Chopped it off,' says Pan. 'Can't go to war tripping over my hair.'

She looks, thinks Fox, like the Botticelli angel in the painting he found caked in mud, as he once found Pan herself.

The helmet and weapons hooked on to her belt clang against her pangolin armour as she jumps into the canoe and sits facing him, flushed and ready. Fox ruffles her sweaty curls – then remembers her betrayal and his hand stiffens on her head. His heart and his mind are burning. What he discovered last night in the Weave has changed the world for him.

'Ready?' he says, trying to focus on the moment.

Pan straps the skateboard on her back and checks the lethal armoury of small weapons hooked on her belt. The little brass bugle is strung on a rope around her neck.

'I was ready moons ago,' she retorts, and points to a sinister ripple in the water. 'Dragon!'

Fox digs his paddle into the murky sea and speeds the canoe through the forest of towers that have begun to sparkle with lumenergy, as if the dusk has sprinkled them with frost. He stops at one of the spots where giant swamp creepers climb out of the water into the spiregyres – the air chutes that coil down the sides of the towers, expelling stale air from the sky city into the netherworld, like great lungs.

Nature has forced its way up into the city and no one has noticed.

Fox cranes his neck to map a path up the strongest limbs of the creeper then hauls himself on to the first branch.

'Come on!' he urges Pan, who is staring at the city walls.

'I want to see the walls come down!'

'It's not a game, Pan. Climb!'

Fox's nerves are strained to breakpoint. He rains a ferocious stream of curses down on Pan's head and she grips the creeper, staring up at him with a look that makes him take a steadying breath. She knows nothing of the world. Now that the world is bursting in, of course she wants to see.

'Wait till we get into the spiregyres,' he urges.

'Just *one* bomb,' Pan pleads.

Her wish is granted as light splashes across the dark water

and a thunderous noise fills the netherworld.

'Get above the waves!' Fox yells.

His ears pop. His heart booms. His skin prickles as the blast from explosion after explosion washes over him and bombs tear holes in the night. He takes a stunned second to look back down at the netherworld and sees ragged gaps in the city wall, as if giant fists have punched through.

The ocean crashes in with a roar. Waves break against the towers, soaking him in great thrashes of sea. His eyes sting, he can't see.

Where's Pan?

Fox shakes saltwater from his face. But there she is, clinging to the creeper below. Is she high enough to be safe from the surge?

'Hold tight!' he yells down.

She looks up, face dripping, eyes full of sea. The incoming ocean is too loud for him to hear the sobbed words on her mouth. She points across the water and in the flash of an explosion, he sees.

The old tower has crumpled and fallen to its knees. The huge cone of the spire tilts forward then breaks off the tower with a death-moan. The spire splinters into pieces and crashes into the water as if made of twigs, not ancient stone.

Sea rushes upon the fallen tower and raids it. A torrent of books spills into the netherworld. The surge reaches deeper into the museum halls and drags out a motley wreckage of paintings, an exodus of stuffed animals, suits of armour and dinosaur bones. The bright tunics from the Chinese room swirl like water lilies on the seething waves.

Pandora begins to climb furiously now, rushing away from the terrible wreckage of their home. Fox lets her go ahead. Her face tells him what's wrong. Her imagined fantasy of war has been trashed by ferocious reality.

They climb until Fox's head crunches into Pandora's feet. She has come to a sudden halt above him.

Fox reaches out and touches the only part of her he can reach – her foot.

'Steady now, Pan. We've got allies in the city, remember. We'll get through. There's a new life ahead.'

'Where?' Pan demands. 'With me or with *her*?'

'Who?'

'You know who,' Pan hisses. 'The Lily girl.'

Fox stares at Pan's long, webbed toes as they curl around the creeper stem. What happened last night in the Weave still seems like a dream. There's been barely a moment to think about it but there will be time a-plenty in the long climb ahead.

Pan is scrambling up the creeper again.

'You said they were *dead*,' she cries over her shoulder. 'But I saw you in the Weave. I followed you. I saw you on the bridge with her and I heard what you said. You're going to dump me in the city and go North for *them*.'

Fox slips on a slimy limb of creeper. He clutches at the sinewy branches with a yell, unable to get a grip. Pan's heel juts in his face and he grasps hold of it, steadying himself as he looks up at the girl's hurt, furious face.

'I said our *connection* was dead. I thought they might be. There's been no time to talk since –' He secures himself on the creeper. 'But you've had time, Pan. When were *you* going to tell *me*? You found my daughter, Lily, in the Weave, didn't you? My *daughter*. Yet you never breathed a word.'

Sirens scream. Flashlights sweep the sea below them. Sky patrols are swarming down from the towers. Gunners on skybikes let rip on the mass of vessels from the boat camp that are now surging through the bombed walls.

Light strikes their tower. An angry buzz fills the night as sky patrols drop from above.

'Into the spiregyres!' Fox yells. 'Quick!'

Startled owls flap in their faces. A dark rush of bats and reptiles scatter in fright as he and Pan scramble up into the shelter of the air chute. Once out of the reach of the searchlights, they pause for breath. Fox wipes the sweat from his face, emotions colliding as he watches the invasion of the netherworld.

Leaves shred and scatter as Pan slithers past him. Horrified, he sees she's let go of the creeper.

'No!'

Fox lunges for her. Clinging to the creeper with one arm, he grabs her round the waist. The pangolin scales cut into his hands but he grips her tight.

'You don't love me,' she whispers. 'You lied. You want Mara and the Lily girl.'

'We've come this far together, Pan,' he says gently, feeling all her hurt and fear as she trembles against him. Whatever she did, what does it matter now? 'Don't give up when we're so close.'

She buries her head in his neck. 'I want to stay close.'

He meant *so close to our goal*, but never mind.

'Come on then,' Fox urges. 'Let's go.'

The world below explodes into war as they climb inside the dark jungle that tunnels up to the city in the sky.

DISTURBING THE ETHER

Just hours before, escaping the seething panic of the Noos, Fox had surfed across the empty blue static of the Nowhere to the forlorn edges of the electronic universe where the virtual ruins of the Weave lie.

It was to be his last-ever visit to the place he'd bequeathed to Pandora. Since she'd taken over Surgent meetings in the Weave, freeing him to fire up revolution in the Noos and the world's soundwaves, he'd had no reason or desire to go there. A final gathering of the avatars of Surgent leaders from all across the Earth had brought him back, at last.

No one knew if they'd survive what lay ahead. As they gathered in the wasteland behind the Boulevard of Dreams, a scream tore through the ether like an omen of the battle to come. Fox saw what looked like a flame of his own fox tail streaking through the Weave-sky. No sooner had he glimpsed it than it was gone. The boulevards were checked but no threat or snooping presences were found. Fox urged his Surgents to keep strong and true in their hearts and the meeting broke up in a sombre, determined mood.

His life might end in a matter of days or hours. So Fox reckoned it was time to say goodbye to the past, once and for all. In the guise of the very same fox avatar of his youth, he roamed old haunts in the electronic boulevards, his wanderings ending where they always did, once upon a time.

But when he padded on to the broken Bridge to Nowhere his cybersenses tingled. Someone else had been here, recently. The disturbance left in the ether was like fresh footprints in dust.

Pan liked to snoop, he knew that, but her snaky presence left barely a trace. These were not Pan's slithering Weave-tracks nor the furtive stalkings of a rogue presence. Neither was there the litter of rotting data the creatures of the junk heaps always left in their wake. These cybertracks were frantic, circling and back-tracking, treading this way and that across the broken bridge. Yet the guard he'd left here years ago, a fox twin on a neverending bridge-watch waiting for Mara if she ever came back, had not sounded its alarm.

He found the fox guard muzzled and useless, hidden under ether dust so thick he knew the creature hadn't stirred in years. Who had muzzled it and put it to sleep? Pan? A rogue Surgent? How long had it been silenced? How many years . . . ? If Mara had ever come here looking for him, he realized with a sick jolt, he'd never know now.

Fox unmuzzled his fox twin and awakened it from its enforced slumber. Back in realworld, suddenly exhausted in body and mind, Fox flopped down on his pulpy bed in the tower room and fell into a blank sleep of his own.

Jolted awake into throbbing darkness he couldn't tell if he'd slept minutes or months. He'd fallen asleep with his godgem on and woke up still on the Bridge to Nowhere at the edges of the Weave. The fox guard was on its feet yipping and yapping at the avatar of a girl scrambling across the rubble to clamber up on to the broken bridge arm. As she spied the two foxes on the bridge she stumbled to a halt.

Fox silenced his yapping bridge-guard. In realworld, he could barely breathe. The skin of his human body prickled with shock. The name formed on his lips but it couldn't be . . .

'Mara?'

The girl was trembling so hard the ether rippled around her.

'I – I'm not Mara.'

Her voice was as incredulous as his own.

It was not Mara. He saw that after the first shock passed. Yet, there was something about the girl's intense gaze and burning presence, that was . . .

'Who are you?' Fox demanded, all his Weave-senses super-charged.

'I'm Lily,' she replied with a gasping cry. 'I thought I'd never find you.'

Fox stared harder and padded towards her until they were a footstep apart. She watched his every move with wide, fiery eyes.

'Once upon a time there was a fox,' she said, quick and breathless, 'who liked to sneak through the ruins of a beautiful, broken world on to the Bridge to Nowhere. My mother used to tell this tale when I was small.'

'Who,' Fox whispered, 'is your mother?'

'Mara,' said the girl.

Reality seemed to bend and crumple. The eyes that stared back at him were, he now saw, a mirror of his own.

'You are *Fox?' It was a desperate plea. 'My mother's Fox?'*

'I am Fox,' he replied.

'Then – then you're my father,' she said, her tentative young voice reaching out to him across a footstep of cyberspace, an ocean of lost time.

It was the violent tug of her voice on his heart that made him believe beyond doubt.

Back in realworld, Fox whispered a Weave spell into the godgem, while on the broken bridge . . .

A tiny tornado began to whirl around the cyberfox. He was breaking up, vanishing before Lily's horrified eyes.

'No!' A cry tore from her. 'Please don't go!'

Unable to breathe, she could only watch as the cyberswirl slowed and the electronic matter rearranged and settled into the shape of . . . a man. A man who was a stranger – yet he belonged to her, she knew that right away. His face was so like the one she has studied in the cracked mirror inside the lid of Granny Mary's wooden box: her own.

Lily wanted to rip through the virtual skin of the Weave, to reach out and touch her real, human father.

The ether crackled and sparked around them as the man and the girl stood together on the broken bridge.

She was a heart-wrenching mixture of Mara and himself. And there was even, Fox saw, a ghost of his own mother in Lily's face. But there was something more, something beyond all that, which was her very own self.

This is my daughter, *thought Fox, amazed.*

'But Mara,' he blurted out, 'is she . . . ?'

Lily sighed and his heart sank.

Dead, *he thought. She's dead, after all.*

'She's on the far side of the mountain,' said Lily.

'She's alive?' The throb of emotion in Fox made a violent ripple in the ether.

Lily nodded. 'But she doesn't know where I am. I ran away to find you.'

Fox studied his daughter's face, lost for words.

'I never knew you existed,' she burst out. 'I thought Rowan was my dad. The wizz globe was stolen before I was born so Mum lost contact with you. I came through the mountains to the ocean to search for you. I found the globe and now I've found you, but I've lost everything else.' The girl's face quivered. 'My best friend is dead and I'm a prisoner in Tuck's ship in the city of Ilira. He's a brutal man, he – ' She gasped, glancing upwards at something Fox couldn't see, frightened by something in her world. 'I don't know what's happening. There's shouting and screaming up on deck. Help me.'

Fox stepped as close as he dared. The slightest touch would tear the ether and leave a gash like a wound in the skin of the Weave.

'Lily, I'm an ocean away. You must help yourself.'

Her eyes were desperate. 'I had to see you, I had to. I was sure that snake-girl, Pandora, knew who you were. I told her you were my father but she chased me away.'

Pandora found Lily here and never told him?

Fox controlled a surge of rage at such betrayal. He felt he was furiously trying to fit together the lost pieces of a puzzle in the dark. The only parts of the puzzle that mattered were Mara and Lily. Mara was alive. But his daughter's life was in danger because of him.

And within hours his own life might end.

Emotion whirled inside Fox as he thought of the coming cyclone he had stirred up around the world. Yet here they were, he and Lily. Somehow they'd found each other in the virtual universe. It was as unlikely as two bits of flotsam from a storm-wrecked ship coming together, years later, in the eye of another storm.

His war was about to burst through the walls of the

WIZZLOG TO THE WORLD

Fox uttered a cybercode into his godgem – a Weave-spell he treasured years ago, found in the wreckage of a Weavesite and saved in the godgem's memory banks in case Mara ever came back.

On the Bridge to Nowhere a dark-haired young woman appeared like a genie from the ether.

'Mum?' Lily gasped.

'It's her grandmother,' Fox told her. 'Your great-grandmother, Mary Bell, when she was young.'

'Granny Mary?' Lily gaped in amazement.

'A lumen image of her I found in a newsgram,' Fox quickly explained. 'She logged the plight of her islands when the seas first rose. Her wizzlogs once had a worldwide following.' He started the lumen. 'Watch.'

'Wizzlog 47,' said Mary Bell. 'Last night the sea took one of our islands – whole families wiped out as they slept.' Her voice broke. 'Our land is vanishing around us. This is an SOS to the outside world.'

Mary Bell raked dark hair from her face in a gesture that is now Lily's and Mara's. She gazed out across the years. 'The people of our islands are survivors. Please help us. But if you don't, we'll find a way through this somehow.'

Her defiant dark eyes widened and she cried out in sudden joy to someone in her world that they couldn't see. 'Tain! You're safe!'

Mary Bell vanished.

Fox turned to her astonished great-granddaughter on the broken bridge.

'Don't give up. Do what Mary Bell and Mara did. Save yourself!'

Lily began to cough.

'Smoke,' she gasped. Then, 'I'm getting out.'

Fox heard the defiant tone. He glimpsed the bold spirit that had taken Lily through a mountain to track him down.

'I'll find you,' he promised.

'Look for the shining bridges of Ilira,' she cried, as she faded into the ether. 'A mountain city, deep in a sea fjord . . . find me there . . . !'

Then she was gone.

Moments later came Kitsune's call to arms.

CREEPING INTO HISTORY

'Will it hurt?' asks Pan.

She unhooks the metal helmet from her belt and pulls it on to her head.

'Not as much as it did on the way down,' Fox remembers. A wry smile breaks on his tense face.

Excitement pulses in him now that he's out of the netherworld, heading back up into the sky city he abandoned years ago. Back then, he almost drowned when he hurtled down these twisting air chutes and crashed into the netherworld sea.

Pan's green eyes glint at him through the visor slit. Clinging to the creeper, the helmet of a medieval knight on her head, skateboard strapped to the back of her pangolin-scale armour, she could be an exotic giant beetle among the jungle of leaves.

Fox pockets his godgem. It wasn't easy to Noosjump with creeper creatures fluttering and scuttling all around. But he just did. He shot a flare deep into the Noos. It's the signal for Steerpike, a secret Surgent at the heart of the sky city above, to set New Mungo's air systems to extreme power – in reverse.

It starts like a welcome breeze in the muggy jungle of the air tunnel. Then wind fills the coiling chute as a great rush of damp air is sucked up from the netherworld. Creeper creatures sweep past them in a flurry of leaves.

'Let go!' Fox yells, when it feels impossible to cling on any longer.

And up they surge, sucked higher and higher into the dark spiral of the chute. Pan screams like her crazy old self as they helter-skelter up towards the sky city in a blast of wind. Fox has forgotten the sheer joy of moving so fast that reality blurs. He doesn't want it to end, but it will, any moment, in a great –

CRASH!

They blast in a spray of filthy water into unearthly light. Fox lies in a wet heap for a long, dizzying moment, insects and swamp creatures raining down on him.

He sits up and looks around at an intersection of tunnels. He sees the movement of skaters at the distant end of one tunnel, feels the rumble of a sky train overhead.

We're in!

Creeper debris keeps spouting from the opened air vent: swampwater choked with newts and salamanders, frogs and lizards, bats and beetles, water snakes and rats, a saltwater otter, a squabble of mudcats, blizzards of butterflies, mosquitos and moths, a hooting volley of owls. The invasion of netherworld creatures swarms into the tunnels. Fox staggers to his feet, remembering himself among a flock of youths, speeding across the city through these silver sky tunnels . . .

A moan of pain brings him back to the moment. Pan is slumped awkwardly, crushed against a wall. He hurries over. Dazed green eyes blink at him through the helmet visor. Then she wriggles and jumps to her feet with a scream, tearing off the helmet, shaking out insects and lizards.

'Dragon!' she yells, and aims a brutal kick.

A baby swamp dragon, sucked up from the netherworld, hurtles through the air.

'You're all right then?' Fox judges, with a grin.

Pan nods as the swamp dragon scampers off. All of a sudden the blast of muddy debris from the air vent stops. Now they can hear terrified shouts and screams as bombs shake the sky city. Fox shoves his feet into the zapeedo boots that have been carefully placed beside the opened vent, as Pan unstraps the skateboard from her back.

'Come on!'

Impatient as ever, she is off.

'It's a while since I've done this,' Fox shouts after her, unsteady at first as the zapeedos power up. Then the joy-rush of speed and momentum, missed for so long, consumes him again and he remembers how to skate.

No longer is he creeping along the edges of history, now he's hurtling towards the future, deep in the heartbeat of the world. He can hear it booming through the towers . . .

All the stagnant years in the netherworld fall behind Fox as he races towards the centre of New Mungo, sparks crackling from the blades of his zapeedos as he zips round a bend.

I am the storyteller, he is thinking. *I can tell this tale any way I want. I will not die.*

He won't think of his promise to the Surgents, now at war in every sky city across the planet, in the rebellion that's taken him half his life to plan – the promise that he is ready to sacrifice himself, as they are, to break the empire's hold on the world and reclaim the Earth for all its people. For the first time in years Fox is not thinking of the rest of the world. He is thinking of himself, of Lily, the daughter he must reach, and of Mara.

He must create the right end for his own story. Now.

THE GHOST TRAP

Every sky city of the New World is under attack. The walls that make every city a sea fortress, the spiregyres of the vast sky towers, the Noos, the trade empire and, most crucially of all, the imaginations of the Nooworlders – the Surgents have invaded it all.

There is an added shock that Fox means to detonate: his own return from the dead.

His parents have always been strangers to him. Their work as empire builders meant constant travelling among the cities, so the bonds between parents and son were already stretched over thousands of ocean miles before Fox made the final break.

The vanishing of David Stone, grandson of Caledon and son of two of the empire's most powerful Guardians, is a mystery that has never been solved. Fox means to solve that mystery today.

The original plan was for the boat-camp Surgents now crashing through the city walls into the towers of New Mungo to band together with rebels inside the city to seize the Guardians and wrench power from their hands. With the Guardians under arrest Fox would take control of the city as

Caledon's genuine heir, and reveal himself through the Noos as the beloved global superstar of the Midnight tales. Fox's great hope is that the sky people, thrust into chaos, but with hearts and minds newly opened through the stories he has told, will seize the moment as a chance to re-imagine what they can be, what kind of world they want, and how it might be remade for *all* its people.

Second by second as he speeds through the sky tunnels Fox is redrafting his plans. Finding Lily has changed everything.

Skaters zip up the sides of the tunnels, looping overhead, whizzing in cascades of fear. The thunder of the bombs and the invasion of netherworld creatures allow Fox and Pandora to skate through the mounting panic unchallenged while the Nooworlders, desperate to find out what is happening to their world, try to Noos-connect on the move.

'Look, look!' Pan yells, as they zap past bright, airy arcades full of shops and entertainments that seem a universe away from the harsh gloomy grime of the netherworld below. 'You never told me it was all so beautiful. Ow!' Pan's quick reflexes send her looping up the tunnel wall to avoid a skater who has skidded to a halt.

'What's up?' Fox asks, skating around the bewildered youth.

'Something's wrong with my godkin. My Noos connection's gone.'

'Mine too!' a passing girl shrieks.

'And mine!'

'What's happening?'

'All the godkins are dead . . .'

'The Noos has crashed!'

Fox and Pandora exchange glances. It's as they'd hoped. Under attack from all fronts across the world, the empire has panicked and blocked connections to the Noos. Now the sky citizens are disorientated and at the mercy of the Surge.

'Junction 237.' Fox glances at an overhead sign. 'Steerpike's package should be here.'

'There!' Pandora points to a green litter bin on the wall.

Fox rummages among a mush of litter and finds a bento box. Wrapped in seaweed rolls inside the edible box is the equipment he needs: a soundwave connector and a sharp sliver of metal the size of a baby's fingernail. Fox inserts the earplug that will connect him on a soundwave to Kitsune at the helm of the global Surge. He looks at the tiny blade in disgust.

This is what a godgem has become. A godkin. A bland metal chip. Not voice-controlled as his trusty old godgem is but by thought, sensation and mood. Fox's Noos-trawls have kept him up to date with a technology that's now a world away from what it was in his youth. Each Nooworlder is a dynamo of sensor chips and connectors embedded in skin and clothes; a human techno-hub tuned in, even in sleep, to the pandemonium of the Noos. Sudden disconnection must feel like amputation, as shocking as if Fox had sliced his sword through the ankles of skaters as they zip past.

It's a miracle so many were ensnared by his Midnight broadcasts. Fox's secret was to awaken a buried need, one embedded even deeper in their circuitry – the hunger for a good story, told by a human voice.

In the absence of a Noos doctor, Kitsune has told him how to implant the godkin – by slicing it into the skin behind his ear. Then, when the Noos is reconnected, Fox will be ready to lead.

But Steerpike and Kitsune don't know that Fox has shredded that part of the plan.

Fox stuffs the godkin back inside the sushi. He unwraps another seaweed roll and finds two sleek weapons. With his back to the skaters, he slips Pan the stun gun and keeps the laser for himself.

'Just point and press with your thumb here.'

He shows her; she nods.

Fox chucks the bento box in the bin. He checks the tiny godbox pinned to the leather collar of his armoured vest then feels for the green gem in his pocket. Fiddly it might be, but he'll stick with his old godgem.

The soundwave crackles in his ear.

'Kitsune?'

'The Noos is down. Walls breached in thirty-eight cities, Fox – and more to go. Where are you?'

'Junction 237. Tell Steerpike thanks for the godkin, but no thanks.'

Kitsune chuckles. 'Thought so. Remember the way to the Nux?'

'I remember.' Fox has travelled these tunnels endlessly in his dreams. 'Steerpike still safe?'

He hopes so. So much depends on Steerpike, his unknown guardian angel. Over the years, Fox has learned to trust this mysterious friend whose Noosname is stolen from a Midnight tale. All communications are passed through Kitsune and his accomplices in the Far East. Direct messages between Steerpike, a traitor at the heart of New Mungo, and Fox in the netherworld ruins at the feet of the city, was too risky in case police rooks in the Noos ever tracked the message trail.

'All safe, so far,' Kitsune whispers in his ear, as Fox zips through chaotic throngs of skaters towards the great hub at the centre of the towers where all the sky tunnels meet.

And there it is! Fox's heart gives a nostalgic leap as he sees the majestic doors of the cybercathedral, the hive of business and industry where he once worked.

'Approaching the cybercath,' he tells Kitsune. 'Where exactly are *you*?'

'Never mind me. Watch out, Fox. There'll be traders in the cybercath who knew you before. Steerpike's set up the tok-check. Head straight for the Guardians' main chamber. Armed Surgents will meet you there.'

Fox glimpses a tall, weather-tanned, bruisedly handsome warrior skating towards him through the crowd. His face is alight with adrenalin and the brown eyes that lock with his are flecked with a dangerous fire. *Who is he? Does he know me?* Fox's heart quickens until he realizes he is looking at himself in the soaring wall of mirror outside the cybercath. In a flak-jacket made from the armoured leathers of an ancient soldier and his second skin of netherworld grime, he is unrecognizable as the young Noosdreamer who was David Stone.

He gives a husky laugh.

'Don't worry,' he tells Kitsune, as the warrior in the mirror gives a wry grin. 'No one will *ever* know me.'

Workers rush from the cybercathedral into the city as the bombing of the walls shakes the very core of New Mungo.

'Pan – here!' Fox shouts through the oncoming crowd. She skids to a halt on her skateboard at the giant doors of the cybercath, her green eyes widening.

A lumen, a virtual door guard with hair and clothes like starlight, greets them with an enthusiastic 'Hello!'

'Hello,' Fox responds brusquely to the tok-check, his hand on the gun in his pocket.

'Hello!' Pan echoes. 'You're beautiful!'

The lumen quivers as if delighted at the compliment – but it's an electronic quake, anticipating the blast that now rips through the tunnels. A series of blows rocks the city, one after the other, as if a demented giant is chopping at the

232

limbs of the empire with an axe.

The crowd stills in shock.

The lumen's eyes beam like lasers – which, Fox knows, they are. They can't duck or move or the tok-check will fail. They must stay in the lumen's eyebeam. A failed voice recognition means an instant stun ray from its eyes.

Fox's fingers grip his gun. Though what can his laser do to a girl made of lumenergy? Has the tok-check failed?

In a moment of searing stillness between explosions, the shimmering girl steps aside.

'Work well and prosper!' she urges, oblivious to the mayhem.

Pandora returns the lumen's brilliant smile as they pass through the tall doors into a large, domed arena. A rabble of Noostraders are rooted to the spot, ignoring the mayhem in the world outside. They stare aghast at the flashing data on the huge walls – trading updates from sky cities all around the Earth. But the trade alerts have stuck in the moment the Noos connections were cut.

The traders seem to bellow into thin air but the godkins embedded in their skin are relaying to their Trade Lords a double catastrophe – not only are the businesses they sunk their wealth into still vanished from the ether, now the Noos itself has disappeared.

Fox grabs Pandora's hand and they race through the crowded work pods towards a hidden door he remembers in the mirror walls.

'Trillions of Noo$dollars!' a purple-cheeked trader is hollering. 'All gone – and now there's no Noos!'

A woman stares aghast at the data walls. 'But I – I can't explain, Lord Edin. It's just gone.'

The cacophony of disbelief almost drowns out the

sound of the bombs outside.

'Great work, Surgent Fox,' Pandora whispers.

'What,' says an appalled voice, 'is *that*?'

The smile dies on Pandora's face as a group of young traders recoil from her as they might if they found a swamp dragon scuttling through their shining cathedral. A horrified woman looks her up and down and screams. Fox pulls Pandora away through the chaotic crowd until they are face to face with themselves in the mirrored wall.

Pan stares at her reflection with a shattered look.

The dead alerts of the trade screens spark in her eyes and on the scaly armour of her tunic. Amid the crystal brightness of New Mungo and its groomed sky citizens her sleek-haired skin, webbed feet and fingers, even the grimed features of her fiercely angelic face, are dangerously alien.

Get her out of here fast, thinks Fox.

'David Stone,' he snaps at his reflection and sees the flicker of the eye-scanner behind the mirror.

Behind him, a young trader approaches, his eyes fixed on Pan, the blade of a skate boot aimed at her head. Fox sees the zapeedo blade flash as the concealed door slides open in the wall. He yanks Pan through. The door shuts and the tumult of the cybercath cuts dead.

They are safe. For the moment. Unless the violent young Noostrader has security clearance for the Nux.

Luckily, the private door in the mirrored wall stays sealed.

Steerpike couldn't believe it. Though Fox vanished from New Mungo over fifteen years ago, his identity was never erased from the security systems. No one ever knew what happened to young David Stone. How could they have guessed? He was assumed dead, said Steerpike, though there was no body to be found. But instead of instant deletion, upon death, his identity has lingered in the system like an electronic ghost.

Did they forget to delete him? Or did his parents hope that one day he would return as mysteriously as he disappeared?

They have entered a softly lit inner corridor. Deep in this hidden area beyond the cybercath are the city Guardians' chambers of power. Fox remembers it all as if he has never been away.

Pan hisses a warning. He sees a flash, like a red alert. A Nux guard has appeared among the mirrors. Out of the corner of his eye, Fox sees the pincer movement of yet more guards in the empire's scarlet jackets.

The stun blast hits him like a giant's punch. Too late, he realizes the mirrors have tricked him into seeing six guards where there's only one – and that one was right behind him. His legs crumple; he slumps to the floor. With a groan of despair he sees that his ghost might have been left in the system as a trap, in case he ever dared to return.

The ancient armour in his flak-jacket has saved his upper body from the blast but his legs are dead. They might as well be chopped off.

'Been stunned,' he replies to Kitsune's frantic query on the soundwave. 'No legs. I need back-up, fast.'

'Surgents are heading to the Nux but there are battles all over the city – hold on, Fox.'

'Too late.'

Kitsune groans now. The guard advances, his eyes flicking from Fox to Pan.

'What – what *are* you?' he gasps, as if he has stumbled across creatures from another world.

For a split second Fox's heart leaps as the nervous young guard fumbles and drops the stun gun. But now he grips another gun, a laser, and takes aim at Fox's head.

235

ROGUE SURGE

'Run!'

Pan ignores Fox's order.

She's taken one of the medieval weapons from her belt and whirls the chain around her head. On the end of the chain is the Morning Star, a vicious little ball of spikes that can strangle a dragon, the deadly star embedding in the beast's throat as the loaded chain wraps around its jaw.

A tornado of Morning Stars seems to fly around the corridor, the mirrors multiplying the spiked metal ball into a whirling storm. The guard panics, ducks and runs to escape the onslaught – but his confusion takes him right into Pan's stun blast. He gives a strangled scream and drops to the ground as the spikes sink into his neck and the loaded chain lassoes around his throat.

Pan's skateboard clatters on to the floor. She heaves Fox on to it and retrieves her spiked ball and chain from the unconscious guard. Fox lies on his stomach and grips the edges of the skateboard, his stunned legs a dead weight.

'The lift,' he gasps, pointing. 'Over there! Red button . . .'

Shouts and footsteps resound in the corridors as Pan pushes him towards the lift. She slams her fist on the red crystal button. A door opens in the wall and Pan pushes Fox into the lift capsule. Then she rushes back out.

'Get *in*,' Fox yells.

She is dragging the unconscious guard towards the lift. She hauls him in and the lift doors slide shut as a flash of red-jacketed guards appear at the edge of the corridor.

'How long till you get your legs back?' Pan demands breathlessly.

Fox wiggles his toes. Feels a tingle as the lift speeds upward.

'Not long – but the second I do, you're going to use *your* legs and get to the top of the towers. Plans have changed,' he responds, as she argues. 'Get to a rooftop and wait for the ships. There's something I have to do on my own.'

'Ship? Since when was I going on a ship?' Pan is searching the young guard's jacket, having already pocketed his gun. She pulls a second gun from his belt and hands it to Fox. 'You need me. I just saved you. We're fighting for this city. You said we'd be king and queen of the empire once the Guardians were gone, that we'd change everything. How can we abandon all that?'

'Not king and queen, Pan, I never said that. Not rulers. A different kind of guardian. But that was before I found Lily. What do you expect me to do? Abandon her?' he retorts, torn between duty and desire; what he should do and what he must. 'It's not only our fight. Others can take over here. I can still be a global force once we've rebooted the Noos. We can still do what we said, make a new kind of world – just do it from the Northlands.'

He grinds to a halt, overwhelmed by guilt, by the enormity of abandoning the plan he has worked towards for years. Then Lily's face flashes up in his mind's eye and he hears her last, desperate cry and his decision becomes clear and pure. His daughter needs him. Nothing else matters more, nothing in the world.

'Maybe I don't want to go North,' says Pan sullenly. 'Maybe I want to do what we always *said* we'd do, right *here*.'

She works fast as she speaks, binding the guard's hands with a rope from her weapons belt. The lift stops and the door slides open. Guns ready, they listen to brutal echoes from somewhere deeper in the Nux. But the corridor outside is clear.

'Pan, what happened in the cybercath –'

Fox staggers to his feet, struggling to make his dead legs work. They tingle fiercely, as if embedded with spiky Morning Stars. The near-attack in the cybercath convinced him that Pan would not be safe here.

'They looked at me like I was a – a *snake*. Maybe they'd think I was a freak in the Northlands too!' Fox's heart turns over as Pan's voice breaks. 'So where am I supposed to go?'

'You're coming North with me.'

Fox leans against a wall and pulls a folded paper from a pocket of his armoured jacket – the map of the city he has drawn in charcoal to show the network of sky tunnels with the cybercathedral and the Nux like a fat spider at the heart of a great web.

'Look.' Fox trails his finger across the map. 'Each of the sky tunnels leads to a tower. Elevator shafts lead to the roofs. They all say *No Access* – ignore that. The tok-checks are all set up for you.'

In his mind's eye Fox sees air fleets from the east surging across the globe, each one headed for a sky city.

'I want to stay with you.' Pandora's mouth trembles.

'Why can't I come? What is it you're going to do?'

'I need to fix a broken bridge,' says Fox. 'I need to do it alone. Go and help the boat refugees find their way to the roofs. They should be battling up through the towers now. Keep yourself safe and head for the top of Aspen Tower.' His grandfather named the first towers of his New World after the lost trees of the Earth; Fox only realized this when he explored the old books. He shows Pan the route to Aspen, the northernmost tower, on the map. 'I'll meet you there.'

Kitsune is muttering on the soundwave, asking him what's happening, where is he, what's he doing, why's he heading for Aspen? Fox extinguishes his old friend with a tug on the earplug and gives the connector to Pandora.

'Promise?' Pan holds his gaze.

'Promise. Kitsune will keep you right.'

'Because you need me,' Pan murmurs, doubtful still. 'You do.'

Her green eyes burn into him. Then she slams her skateboard on the ground and speeds off.

The city sways and shakes in ocean-blasts and bombs. Fox staggers through pillared corridors, stamping the last numbness from his tingling legs, imagining the towers and sky tunnels as giant trees in a global storm.

The thunder of feet makes him halt. A gun in each hand, Fox flattens himself behind a pillar. Guards rush past. One trips and sprawls on the ground. Fox takes aim but the guard lies stunned. Another man crashes down, then another, and Fox sees the rogue guards at the tail end stun-blasting their comrades.

His spirit leaps. It's really happening! The Surge is bursting into the cities and now the secret Surgents inside the empire are breaking loose. Maybe this *is* his true legacy –

to break the grip of the Guardians for the new imagineers. There must be other young dreamers in these cities who will rise from all this with a new sense of the world, of what might be possible, what could be . . .

Adrenalin speeds him round a last bend in the corridor towards the private chambers that were once his grandfather's and now belong to his father, Mungo Stone.

The last time he entered these chambers he was with Mara. Hours later, she escaped on a ship and he crashed down into the netherworld, a teenage dreamer who planned to change the world. How could he have known how many hard years it would take, how much he must lose before he returned?

Fox stuns the two guards on duty outside the chamber and steps over the crumpled bodies.

He pulls out his laser gun to disable the tok-check and his eyes fall upon the blood-red jackets of the guards with the dark lilies, the emblem of the empire, emblazoned at their hearts. A bolt of emotion hits like the gentlest stun-blast at the memory of the old woman who lived in a tree, the ancient guardian who showed Fox how to survive in the netherworld and guided him as he sowed the first seeds of his revolution: the Lily his grandfather once cast down into the netherworld and years later, ridden by guilt, enshrined as the emblem of the empire; the same Lily remembered by Mara in their daughter's name.

The door to his father's chamber slides open with barely a whisper and Fox steps inside.

THE GHOST OF CALEDON

An enormous blue globe floats in the middle of the room.

Inside the slow-spinning lumen stands a man, engulfed by a storm of newsflashes from a hundred points within the globe's oceanic skin. Fox watches, mesmerized by the computerized lumen of the planet and the sky cities.

Fox peers through the flashing alerts and watches the elderly man select news with his fingertips from around the globe, absorbing it all into his personal circuitry. The man sighs and rubs his hands together as if cold, though the room is hot.

Fox knows the gesture is his father's – but this man could, almost, be his grandfather, Caledon. The smooth-as-glass dome of the head, edged with a frost of hair. Stooped shoulders. Papery, pale skin. Smooth white hands. An elderly yet unnaturally ageless man.

Fox looks at the dark, callused skin of his own hands and remembers how soft and unweathered they once were. When he lifts his gaze to the older man in the ghostly light of the globe his father seems to be a phantom of the man Fox will never now become.

Fox remembers his father as a robust presence who wore

his hard-edged energy like armour, forever travelling the planet's sky cities, a dynamic knight in Caledon's realm. Age has shrunk and stilled Mungo Stone. Now he travels the planet by cyberspace, Fox sees, troubleshooting from within his globe. His power base, once the steel axis of the empire, has been stolen by younger, stronger rivals across the world. The invasion of the Northlands is Mungo's last, desperate gamble for lost power.

Fox steps closer. At last his father sees him. Mungo's shocked eyes meet his son's.

'What are you doing here? How did you get in?' Mungo Stone emerges from the globe. 'Security!'

There is no recognition on his father's face. So the tok-check didn't alert him? Was his identity just left there, forgotten?

'No guards. No security,' says Fox softly. 'Dad, it's me.'

The young man holds the shocked gaze of the older one. Mungo Stone gives another useless shout to the disabled circuitry of his personal Noosguard.

'It's me, David,' says Fox.

His father's eyes widen a fraction and there's a tremor of the papery eyelids.

'I don't care who you are,' he says. '*No one* enters my chambers without—'

'I'm your son.'

'My son,' says Mungo Stone, and now his voice shakes, 'is dead.'

Fox watches his father's right hand slide into a pocket. He pulls out a gun.

'I'm not dead,' says Fox. *Not yet*.

He looks at the gun in his own hand. Slowly he slips it back into his belt and faces his father with bare hands. All

242

his nervousness has gone. For once in his life, Fox intends to be the most important thing in his father's world. And for the first time, Mungo will know who his son really is.

'My son,' says Mungo Stone, the gun still in his hand, 'was killed in the 2100 Uprising.'

'You saw his body?' says Fox. 'But you couldn't have, you weren't here. You were at the other side of the world.'

Mungo's pale face bleaches to white. 'My father, Caledon—'

'— lied, if he told you I was dead. I vanished in the slave breakout but I didn't die. No body was ever found.'

Mungo Stone brushes his hand across his brow, wiping away beads of sweat. The atmosphere is stifling, though the city air should be mellow and fresh – another sign that all systems are in breakdown, even the air con. All of a sudden Fox longs to be standing at the top of the old tower with the North Wind in his face.

'Who are you?' demands Mungo Stone.

'The last time we met in the Noos,' says Fox, 'we had a row because you forgot my seventeenth birthday.'

'I never forgot, I . . .' Mungo stumbles to a confused halt. The gun droops in his hand.

'You had important business in New Jing.'

Mungo Stone takes a stumbling step backwards. Flashing alerts on the globe spike all around his head like a silent lightning storm. He makes a fumbling gesture as if to brush the planet aside.

'End,' he orders.

The lumen fades and disappears.

'It can't be you,' Mungo murmurs. But recognition sparks at last in the stricken eyes that study Fox's face. 'Where could you have hidden all these years? How could you do this to your mother – no, this is *outrageous*, impossible.' He shakes his head, takes another step backwards.

'You left my identity in the system,' Fox reminds his father. 'Why do that if you believed I was dead?'

'That would have been your mother,' Mungo says, after a pause. 'She never accepted your death.'

Fox hears pain in his father's voice. They seem to stare at each other across a gulf of time.

'If – *if* it's you – where have you *been*?' his father demands. 'Which city? Why did you disappear?'

'I've been living in the drowned ruins at the foot of *this* city.'

'Don't be ridiculous! No one could survive there.'

'Look.' Fox holds out his begrimed hands. 'This is dirt. Earth.' He pulls open the leather collar of his jacket to show his father patches of infected skin on his neck and chest. 'Insect bites. You know there are flood refugees surviving outside the wall. You *know* what's outside. I survived – just as they do. Some of them.'

'David,' murmurs his father. 'What are you? What have you become?'

Fox looks into his father's bewildered face. Mungo's power struggles in the empire have fascinated his son as he tracked all his doings, stealthily, in the news stations of the Noos. With a clench of his heart Fox now sees in his father a glimmer of his own self: the same dream-chasing spirit that drove Caledon to create the sky empire is behind Mungo's plots and schemes, and drives Fox now. That spirit lives on in Lily, who chased her dream through a mountain, risking her young life to find him.

The dreamers of the day are the dangerous men, his book of rebel wisdom said. They are the ones who act with eyes

244

wide open to make their dreams come true.

A family of dreamers, all of us, Fox sees; *for good and for bad*.

'Your David *did* die,' he tells his father, 'but I lived on. I am Fox and I lead the Surge – the last survivors of the Great Floods. War is on your doorstep, Dad. My Surgents have amassed all across the world. We are breaking through your walls. We are outside and inside every city. We are in the Noos. We are *here*,' he says as the tremor of an explosion vibrates in the room. 'There are Surgent fleets in the Northlands and other high lands of the Earth, all ready to fight the invasions of your empire. How many fighters do you have? How many thousands? Do you know how many flood refugees there are in the world? Millions, Dad. And I have roused them. The empire will ultimately lose.'

'*Your* Surgents? *We* are your people. In the name of Caledon!' The words burst like a curse and Mungo sweeps his arm around the room in a grand gesture, as if he stands on a mountain top with all the world before him. 'This was yours to inherit – why do you want to destroy it? And me?'

'I don't want to destroy,' says Fox. 'I want the sea-broken people to reclaim their share of the world. The empire blocks us. *You* block us. You can choose to stand aside and we'll call off our Surge. Listen to me, Dad. There isn't much time.'

A SON DEAD AND FOUND

'You're declaring war on the empire your own grandfather created?' Mungo paces the room. 'These cities saved a generation from the floods. We house millions of happy, productive citizens. We can't look after everyone. You would ruin all those lives just to share out the misery? Wreck the future of our innocent children? Kill your own people?'

'There are millions of innocents abandoned in the world outside,' Fox counters. 'Aren't they our people too? I don't want to wreck or ruin or kill. I want—'

'You're bombing us!'

'We're bombing the walls and the entrances to the towers. Not the people.' *Make war on places not people*: a crucial pillar of wisdom for the Surge. 'I'm not asking you to house the refugees,' he tells his father. 'Just let them have the high lands of the world. Let them *live*.'

'It took two generations of the best human minds to create this empire,' Mungo rages. 'Blow it all up then – let's *all* live in boats!'

He never could listen, Fox remembers. His temper always got in the way.

Mungo stops his furious pacing. 'You ran away from your destiny, David.'

'I'll decide what my destiny is,' Fox growls back.

'So tell me about that? What kind of future will there be after you ruin our world?'

'The planet does not belong to the empire,' says Fox. 'It belongs to all the people of the Earth. Share it with us, Dad.' He pauses, feels a bead of sweat trickle down his neck. 'It belongs to your granddaughter too.'

Mungo Stone blinks. 'Granddaughter?'

Fox hears a soft cry behind him. He spins around. An elegant woman dressed in the silken finery only afforded by the ruling powers of the empire stands just inside the doorway with a guard on either side. Her face is a faded version of the image Fox has burrowed away in his memory.

'Security – at *last*,' Mungo rasps. 'This intruder is armed – deal with him fast. Sarah, my love, stand back.' He glares at the unresponsive guards. 'What are you waiting for? Stun him!'

'Sorry, sir,' the female guard replies, 'but we will stun *you* if necessary.'

The male guard turns to Fox with an awestruck expression. 'Steerpike sent us. The Surge has broken all across the city and the Guardians don't know which citizens and guards are loyal and which are not. The boat people are now in the towers . . .' He pauses breathlessly as Fox – his eyes fixed on the silver-haired woman brought by the guards – does not reply. 'Er, what do you want us to do here, Surgent Fox?'

'Take my wife away,' Mungo Stone cuts in, but his voice has lost power. 'Sarah, go back to the apartment. I'll deal with this.'

'They said my son was here,' says Sarah. Her hands are clasped together, the knuckles white.

Her eyes meet Fox's across the space of the room. It feels to him as if they stare at each other down a long tunnel of time.

'David,' she whispers. 'Is it really you?'

247

DREAMERS OF THE DAY

'It's me,' he replies softly.

His mother takes three quick steps towards him then stops an arm's length away. She studies his face, a world of emotion in her eyes. She takes another step as if to embrace him then stops, shaking her head in disbelief, glancing from son to husband and back.

'What's happening? I don't understand.'

'There isn't much time . . .' Fox begins.

'You won't upset her with your madness,' says Mungo. 'Sarah, we don't even know if it's really him.'

'I know my own son,' Sarah retorts. 'Let him speak.'

In the gaze of her fiery, commanding eyes Fox tries to spill out the story of his missing years. Yet as he speaks he is overcome by despair. Coming here was all wrong. What is he trying to do? Make them see the world as he sees it? His father is a lost cause and his mother seems to look at him through a haze of bewildered anger and hurt. How can he make her understand the enormity of things in a few, rushed moments, amid this welter of pain?

He has been so stupid. This was never part of the original plan. He has risked his chance to escape because of a ridiculous fantasy of a happy-ever-after ending to the wreckage of his own life. Finding Lily brought a sudden urge to mend his broken family, just as he is trying to fix a sea-broken world.

'But I know this story!' His mother puts a quivering hand on his arm. 'It's what happened to Mara in *Exodus*.'

'You listen to the Midnight Storyteller?' Fox is stunned because that's the only way she can possibly know.

'That was outlawed,' Mungo interjects. 'Years ago.'

His mother, Fox realizes, is grasping towards under-standing while his father has shut down his mind.

'*You* are the Midnight Storyteller who lives in the crumbling tower?' Sarah is now oblivious to the bombs and her blustering husband. 'I thought he was just a Nooscreation. I never imagined he was *real*.'

Fox nods as his amazed mother tries to absorb the reality of her resurrected son.

'*Beowulf*, *Brave New World*, *The Time Machine*, *Gormenghast*, *Wuthering Heights*, *The Tempest*, *Frankenstein*, *Gulliver's Travels*, *The Grapes of Wrath*, *War and Peace*.' She reels off so many of the magnificent stories he has told. 'But the story of Mara,' she remembers, 'has no ending. You said that the ending is to be made by the people of the world – by us?'

Fox nods again, holding his mother's searching gaze.

'It's all true? Then *Exodus* is your story too. And this Mara,' she whispers, full of wonder, 'is the mother of – of my own grandchild? She set sail on the oceans to search for a new home for her child and her people at the top of the world, while Fox . . .' She pauses, understanding now.

'You,' Fox urges his mother, 'can decide the ending for your granddaughter, right now.' He looks up at the lumen star

249

constellations in the domed ceiling above. 'You people, you own the oceans, you want to colonize the stars, everything. Can't you spare the Northlands for your granddaughter? Let that be a land for all the people. Leave the high lands of the world for the flood refugees – *help* them settle there.'

'If there is a granddaughter, she should be here safe with us,' Mungo declares.

'Safe?' Sarah replies scornfully as yet another explosion rocks the city. 'Does this feel safe?'

'Put a stop to this, David,' Mungo persists. 'We'll bring the child and her mother here. The colonization of the North is necessary. You can't stop us, so why not work with us?' he cajoles. 'Let's see what we can do together! This world can still be yours.'

It was his original plan. Take control of the city and transform the empire from within. And a chance to do that is being offered to him by his father. But as he looks into Mungo's cunning eyes and hears the slippery promise his father is trying to bribe him with, Fox seems to see his future self when his bold dreams have been fretted and frayed and diminished, his one chance to unlock the future held hostage in this moment. He doesn't trust a word.

'I don't want your world,' Fox decides. 'Not this way. I want something better.'

'I won't let you destroy us,' his father warns.

Something is unravelling in Mungo. Fox sees it in a pulsing vein at his temple, in a spasm of his face. His father's whole existence has been built on a blind madness for power. *It's all he knows*, thinks Fox, *and he will not let anything or anyone stand in his way*.

'My true son,' Mungo Stone mutters, '*is* dead.'

The shot comes before Fox can react. A sword of light

that blasts the young guards then knocks him flat on his back as his hand reaches for his gun. He hears his mother scream.

He is in agony. The shoulder of his armoured jacket is melted and warped. The flesh underneath is a burned and bloodied mess. But the ancient armour has absorbed the worst of the laser blast. He'd be dead otherwise.

He raises his dazed head from the ground. Mungo stares down at him, a man lost in his own nightmare.

He aimed for my heart, thinks Fox.

In the blaze of pain that engulfs him, Fox seems to feel all that his father and the empire have cost him. It's the emptiest, most searing moment of his life. Fox has no thoughts at all as he draws his own gun . . .

Only to find it blasted out of his hand – by his mother, who in the same smooth second turns her gun on her husband.

Mungo falls to the ground.

'On your feet.'

Sarah pulls Fox upright. All her gentleness is gone.

'What kind of people *are* you?' he says through gritted teeth. His shoulder feels on fire, his hand and mind are numb.

'Not the kind who would let my husband and son kill each other,' his mother replies in a voice as harsh as his own.

Fox looks down at the gun she blasted from his hand. Not a stun gun but a laser. He would have killed his father had he shot back.

Sarah drops to her knees beside Mungo.

'According to his pulse he's alive. Though I'm not sure,' she says, harsh and dry, 'that he *has* a heart. He's badly stunned but otherwise conscious. He will survive. But will you?' She glances at her son with an unreadable expression and motions to the door with her gun. 'Come with me.'

She walks towards the door of the chamber, stopping to check the rogue guards.

'Dead.' She turns again to her husband with a furious cry. 'That was not necessary, Mungo,' she exclaims. 'Like so much that you do.'

'Am I your prisoner?' Fox asks his mother, as she hurries him out of the chamber and along the corridors of the Nux, her gun poised to fire. Bewildered, the pain in his shoulder searing, he does as she bids him. If she meant to kill him, surely she would have by now?

'You are only bound to me by blood,' she responds.

'My shoulder.' Fox staggers, hit by a spasm of pain.

Sarah pulls a handkerchief from a pocket to staunch the bleeding, but the cloth is soaked right away.

'What's your plan?' she asks, ripping at the sleeves of her graceful clothing and bandaging his wound, firmly, gently, as best she can. 'To break us – then what?'

'To break your stranglehold on the world,' Fox corrects. 'You know that your city wall is thirty boats deep in refugees? You're a Guardian of the empire – surely you know.'

'The wall is down,' Sarah corrects him, avoiding the question. 'The boat people have invaded the towers. The city guards are overwhelmed. Cities all across the world are in crisis too. So what happens now, David?'

'The refugee boats are junk heaps, they'd never make it across the Atlantic.' He gasps as she loops the silken material over his shoulder and under his arm, bandaging the wound tight. 'There are sky fleets heading to every city to take boat refugees to the Northlands and other high lands. Surgent leaders all across the Earth are in charge of local forces that will fight for the high lands of South America, the Tibetan plateaux, Siberia . . . and more. The empire can't take us all on. The guard forces you have in these high lands are not enough to overcome an organized Surge. The refugees are focused and desperate. They'll fight to the death. This is their only chance for a foothold on the Earth. We will break the empire.'

Machine-gun fire from the sky patrols batters the world outside. The zip of lasers flashes deep in the corridor. Sarah pulls her son to his feet.

'My daughter, she's in trouble.' Fox clutches his bandaged shoulder and tries to run. 'Her life is in danger. I must reach her. She's in Ilira, in the North. Mara too. It's where I need to be. I planned to reclaim the cities . . . start here, change the empire from within . . . help the flood refugees . . . now people's eyes are opened to the world . . . but Lily needs me . . . I must go North . . .'

He trails off, weak with pain and blood loss. His head reels. The strangeness of being reunited in the most critical moment of his life with the intense, commanding woman who is his estranged mother, and his longing for something that is surely unreachable now, overwhelms Fox. He wanted to break down a world but he is breaking down instead.

A guard patrol thunders along the corridor towards them.

Sarah raises her gun to his head. 'Do as I say or you're dead.'

THE MOST SECRET
SURGENT OF ALL

The guard patrol halts. Seeing Fox's blasted, bloodied armour and the ripped clothes of their revered city Guardian, Sarah Stone, with her gun pointed at her prisoner's head, the entire patrol aims their guns at Fox.

'Commander Stone wants this man for questioning,' Sarah says briskly. 'He is one of the lead rebels. You two,' she tells the patrol leaders, 'take him to the cells. The rest of you head for the cybercathedral and secure it. They need reinforcements there.'

Fox cannot catch his mother's eye. He must trust her. There is nothing else he can do.

As the patrol turns and heads for the cybercath, the guards at either side of him drop to the ground, stunned by the gun of Guardian Stone. Fox grins through his pain.

Never in his wildest dreams did he imagine his own mother as the rogue Guardian at the heart of the empire who would be his greatest ally in his moment of need.

'What do you need from me?' she asks him. 'Tell me, quick. What can I do?'

'I must get to the top of Aspen Tower,' he says, thinking of the other ally he has had to place blind faith in: Kitsune, the sly trickster, who has always refused to disclose how he will organize the fleet that Fox trusts is flying towards the sky cities of the world.

In a moment of pain-flooded disorientation, Fox wonders how wise he has been to trust a sly trickster he has never met with such an immense task, a seeming impossibility. Is this the moment where his grand plan comes crashing down around him? He can only hope not.

Sarah has wrestled one of the stunned guards from his red jacket.

'Put this on, quick.' She helps ease the jacket over his injured shoulder. 'If anyone asks, you are my personal guard.'

They rush through endless corridors that are strangely still. The Guardians would have fled the Nux for their penthouse sky castles and will be trying to restore order by diktat from behind personal guard patrols and barricades.

'Come with me,' Fox urges. 'Leave and come North with me.'

His mother doesn't answer. Glancing at her as they hurry on, Fox sees anguish on her face.

'Help me find your granddaughter,' he persists.

'What's her name?' asks Sarah, as they leave the eery emptiness of the Nux at the hidden heart of the city and enter the ringing panic of the sky tunnels.

'Lily,' Fox replies.

Sarah's eyes warm and soften; the same deep brown as her son's, full of the same amber fire. She touches the dark lily on Fox's scarlet guard's jacket. 'The emblem of the empire. How strange.'

'A girl needs a strong grandmother in a broken world,' says Fox, thinking of his cybergift to Lily of a virtual grandmother. But if he could bring her a grandmother for real . . .

Sarah bites her lip as if to stop herself uttering an impulsive 'yes'.

'That,' she says, 'is exactly what I mean to be.'

'You'll come?'

His heart leaps. Is a happy-ever-after ending possible after all?

'If I come,' says his mother slowly, 'then I can't be the grandmother she needs, I can't do everything that is within my power to get you to her. And you must find her.' Sarah turns her face to the wall and speaks into a tok-check. Next to Fox a door springs open in the tunnel wall. 'A service entrance,' Sarah tells him, 'a safe shortcut to Aspen. You'll avoid the patrols. The stairs will take you to the roof.'

Gunfire cracks in the tunnels. Not the zip of lasers but the sound made by the old-style guns and bullets he and Pan practised with in the museum. The boat Surgents must have made it up through the towers. There is no time to waste; he must go.

He grabs his mother's hand. 'But what else can you do here?'

'I am at the heart of things,' says Sarah. 'I am trusted. I can confuse the orders of the Guardians, I can redirect sky patrols, send out false communications from the high command. I can give you the best chance you have of getting out of here alive. I can help give the right ending to your story.'

She holds his gaze.

'I was hardly a mother to you. I was never really there. I thought other things were more important and I've had years to regret that. But I'm here now and I will do this.'

Screams erupt further down the tunnel. Sarah pushes Fox through the door into the service shaft. Mother and son look at each other one last time.

'What about Dad? He won't let you get away with this. You won't be safe.'

'Your father's weaker than you think. He's ill and he needs me. He might not live long. The invasion of the North was his last venture. So you must continue it for him,' Sarah smiles, 'in your own way.'

'The Midnight Story isn't finished,' he reminds her. 'Listen out for me. You haven't heard the end of the story yet.' A wondrous idea strikes him. 'Far beyond the Noos, across the empty seas of static, is the Weave, the virtual world people used before the floods. On the edges of the Weave is a broken bridge. Your granddaughter knows it. We'll meet you there.'

Sarah's eyes turn to molten amber. The door closes between them and his mother is gone.

WARRIORS OF A WOKEN WORLD

Earth spins, hurling the sky city towards the dawn.

Fox steps out on to the top of Aspen Tower as first light streaks across the eastern sky, revealing the awed and stricken faces of the people amassed on the roof.

People from the sky city have walked out into the first real morning they have ever known and take their first-ever breaths of the world's wind. Curious citizens have joined the rebel Surgents on the roof and now gaze like woken sleepwalkers at the spectacle of the outside world. Weather-ragged boat people stand dazed and exhausted among them. All across the city Fox sees the gatherings on every tower roof, the people tense and still like solemn wraiths in the misty dawn.

Dark against the dawn is a strange swarm. As it draws closer, Fox sees it's an air fleet. The deep scarlet emblems of the empire's lilies glow on the tails of each ship. The golden names of the eastern sky cities glow on the whale-like bodies. Kitsune has been as good as his word.

Fox imagines all the unknown masses he reached out to on the Zenith radio and in the Noos breaking out in wonder on to sky city towers all over the Earth: the warriors for the future he appealed for in his last broadcast to the global Surge.

Air turbulence blasts the vast open space of the rooftop as the giant fleet spreads across the sky. The spiregyres at the edges of the tower whirl and whoop in the sudden wind. People cling to each other against the gale.

The wind rips at Fox, tearing his makeshift bandage. The blast of air burns like fire on the raw shoulder wound. The fire seeps, warm as honey, across his chest. Faces stare at him in alarm. Glancing down, Fox sees why. His upper body is soaked in blood. It spreads in the shape of a huge dark lily all across the scarlet jacket stolen from the guard. Suddenly, he feels dizzy. Nooworlders surround him; faces young and old, full of awe.

'Fox!' a voice is calling.

A bugle call sounds. Fox turns towards the voice and the urgent, musical blast.

'Pan!' he calls back, but his voice is weak with pain.

Is this the Fox? people whisper. Hands reach out to help him; he is given a sip of water from a flask. He is among friends, he realizes, with a stab of shock.

Pan finds him at last, pushing through the crowd.

'You came!'

She is about to grab him in a hug when she sees his wound and stops, placing her hand tenderly over the dark stain.

Her relief shames him. He can hardly meet the blaze of love in her eyes.

'Who tried to kill you?' she whispers. 'Your father? You went to find him, didn't you? Did – did you kill him?'

Fox gives a shaky smile. 'My mother saved us both.'

The question on her lips is lost. Pan's mouth drops open and her head falls back, her green eyes widening, as one of the airships pauses overhead. The turbulence calms now as the vessel drops towards the rooftop, quiet and gentle as a cloud. It doesn't land, but hovers just above the tower on a cushion of air.

'The soundwave,' Fox gasps through a spike of pain.

Pan pulls the connector from a pocket and puts it in his ear. 'I unplugged. Got fed up with Kitsune yelling about you going off-plan.'

'Kitsune?' Fox cries, hoping the connection is still live.

'At last!' the voice in the earphone erupts. 'We've been frantic – get on the ship!'

A pulse of adrenalin overrides the pain of his wound. Fox takes a deep, reviving breath of air and begins directing the exodus of people to the air chute that will suck them up into the huge round belly of the ship.

The soundwave crackles.

'Never mind the rest of the world now,' Kitsune insists, as if he knows Fox will be herding people on board before himself. '*You* get on the ship! Move!'

Dazed Nooworlders and refugees keep pouring from the elevator shafts. They stand blinking like newborns in the grey dawn. Pan weaves her way among them, ignited by their stunned excitement as they look at the wide sky and the mass of airships. They barely notice Pandora. She might be a chattering ghost wafting among them. She touches their arms, their hair, a stunned face or two, as if they are statues from the museum.

'You can still see a few stars. Look! The bright one is Venus, the morning star,' she tells a throng of excited children. She might be a guide introducing them all to the world. 'That was the city wall down there. It wrapped around the towers and stopped the outside getting in. See how it's all bombed now and the boat people poured in. See all the boats and the ocean!'

'Empire guards advancing up the towers,' Kitsune warns Fox. 'Everyone on board, now!'

'They're alive, Kitsune,' Fox shouts into the soundwave connector, still herding frantic refugees. 'Mara and my daughter . . .'

He stumbles over the word.

'Your daughter!' Kitsune exclaims. 'But you thought they were dead. Fox, your *daughter*!'

'I found her in the Weave,' says Fox. 'Lily, Mara's child. She's in a mountain city in the North with shining bridges, deep in a sea fjord . . .'

'In the Northlands?' Kitsune breaks into his soft laugh. 'Well, what do you know – that's just where we're headed! So can I assure Steerpike,' he adds in a dry tone, 'that it's not all pirates up there?'

The Arctic pirates on the radio waves have told all about the burgeoning trade ports of the North. But the propaganda of the empire tells the sky people that the land at the top of the world is empty, just a handful of savage tribes to reorganize, resettle, or where necessary, reduce – the empire's code words for exile, enslavement, extermination.

'But you have a daughter!' Kitsune cries again and a smile breaks on Fox's face as he hears his friend's astonished delight.

'I have a daughter,' Fox repeats. It's still such an unbelievable thought. 'I have to find them, Kitsune. They matter more than anything now.'

He motions to Pan to get on the airship. She doesn't move.

'You go,' she says bluntly. 'Go and find them.'

'What?' Fox snaps at her impatiently. He is trying to hear Kitsune and organize an exodus of people; this is no time for Pan to be awkward and childish. Then he sees the flash

261

of tears in her eyes and, stricken, recalls the words she just heard him say.

'I said get on this airship now!' Kitsune sounds just as he did when they were young wizzers, racing through glittering speedlinks of the Noos, breathless, on the edge of time. 'Move, Noosrunner! There's a gun patrol on its way to the roof. Your battle's done here, Fox.'

An electric sizzle cuts through the soundwave. Kitsune's voice is snapped off. He is gone. Fox is on his own.

'Hurry!' he roars, and begins pushing people two and three at a time up into the airship's entry chute. 'Pan! Come on! Get in.'

Someone screams. Fox spins around and sees armed guards rushing from an elevator shaft.

'Do not move!' a voice commands. 'Do not board the airships. Anyone attempting to board the airships will be shot.'

Time seems to freeze as the crowd stills. A mass of instant calculations are made. Chaos breaks out as some obey the order and others rush for the ships. Warning shots fire overhead. The police scan the crowd. They are looking for him, Fox knows. His father's stunned state will have worn off and an order will have been given to stun or shoot him on sight. Though Fox still wears the scarlet jacket, his weather-rugged face stands out like a barnacle among the fine, indoor skins of the empire's guards. He ducks, glancing around for Pan. The sudden movement attracts a policewoman's glare.

'Here!' she shouts. 'I've got him!'

Her gun points straight at him through a gap in the crowd. She's too close to miss. He is pinned to the spot, his chance to escape lost.

It's all over now, thinks Fox.

CANDLE COMMANDS

This is what speed feels like! This is what running is!

Never in her life has Candle moved so fast. Never has she needed to; there has always been a slave to run for her and do whatever she asked.

But the glass walls of the palace are full of flames and no one has answered her cries. All the guards and slaves have vanished. *Where are Broom and Clay? Where is Tuck?* The rooms and corridors are empty.

Candle runs through the maze of the palace until she is out of breath. Adrenalin deadens the pain of her maimed fingers. She pauses, heart drumming hard as she stares at the flames that seem to blaze through the walls. Surely the palace will melt! She touches the glass but it's cold and hard. The fire is outside. She is safe. But where has everyone gone?

'Broom! Tuck?'

She stares down empty glass corridors, feeling blank. And annoyed. Annoyance burns into anger. She is the First Lady of Ilira, the wife of the Pontifix. The brutality of her husband is something she cannot yet see a way around, but how dare everyone else forget about her?

But of course they have not. Here they come. She listens

to the tramp of heavy feet in the corridors.

'What's happening?' Candle demands of the guards who rush towards her. One seizes her roughly by the arm. Aghast, she tries to shake him off – and freezes as he pulls his cutlass. The blade glistens as he points it at her throat. She sees the emblem of the Vulture's claw on the guard's helmet, and screams.

A mass of invading guards rush past and Candle sees they all wear the Vulture's claw.

'Put your cutlass away!' bellows a voice. 'That's Rodenglaw's daughter, fool!'

The guard drops Candle's arm with a stricken look. He gives a sharp little bow and runs off.

A burly figure with a red, weathered face that Candle knows from her childhood, the owner of the bellowing voice, takes off his helmet, grabs her hand and plants a rough, wet kiss on it.

'Strozzi!' Candle is dizzy with relief.

Strozzi, the long-trusted captain of Rodenglaw's fleet, gives her a smile that steadies her heart. Candle throws her arms around the neck of the fatherly figure who always brought her tales of his adventures in the Arctic seas where he would famously outwit pirate fleets and storms, along with tasty treats and trinkets for her from the port cities he sailed to in her father's ships. Strozzi could even jolly Rodenglaw out of his dark moods with reports of lucrative trade deals struck on his master's behalf.

'The very lady I was searching for!' The burly sea captain winks at her, a shrewd look in his eye.

'Strozzi, what's happening?'

'Your husband lies dead on the harbour,' cries the wily captain, never one to waste money or words. 'Struck down by the Vulture's claw – as I will be if I don't keep

264

my wits about me, and you too.

Candle gasps.

'Now don't panic, and don't tell me it was love at first sight,' says Strozzi. 'Tuck Culpy was as blind and dangerous as I am fat and you were hardly married a minute. So no tears. Listen to me, Candle. I have a deal to put to you and no time to waste.'

'A deal? Now?'

'The deal of a lifetime . . . No looting! Put it all back! Every last bit!' he bellows to a bustle of guards trying to sneak past with Tuck's treasured relics under their cloaks. 'That is the property of your new sea commander. Quick, now!' he urges Candle. 'Let's get you ready for your big moment.'

He stares at the bandaged stump of the hand he was about to seize.

'Just as well he's already dead, my little Candle,' he murmurs after a pause.

Candle shoves the bloodstained stump behind her back.

'What big moment?' she demands.

If Strozzi's deal is to marry her off to whoever is the new commander of the combined fleets of her dead father and husband, then she will fight against it with her teeth and the nails of her one good hand. She will never again be at the mercy of a power-crazed brute.

'Who is the new commander?'

'Commander Candle, of course,' says Strozzi. His clever eyes twinkle at the stunned girl. 'Why not? Who better than you? These are your father's guards, this is your husband's palace. I am your most loyal sea captain, always at your command. Our lives hang in the balance, Candle. Yours too. Ilira's Sea Lords have scuttled into the shadows like sea rats. Who else can unite us and save us from the Vulture's claw?'

THE HEART OF A WOLF

The burning masts of Tuck's ship fall with a tremendous groan. The ship gives a *boom* as the flames consume the *Great Skua*. Mara plunges off the rocks and swims through cold waves towards the inferno, choking on seawater as she shoutes for Lily until her throat is raw. Her eyes stream. She can barely see through the thick smoke and the litter of burning debris on the waves.

Did Lily jump into the sea and escape the falling masts? Or was she trapped in the blaze?

Panic screams through her, propelling her towards the sea of flame. Mara's heart feels ready to burst when she spots Wing's wolfskin, swimming towards her.

Alone. Without Lily.

Don't let her be gone, she prays. *I couldn't bear that.*

The wolfskin grabs her. But it's not Wing. She hears the ragged, sobbing breaths inside and knows the sound. She'd recognize her own child's cry from a million others.

Mara catches the wretched bundle that is Lily. Clasping her with one arm, Mara struggles to swim back through the seething sea. But the relief of finding Lily alive gives her the strength to steer them both back towards the harbour where dark figures are waiting to haul them on to the rocks.

Shivering, she and Lily cling together as the *Great Skua* gives another monstrous groan as it breaks apart upon the dark sea.

'Wing found me!' gasps Lily. 'He threw his wolfskin over me then the fire caught him. Oh, where is he?'

Mara looks out at the fire-strewn waves. She looks along the harbour rocks. Lily screams his name again and again but there is no sign of Wing.

'I thought he was dead and now he really is,' Lily sobs. 'I'm sorry, Mum, so sorry. I never meant all this to happen . . .'

Mara can only hug her daughter. 'He saved me once and now he's saved you. Don't give up on him yet. Wing has the heart of a wolf.'

Bodies are being heaved from the sea. Lily and Mara rush to see if Wing is among them. Some are alive, burned, others have drowned; all wear the silver crescent emblem of Tuck's guards.

Lily sees Tuck's body. 'His heart was ice.'

A ragged heap is dumped on the flat harbour rocks. Some grotesque, wizened creature. Lily pulls away from Mara with a cry and throws herself down beside the poor, drowned thing. Gently, she cradles the head and Mara sees that one side is burned, horribly, the hair razed away. But the unravaged half of the face is Wing's.

Lily puts her ear to Wing's chest and listens.

'He's alive!'

She pulls the wolfskin from her shoulders and lays it over Wing, placing the wolf head tenderly beside his. Mara hears her daughter beseech the spirit of the dead creature to help Wing.

She pulls herself together. There are far more practical

things than wolf spirits. Mara takes the flask of milk from her backpack that curdled days ago. Ever so gently, she pours the soothing curd on to the burns. Wing squirms in agony but makes not a sound. Years with the wolves have taught him the contained energy of silence, even at the point of death. Now Mara tips a small flask of pine wine, brought to clean wounds, to Wing's mouth to numb his pain. Lily soothes him, murmuring in wolf-tongue, until Wing relaxes into a daze of alcohol and pain.

'All that matters is that he's *alive*,' Lily declares.

There are a thousand things to say but it can all wait. As the last of the *Great Skua* breaks up in a series of fiery cracks and booms, Mara can only agree with a shuddered '*yes*'.

THE PARADISE DEAL

At first Mara thinks the girl on the steps of the palace is on fire. But it's a dazzling necklace, reflecting the last sparks of the burning ship, that seems to flame and sizzle upon her chest.

The small, sturdy girl walks down the rocky steps of the palace, wrapped in a white fur cloak. On the harbour, Oreon watches her approach with a look of relief. Just a girl, says his face. The girl stops at Tuck's lifeless body with an unreadable expression. Then she turns to Oreon with a hard, insolent look.

The look throws Oreon. He was, thinks Mara, expecting tears.

'I am sorry,' he begins.

'Not as sorry as you will be,' says the girl, 'when your brother hears how you bungled his plans. Captain Strozzi, *my* captain, has told me everything.'

'You are the new bride of the Pontifix?' asks Oreon, in the manner of someone suddenly struggling to find his bearings.

'I am Tartoq Rodenglaw, known as Candle, the Light of Ilira. These guards are my father's men and women. This is my palace, my city, my land. I hold the reins of power in

Ilira now my husband is dead. What's your business here, gypsea?'

Oreon blinks, taken aback. Then he laughs.

Mara leaves Lily to tend to Wing and steps closer to the power tussle between the bemused gypsea scholar and Tuck's unexpected young wife.

'I am Oreon,' says the gypsea grandly, 'a *scholar* on a mission from my brother, the Vulture of the North. These guards have sworn allegiance to him. As you can see, many now wear the Vulture's claw. Tuck's guards – those still alive – will doubtless join us too.'

'Ah, but what *I* see is that many haven't swapped their emblems at all!' Candle shakes her head as if Oreon has made a silly mistake. 'Look closer. See how many still wear my father's emblem, the *Rodenglaw* claw – which *is* similar, though somewhat smaller than the Vulture's. But sharp and deadly, I promise you. Now they have no need to swap allegiance. They will not take second place in the Vulture's fleet because I, Tartoq Rodenglaw, will take control of Ilira's fleets with my loyal Captain Strozzi. And my men and women will continue to wear the Rodenglaw claw!'

Now Candle addresses the mass of guards gathered on the rocks who have turned from the burning ship to hear the commanding young woman in the antique fur and jewels.

'My people have lived on this land since the White Age of ice and snow,' she declares. 'I am the daughter of Sea Lord Rodenglaw and my mother was a Hakan from Eagle Heights. My cloak,' she grabs a handful of the heavy fur, 'was made from the last white bear ever seen in Ilira, killed by my mother's mother when she was hardly more than a girl.' Candle puffs out her stout body. 'And who knows if I am already carrying the heir of the Pontifix?'

All eyes fix on her round stomach. Candle's eyes glint.

'Guards of Ilira, we must not betray our ancestors or our children,' Candle urges them. 'Or ourselves. And that's what we would do if we give the Vulture control of our land and ships. So, I will tell you of the plan Captain Strozzi has put to me. We will fight with the gypseas to defend the North from invaders from the sky cities who want to steal our land – but we will not live in the grip of the Vulture's claw. All of Ilira can unite through me!'

Captain Strozzi strides forward.

'Pledge allegiance to the new Commander of the Fleet – the Light of Ilira!'

The cheer that erupts from the mass of guards is a roar of relief. Captain Strozzi looks surprised by the strength of the vote and his round face crinkles in a satisfied smile.

'What are you a scholar of?' Candle asks Oreon, helping herself to the silver gun stuck in the belt of his windwrap.

The young scholar is struggling to keep his dignified composure. He looks as if he wants to dive into the sea and swim for his life.

'Oh, everything,' Oreon mutters desolately. He looks at his watch with a sigh, as if to check whether he has run out of time. 'I am a scholar of the world,' he adds.

Candle studies the handsome gypsea intently. Her sharp little eyes flicker over his long limbs and fine, clever face.

'I want to make a deal with you, Oreon, scholar of the world,' she says. 'The deal of a lifetime.'

Captain Strozzi hurries over, looking alarmed.

'Now, Candle,' he murmurs, in a fatherly tone, 'that was a triumph. But let us men of the sea handle this business now.'

'*Commander* Candle,' she corrects him. 'Make sure Ilira's

271

defences are strong, Captain Strozzi. That's your business now.'

She dismisses her captain without another glance and Strozzi turns to his guards with the bellow of a man who will not be ignored, even though his young mistress has done precisely that.

'My glass palace is full of *everything*,' Candle murmurs confidentially to Oreon. 'Tuck collected relics and mysteries of the drowned world.'

'Yes, I know,' says Oreon sadly. 'That's the real reason I agreed to do this for my brother. I hoped Tuck might show me those treasures. I wanted to learn, I wanted to see – I wanted to be his friend.'

'You wanted to befriend your prisoner?' Candle eyes him intently. 'Is that possible, Oreon?'

'But if he understood my passion . . .' Oreon looks distraught.

'You must know that the Pontifix was the Keeper of the Globe?' says Candle, moving ever closer. 'The magic wizz.'

'The globe,' breathes Oreon. He gazes at Candle as if she holds the keys to paradise.

'My deal is this,' says Candle. 'I will hold you prisoner in my palace, safe from your brother's wrath, and you can study all the relics and mysteries, everything that was Tuck's and now belongs to me. It's the perfect place for a scholar of the world, and for a gypsea. The glass walls of the palace do strange things to the light and the dark,' she whispers to him, 'and you feel you are under the sea in a sunken ship.'

Oreon looks mesmerized, nervous, tempted.

'Oh, and I'm not *really* carrying the Pontifix's child,' Candle adds, with a shy, sly smile.

Oreon studies her face as he would a map of a mysterious

land. 'But – but what do you get from this deal?'

'You,' Candle says, in an airless voice as if she has been running round and round the corridors of the palace. 'Your knowledge of the world,' she adds hastily, 'would be very useful to me, now that I'm Commander of Ilira.'

Oreon gazes out for a long, wistful moment at the moonlit ocean beyond the fjord. He looks through the drifting smoke from the burned ship to the glass museum of Tuck's palace, crammed with precious mysteries of the drowned world. Finally, he looks down at Candle, who seems to be holding her breath.

'Deal,' ventures the gypsea scholar.

THE TOUCH OF AN OLD FRIEND

'Wait!' Lily bursts through the guards on the harbour and runs towards Candle as she leads Oreon away. 'Candle! Broom and Clay are in danger. They're trapped somewhere under the palace.'

Candle's startled expression suggests she did not expect to see Lily alive again and is not entirely happy to find that she is.

Lily bounds up the palace steps. 'Tuck said they'd drown by the morning tide.'

Candle glances at the eastern sky, at the sea, and gasps.

'Find them, quick!' she orders some guards. 'Bring my husband's body inside,' she tells others. She sees the body lying near to Tuck's on the harbour rocks. 'Is that a drowned *wolf*?'

'It's my friend, Wing,' says Lily. 'He saved me from the ship. He's burned. Please, Candle . . . ?'

Candle sighs. 'Bring him too. Broom has a medicine box.' Her face crumples in sudden fear. She races into the palace. 'Broom! Clay!'

Mara grabs Lily's hand. 'What do you mean, Broom and Clay? It – it can't be.'

Lily nods. 'It is.'

Mara sits down hard on the palace steps. 'They didn't drown when the *Arkiel* sank? They've been here all this time?'

She looks out to sea. There is a sudden definition in the darkness, a soft grey line drawn across the ocean night.

'Dawn,' Mara cries, hurrying into the palace. 'The turn of the tide. They can't drown, not now.'

She races blindly, desperately, along winding corridors.

'Broomielaw!' Mara shouts. Her voice echoes forlornly through the glass maze. The only reply is the hot hiss of a geyser in an alcove. The sea booms softly outside.

There comes an answering cry from somewhere deep in the palace. Mara runs towards the voice until, rounding a final bend, she rushes into the embrace of the friend she thought drowned years ago.

They gather in Tuck's room of relics, among the strange objects nestled in the glass walls and upon rocks. As the lost ones reunite with tears and joy, Oreon picks up relic after relic with the look of a starving man imprisoned at the greatest banquet on Earth.

Mara and Broom tend to Wing and he sinks into a spirit-numbed sleep on a bed of furs, his burns soothed by seaweed balm.

A torrent of conversation rushes around the room, drowning out the gush of the geyser, voices spilling over each other as stories are shared and mysteries explained.

'He's alive and he *will* come, he said he would,' Lily is insisting to her incredulous, wide-eyed mother.

'What was the point,' Broom demands, 'of us surviving everything if you youngsters are now going to lead us into war and—'

275

'Make surviving worthwhile?' Clay interrupts. 'Mum, this war will come and find us anyway.'

'Not if we go into the mountains with Mara,' Broom retorts. 'No one will find us there.'

'Clay is right,' Oreon cuts in. 'The sky empire has already invaded at Fort Aurora, due North of here – and elsewhere. The invasion will spread. They're sure to break into the interior of the island. Nowhere will be safe. Our only hope is to fight with the Surgents.'

Oreon is dragged from his solitary banquet with Tuck's relics to show the radio watch on his wrist that connects him to the Surgents. The global leader of the Surgency is also, he is sure, the Midnight Storyteller who captivates the world.

'Midnight is a different time zone all around the world so I have worked out his rough whereabouts,' says Oreon, looking around Tuck's possessions. 'I could show you if I had a map of the oceans . . .'

'He's in New Mungo,' Mara says softly, and she grips Lily's hand. 'It's Fox's revolution. He did it.'

'Not yet, he hasn't,' says Oreon. 'But it's begun.'

With careful fingers, he picks up something that lies on the wide stone table at the centre of the room.

'A book,' he says, and his lips quiver hungrily. '*Natural Engineering* by C. D. Stone.'

An astonished cry breaks from Mara and she rushes over to look.

'Caledon David Stone. Your grandfather, Lily!' Mara takes the book from Oreon and with Lily hanging over her shoulder she flicks through pictures of spiderwebs and termite towers and nests, all the astounding architecture of the natural world that first inspired Caledon and then, much later, Tuck. 'It's a book for Broom,' she sees, with a smile for her visionary friend. Then her smile wobbles as all the happenings and revelations of this strangest of days overwhelm her.

'The globe,' she remembers, scanning the room. 'We need to look for my globe.'

'I forgot!' Lily begins unfastening the band of netting she has knotted around her waist like a thick belt. From the folds of fishnet she unwraps Granny Mary's carved box and hands the heirloom back to her mother.

'I saw Granny Mary in the Weave,' she tells her dazed-looking mother. 'Really, I did. Fox found her and kept her for you.'

Now Lily unwraps from the netting the prize that almost cost her her life. She disentangles the crescent of the halo and wipes a strand of seaweed from the globe before handing it to her mother.

'Oh, Lily,' Mara whispers. 'You found it. But if I'd lost *you . . .*'

'Don't know if it still works,' Lily confesses. 'It's been in the sea.'

A tingle runs up Mara's arm; a shock of delight at the touch of an old friend. The globe powers up, coloured clouds swirling across the smooth surface, a warm glow at its core. Then it begins to fade.

'It's dying,' Lily whispers. 'It keeps fading.'

'It survived a drowning before, twice,' says Mara, opening the globe. She takes out the small wand inside. 'And a mountain falling on it.' With her nail, she flips up the small screenpad and removes the tiny solar rods. 'It needs some sun.'

'Last night was the final broadcast before the Surge began,' says Oreon slowly, transfixed by the sight of the most famed of all of Tuck's relics, the globe in Mara's hands. 'No one knows if the Fox will survive. But what he's done for the world is – it's *vast*. You should be very proud if the Fox is your father,' he tells Lily. 'Whatever happens now.'

A ghost seems to walk across Mara's skin as she recalls the haunting words from the voice in Oreon's watch.

Someone, I say to you, will think of us in some future time.

They were the words of a poet, said Fox, a young woman called Sappho who lived on an island almost three thousand years ago. Her words had survived all down the ages. If we do the right thing now, Fox urged his listeners, our words and actions will stand like a rock in the ocean of time for our children and all the generations after.

Then his voice was lost as the soundwave died in the sizzle of the spring auroras.

'If he doesn't come I'll get on a ship and find him,' Lily declares.

'You can't just launch out into the ocean,' says Mara.

'Like you once did?' Lily retorts.

'I had to find a home!'

'I have to find my father!'

'You already have a father,' says Mara quietly. 'Rowan has loved you since the day you were born and you know it. He'll be out of his mind with worry. And the little ones . . .'

Mara's voice breaks. Lily looks at the ground and nods.

'You're not going to sea either, Clay.' Broom breaks the tense silence. 'A Treenester lives on the land.'

'There's a future to fight for, Mum. I'll do what I have to.' Clay hesitates. 'And I'm not really a Treenester. This is my home. I love the ocean and I want to see the world.'

Lily lifts her gaze from the ground and meets Clay's eyes.

'I want to see a sky city,' she murmurs.

'Well, isn't there always a future to fight for?' Broom sighs in exasperation. 'Of course you're a Treenester,' she chides Clay. 'You were born in a tree nest! What about *your* father? You have one in Candlewood you've never met. *Some* people risk their lives to find their fathers but you'd rather run off to sea.'

'Well, if our mothers didn't keep *losing* our fathers . . .' Clay retorts.

Lily smothers a giggle as Clay grins mischievously. Mara and Broom surrender to weary laughter as the tension breaks. The sound of the morning tide on the rocks beyond the glass walls is like a sigh of relief.

'Clay won't be running off to sea,' says Candle, who has been watching everything with her acute eyes. 'I need him here.'

Now she asserts her authority, inserting herself between Lily and Clay who seem to be imperceptibly drawing towards each other, moment by moment.

'I won't be your slave, Candle,' growls Clay.

'I want you to be my ocean master. I will have Oreon as my adviser on world affairs and you, Clay, will rule and organize Ilira's fleets and trade. Strozzi will carry out your orders and captain the fleets at sea. And you will be my dreamswoman, Broom,' Candle adds. 'All your ideas of the power that lies in the sun and the weather and the waterfalls – we can make those dreams real now!'

Broom looks torn; Clay unimpressed.

'An ocean master who never goes to sea?' he scoffs.

'I must go home, Candle,' Broom decides.

'This is your home.' All Candle's imperiousness vanishes and she rushes across the room to fling her arms around Broom. 'You're my slave,' she murmurs to the woman who

279

has been her mother. 'You'll do as I say or I'll have you locked up under the palace again.'

Broom kisses her then sets her apart. 'Now that is no way for a commander to behave. And don't you be so cheeky.'

'No more slaves, Candle,' says Mara. She pulls up the sleeve of her jumper to reveal a faded symbol on her arm. 'Your people branded me one once, before I escaped into the mountains. Ilira made Broom and Clay slaves and all their talents were lost. So much is lost when people are not free.'

'But I'll lose Broom if she goes with you,' Candle cries. 'Just when I need her most. And Clay too if – if he . . .'

She stutters to a stop and glares at Lily, her tears dried to flinty sparks.

'Imagine if the way into the interior was opened up,' says Mara. 'There's so much we could do! No one ever need lose anyone again. What about trains, communication links . . . radios . . . all kinds of things are possible . . .'

Her vision is only fragments. She must piece it together before she can see what the world might be. But now she has the globe back Mara has regained all the lost treasures of the Weave. The old virtual world is a cybermuseum littered with crucial knowledge of the drowned world and lost ages. That knowledge can surely help them learn from the mistakes of the past.

'This great island was once called the Land of the People,' Mara remembers. 'Tuck opened up Ilira to the world but we could build on that and open up this whole land for all its people. If war is on its way,' she adds, 'won't a free people fight for their land much harder than slaves?'

'You've been enslaved all *your* life,' Broom says softly to Candle. 'Everyone should be free.'

'Does that include me, Mother?' says Clay with a sly grin.

Broom replies with a rueful smile, trapped by her own words.

Oreon picks up a beautiful relic, full of mended cracks, with a long neck and a curving body of iridescent blue.

'Some kind of weapon?' Oreon muses, puzzling over the wires on the axe-like neck.

'I won't hide away in the mountains or in a palace,' Clay tells Candle. 'Captain Strozzi should master our fleets through a war. He is already a master of the ocean – but I could learn from him.'

The burly sea captain has been sitting in grumpy dejection on a rock, having been insulted twice now by the young mistress he himself just lifted on to a pedestal of power. He gets to his feet, struggling with hurt pride.

'No one is ever a master of the ocean but I am always at the service of Ilira,' he says gruffly, appraising Clay from head to foot, with the expression of a cook asked to create a feast from unworthy scraps, but his eyes twinkle as he seems to spy some essential ingredient in Clay's determined face. 'Well,' he shrugs, 'let's see what the ocean makes of you.'

Lily touches the mysterious blue relic in Oreon's arms. Its curving body is the vivid blue of a twilight sky above Lake Longhope. At her curious touch the taut wires strung from its neck vibrate. A wild thrum fills the air.

'It doesn't kill,' Lily exclaims, grabbing it from the scholar and thrumming it again. 'It makes music.'

'Ah, I saw a weapon but you found music,' says Oreon, looking shamed. 'War has invaded me and it hasn't yet begun. What will it make of us all once it breaks on our world?'

WOLFSCAR

The wolfskin wraps around Lily, steeped in Wing's scent.

'My wolf will keep you safe till the Fox comes,' says Wing.

Lily looks up from the harbour rock she is sitting on, watching the skies. The agony she sees in Wing's burned face is not only from his wound.

'You're going back? But you're hurt, you can't go. You need to rest.' Lily reads the unspoken words in his eyes. 'You're going back to *her*.'

Wing sits on the rock beside her.

'I need my wolves, my mountain,' he tells her.

He leans forward and Lily sees in his eyes all the pain he is bearing. She wants to touch his face but links her arm through his instead.

'Wing is Mara's island,' he says, referring to the name Mara gave him when she found him abandoned in the netherworld: the name of her island home. 'Now I found my own name.' He points to his face. 'I am Wolfscar. See?' he says proudly as Lily stares at the burns that warp the sleek down of his face like the markings of a wolf. 'Like a true wolf now.'

Wolfscar. Scarwell. Lily sees, and has no idea what she can do to keep him.

'She doesn't love you like I do,' she says at last.

He is struggling to use words as he never has before. 'No one love Scar. No one ever. In nederwuld me and Scar was sea rats together, and now we are wolfkin.'

'You're not a wolf. They're not your kin. Only half of you,' Lily gently turns the unscarred side of his face towards her, 'belongs to her.'

'Wolf Mountain is my home,' he insists.

The way he says *home* forces Lily to accept what she knows, deep down. The mountain and the lake and the wolves are his element. Wing aches to be there with them. He doesn't need words there, the human words he finds so clumsy, because he has the language of the Earth, the animal world. He would always be on the edges of the human world. On Wolf Mountain he has a language and a world that he can own.

And Scarwell belongs to that world.

'You'll miss me,' she tells him.

Wing pulls the wolfskin tight around her like a hug.

'I miss you like I miss the sea. I miss Lily all winter.' He sighs. 'But I am Wolfscar.'

It's no good, Lily sees. All she can do is let him go.

'Wing Wolfscar then.' Lily laughs to hide eyes filled with tears. 'One day I'll bring a fox to your wolf cave,' Lily vows. 'He'll find me, won't he, Wing? He won't die?'

'A fox is clever,' Wing assures her. 'Nederwuld foxes never drown. They hunt rats and mudcats and chew off paw to get out of fox trap. Fox not die.'

Wing strokes the snout of the wolf head that lies on Lily's shoulder and grunts a wolfish goodbye in its ear. Then he kisses her hard and is gone.

THE MAGNIFICENT GIFT

'Fire!' comes the order.

Fox waits for the blast of obliteration to come.

The fingers of the guards tremble on their guns.

But people have crowded around Fox like a human wall. The young guards, he sees, can't summon the will to fire on their own citizens, people they know, friends, loved ones.

'Fire!' The order comes again. 'Refusal to fire is a crime against the empire.'

Fox hears the frantic blast of Pan's bugle behind him, alongside echoing screams from an elevator shaft. Heads turn this way and that in fright. The police squad is confused.

Pan's skateboard slams on the ground. He can't see her, but Fox knows the rickety rattle of her skate wheels.

'Pandora says go!' she yells.

Now he sees her. She shoots him a searing glance as she whizzes past and throws something. He catches it and watches her go. There is nothing else he can do. Speeding and swerving, Pan scatters the crowd, distracting the police, luring their lasers, dodging the blasts with her pangolin armour, bewildering them with all the daredevil tricks she learned on the netherworld bridge.

With a gesture as careless as a wave goodbye, Pan lifts her gun and blasts the armed policewoman who is relentlessly seeking out Fox. Pan hits her target with a perfect, deadly fire.

Screams break out. But it's not Pan's kill that sends the crowd scrambling.

'Monster!'

As the crowd parts, Fox sees the grunting creature. Its jaws creak and snap as it lunges across the rooftop at a speed that shouldn't be possible for such a squat, ungainly beast. A small swamp dragon, sucked up by the spiregyres, has followed its snout and sniffed out this feast of flesh on the top of the tower. Fox remembers the screams in the tunnels and the elevator shaft.

A hundred times Pan has outwitted a swamp dragon and she outwits this one too, flipping up the skateboard at the last second to leap over the beast. But the smooth solar sheet of the open rooftop is not the rubbly surface of the bridge. Here, in the gusting wind, speed goes a much longer way.

She's going far too fast!

Fox shouts her name so hard the cry seems to rip apart his wound.

Pan makes a wobbly landing on the skateboard and veers into a deep swerve. Fox holds his breath. Even now, at the lethal edge of a moment, she can regain control. He's seen her do it a hundred times.

A blizzard swirls out of the elevator shaft. The blizzard dances above the heads of the crowd and gusts around Pan. It's a great cloud of moths, drawn to the first flame of the sun, but it seems to Fox that the spirit of the nether-world has sent its creatures up through the spiregyres to the top of the tower to reclaim Pan, who keeps skidding, arms flailing, out of control . . .

Fox moves. He will catch her, somehow. He *must*.

The wind catches her instead. Pan hurtles through the moth cloud, still on her skateboard, free right to the last, right to the edge of the roof.

And beyond.

Fox turns his head away, eyes shut tight, as Pandora falls from the tower.

Her name tears through him again and again. His heart feels like a gaping wound. What he just saw could not have happened. It cannot be real. Fox wants to stop time, to replay the moment, to see Pan spin in the air and land safely back on the tower roof.

He opens his eyes. The moth cloud quivers like a ghost above the spot where Pan fell. For a stricken moment they tremble there then flock towards the dawn. Now, a tremendous energy ignites the crowd as people turn on the nervous and outnumbered guards.

Fox can't fight his way through the wave of anger. He doesn't want this awful, magnificent gift Pan has hurled at him – his own life for hers – but the heaving crowd forces him backwards until he is under the hovering ship where the air chute seizes him like a force of fate.

Fox is sucked up on a cushion of air into the belly of the ship.

He lands in a scarlet spray of his own blood on the entry ramp inside.

'He's in!' someone shouts, and hauls him to the side as people continue to burst into the airship.

'Anyone else?' yells a commanding voice when the flow of refugees stop. 'Last chance to board!'

Fox looks down through the transparent window on the

floor of the airship and sees ragged boat refugees still among the Nooworlders on the roof. Some refugees are choosing to stay behind. There will be a whole new blend of citizens, he realizes, to imagineer a new city from the ruins of the old. And here on board Fox sees, looking around, are excited young sky citizens with their clean skins and clothes, and red-jacketed guards, crammed side by side with the boat refugees.

The future has just been shaken up into a brand-new mix before his very eyes.

The whoosh of air stops; the doors on the underside of the ship slide shut. Fox feels a rapid surge upward as the ship rises in a hail of gunfire from a new rush of guards. But against the impenetrable shell of the airship, it's as useless as a handful of stones.

Strangers stare. A woman leans forward and touches his arm. A face he knows. Someone he hasn't seen since his days as a young Noosrunner.

'Fox, it's me. Steerpike.'

The years fall away as Fox remembers a girl with wispy blonde hair and faraway eyes who was a demon in the Noos.

'*You're* Steerpike?'

Steerpike grasps his hand, her eyes full of tears.

'You remember me? Dolores Dane.'

'I remember you.'

Fox grips the hand of his old friend, Dol, as the ship swerves violently, dodging a swarm of police skybikers. But the buzzing swarm cannot match the speed and power of the airship. Fox slumps against a window and watches the towers of the city spin away from him, as the great ship turns northward.

Far below, sea crashes through the bombed walls of the

city and swirls around the netherworld where his brave, wild Pan has fallen. Fox grips the memento she flung at him, her jade frog good luck charm, tight in the palm of his hand. If anyone could survive such a fall it's Pandora, the warrior queen of the netherworld, who would dive from the great arm of the broken bridge and swim down through the drowned ruins with her webbed feet and feathery gills, dreaming of the lost cities and vanished centuries.

Fox sees her there in his mind's eye. He needs to believe she survived. Otherwise he must live tormented by the grief that she loved him so fiercely she'd die to give him the future he craved.

But already Pandora and the netherworld is behind him as they hit full speed. The sky city recedes until it seems to Fox to be no more than a monolithic rock crop amid the waves, and all he sees before him is the world's ocean and neverending sky.

HOMECOMING TIDE

The sun keeps Tuck company. The red globe slips loose from its night anchor and sails the dark tide of the mountains, trailblazing the path of the fjord for the burning gondola that carries Tuck's body out to the open sea.

News of Tuck's death has blown like a wind through the rockways, up into the mountain caves and halls, and the people of Ilira have gathered in shock on the great bridge that is his masterpiece. Mara has come too.

She pushes through the funeral crowds on the Culpy Bridge and finds a space between the cramped shops. The metal signs above the diamond-dealers and metal-mongers creak and wail and the bridge wires hum against the drum of Ilira's waterfalls, accompanying the windpipers' haunting laments.

The sun climbs into the sky and as a new day breaks over the top of the world Tuck's glass palace becomes a temple of light. It was his beacon, thinks Mara, in a world growing dark to his fading eyes. The burning gondola seems to pass through a cascading green curtain of aurora and, for the first time since he landed in Ilira as a ragged gypsea, Tuck launches back out on to the ocean. A shiver creeps over Mara as the

289

salt wind stings her face and she remembers the awkward kiss of a gypsea boy in a chill mountain cave, years ago.

A soft hand slips into hers. Mara turns and buries her face in the cold hair of the fiery head that leans, heavy and exhausted, on her shoulder.

'I thought you stayed with the others at the palace,' says Mara.

'I was worried about you,' says Lily, and Mara sees how her daughter has grown up all of a sudden, able to understand pain besides her own.

'I'm all right. Go with Clay, I won't be long,' Mara reassures her, and Lily turns back to the tall youth who watches her, tense as a hunter, absorbing Lily as if he must learn her by heart.

As the bridge empties, Mara stands alone and feels a strange pause that she recalls from her island life. It's the lull between the changing tides when the world seems to stand still. The ocean becomes glass. The wind holds its breath. Mara looks down at the stilled water and sees that the bridge and its reflection have joined to make an enormous shining ring in the sea. Silver fish swim up the fjord, nosing towards the ring.

The sea gives a great sigh. Far out, the muscles of the deep oceans begin to heave the waves back to the land. The glassy sea shatters and the shining ring breaks as tide turns and the waves surge up the fjord.

The homecoming tide tugs at Mara. The vast pull of the ocean is unsettling something deeper than memory, like a fragment of glass shifting in an old wound. She reaches into the pocket of her parka, touches the cool sphere of the globe. And suddenly knows what she must do. She will put this to rest forever, here, now, on a seabed cluttered with so many other relics of the past.

When Tuck stole the globe she would have given almost anything to get it back – and that, Mara decides, is why she must get rid of it once and for all. She must never let anyone or anything have such devastating power over her, or Lily, ever again.

Mara searches the shore until she picks out her daughter's tawny head, close to Clay's dark one, in the receding crowd. Lily's future might be here in this lively new metropolis that reaches out to the world. Mara cannot bear the thought of a mountain between herself and Lily . . . and yet . . .

She remembers her earlier vision.

The world can be changed.

Mara looks at the steam gondolas puffing in the fjord, at the buzz of the market shops opening up all along the Culpy bridge, at the rickety cable trains that creep up the mountain in between the thundering waterfalls, a mighty energy that Broom dreams of using to power the city with light and heat through the long Arctic night of winter. If Ilira can transform from the brutal, inward-looking place she once knew to all this, in the space of Lily's short life, what else is possible?

A door swings open in Mara's mind and she seems to glimpse a time beyond whatever battles lie ahead when this vast island that has emerged from aeons of ice has become a pulsing heartland of the Earth.

Is that how it all happened for Tuck? A sudden vision of what could be? Tuck made good on his vision, whatever his demons were. He revolutionized and reinvented Ilira. The city opened up and discovered its power.

Just as Fox and his revolution wants to open up the world.

Is the key to the future *really* to hide away in Candlewood? Or to fight for that future and build on the best of Tuck's dreams? If rickety trains can climb mountains . . . the way to the interior can surely be opened up. The Earth's soundwaves have reconnected its people. Candlewood and Lake Longhope must become part of the world too.

If there were a way to zip through the mountains, right now, Mara would. She aches for the little ones. They'll be crawling out of bed just now with hot, soft, just-wakened bodies and crotchety cries. Her own body cries out for them, but deeper still is the need to unlock their future too. If war is coming, the people of the North must stand together or all will be lost.

And there is Rowan, of course. Rowan, who loves each of the children just as deeply as she does. He longs for the ocean world too. Descended from fisherfolk since time out of mind, his deep calms and sudden swells of temper are like the ocean's moods. She and Rowan grew up like a pair of squabbling barn cats on the island and bonded together in Candlewood, each needing someone to cling to when their lives cracked apart. But there's a deep restlessness in both of them, a longing for the outside world they were forced to abandon so young. What do they each want and need now? The safe haven of Candlewood? Or the risky possibilities of a fast-changing world beyond?

Mara leans on the swaying bridge and stares down at the water where the silver fish glint then disappear under the shadow of the bridge. Who knows what might happen? Who ever knew how their life would unfold?

We must hold the hands of the children yet walk free into the future, she decides. *We mustn't be trapped by a past we didn't create.*

Yet Lily is already trapped, she fears, fixated on the father she has never known. Fox is not coming, Mara tells herself.

How could he, even for Lily, if he is steering a global war?

She must not let Lily be bound to a hopeless longing. Mara can kill that impossible hope now – if she throws the cyberwizz and its globe into the sea. Lily might never forgive her; but, Mara vows, her daughter's future *will* be open and free.

The globe in her hand catches the morning light and glows as if it's a tiny planet fallen to Earth. A tremor runs up Mara's arm as the globe gives an electric tingle, powering up in the sun. Vivid colours swirl around its surface like a tiny aurora storm. She watches, as if in a dream.

Let it go! Now!

Trembling, Mara leans over the bridge to drop the globe into the sea.

ALL THE WORLD'S TOMORROWS

The airship *Wistar* surfs the world's winds, following the frail morning fire of the North Star. Fox is moving too fast for hope or regret, surrendered to the sensation of speed. He's hurtling through a haze of electric blue on the rays of the morning sun.

Here, in the nose of the airship, windows curve all around. Up ahead, the aurora is a sizzling green storm. Far below are hills and valleys of restless sea.

Mountains rise from the horizon, sudden and shocking, as if the huge hull of a sunken ship has heaved up from the ocean deeps. Fox hears cries of wonder from the refugees crammed in the huge belly of the ship as they sight the vast land mass of the North. The *Wistar* heads towards it and Fox is filled with a strange ache of homecoming for a place he has never known. He cannot see an end to the tide of jagged peaks.

'I'm so sorry, Fox, about Pan,' says Steerpike. She has carefully tended to his shoulder wound. Fox relaxes into a haze of painkillers from a medical kit as the sharp edges of agony fade.

'I'd never have made it if it wasn't for her. Pan and my

mother, they both saved me,' he says, seeing how they each hurled him free into the future with gifts of searing rebel kindness.

Fox's composure deserts him. Steerpike grips his hand.

'Steerpike,' he begins, once he's steadied himself. 'I mean, Dol.'

'I'm Dolores these days,' she smiles. 'But *you* can call me Steerpike, Surgent Fox.'

'Steerpike it is,' he smiles back, then remembers. 'What happened to Kitsune? The soundwave cut dead and I lost him. Have you heard anything? Is he all right?'

'I hope so,' says Steerpike. 'He's flying this ship.'

'Kitsune!'

'Our wily trickster fox.' Steerpike laughs. 'He can't wait to see you. Can you walk to the flight deck? Here, lean on me.'

She leads him to the flight deck, an elevated cabin at the nose tip of the airship. Fox follows in disbelief. In all these years he has never met Kitsune in the flesh, only as a bundle of electrons in the Noos and a voice on the soundwave.

'I'd get up and hug you, my friend,' cries a voice Fox seems to have known forever, 'but we're hitting turbulence and one of our engines took a hit from the sky patrol, so it's all hands on deck. Hold tight!'

A pilot at the controls sends Fox a blazing smile. The ship thuds and bounces and Fox winces, but he can't help smiling through the pain. Solid and cheerful, with twinkling eyes in a round face, and a black mop of hair, Kitsune looks nothing like the sly trickster fox of his Noosname.

'Thought we'd surprise you.' Kitsune gives the soft laugh that has kept Fox grounded and calm in so many tense moments. 'Didn't want to get your hopes up in case I didn't make it. And then you nearly didn't. And Pan . . .'

His eyes meet Fox's in wordless sympathy.

Fox focuses on the moment to keep his grief at bay. 'You've flown all the way from New Jing? But *how* . . . ?'

'When you're commander of the eastern sky fleet, many things are possible,' says Kitsune breezily. '*Make maximum use of mobility*, as Lawrence of Arabia would say.'

Fox bursts out laughing. Kitsune always refused to discuss in any detail the plans to hijack a fleet of sky ships. That was his job and Fox must trust him, he said; and because he had to, Fox did.

'It was best to keep all of that top secret and out of the ether, just in case. But here I am.' Kitsune steers the ships out of the turbulence and turns to his old friend with a gentler smile. 'And here you are.'

Kitsune and Steerpike exchange glances.

'We always thought you'd be here, in the end,' Steerpike confides. 'There was always a back-up plan. There are Surgents in New Mungo all ready to take over the reins should anything happen to you. Or,' she smiles, 'should *you* happen to veer off-plan.'

'Lawrence of Arabia's top tip,' Kitsune declares. '*Make a virtue of rebel individuality, irregularity and unpredictability.*'

'The best laid plans of mice and men,' Fox admits with a wry smile, 'often go askew.'

And in so many unexpected ways, he thinks, silently blessing his mother who has rebelled in the most unpredictable way of all.

'Let the Surgency know that Sarah Stone, my mother, has taken over my fight in New Mungo,' he tells Kitsune who absorbs this news in rapt wonderment. 'Tell them to trust her and – and to keep her safe.'

One of the co-pilots turns from the controls. 'We've made radio contact with the Atlantic Surge and located a mountain city called Ilira, a trade port famed for its bridges, deep in the east-coast fjords.'

Fox feels his spirit leap.

'Ilira's fleets will join the Surge,' adds the other co-pilot. 'That's the message coming through. And there's a gypsea fleet at Atlan point, south of Ilira.'

'The Arctic Pirates,' says Steerpike. 'Under the command of the Vulture of the North. With a name like that,' she grins, 'I'm glad he's on our side.'

'Our nearest landing platform is at Fort Aurora, some distance north of Ilira. We're about to begin our descent,' Kitsune announces. He turns to Fox. 'The new settlement at Aurora seems *far* from settled. There are signs that people there will join us, if we give them the choice. We have a chance of taking a major stronghold of the empire, perhaps without too much of a fight. Here's a bit of irregularity and unpredictability that wasn't planned for by your father and his cohorts, Fox! Our people are fascinated by the real world. They're beginning to feel and act in ways the empire didn't foresee now they've been set free from their cages in the sky. We spoke to the command unit at Fort Aurora earlier – from the noise they were making I thought they'd an uprising on their hands, but they were in raptures over the spectacle of an aurora storm.' Kitsune chuckles. 'The empire doesn't know what it's unleashed.'

Fox remembers what he glimpsed as the airship soared away from the sky tower. Some of the unwilling police guards who couldn't bring themselves to fire on their own people were turning on their superiors, while others joined the exodus from the rooftop. All those rebels unleashed themselves from the empire in that moment and chose the risk of the unknown.

'You have Midnight listeners at Aurora,' says Steerpike. 'I tracked their Nooswave in the midnight login. Tell them we have the Storyteller on board,' she suggests to Kitsune. 'That'll cause more excitement than an aurora storm.'

Fox winces with pain as the ship shudders in descent, but his hopes are rising. 'If the Earth itself has stirred the people in the new fortresses of the Northlands and the Midnight stories have awoken their dreams, maybe this war is already half won.'

'Maybe,' says Steerpike. 'But too many still have dreams,' she looks away, 'like your father's. There's a battle ahead yet.'

The airship's tremors deepen. Fox's ears pop and his stomach flips as they lose height rapidly to follow the ragged line of the coast where the edges of the vast island fragment into sea fjords. And now they are flying over an astonishing thing: a network of glistening pathways, woven between the mountains, across a winding path of sea.

Fox's heart jolts painfully, as if tied to an anchor that has just plummeted down to the miraculous world below.

Look for the shining bridges of Ilira, Lily said. *Find me there.*

Fox stares down through the starboard window. In his mind's eye he remembers a dark-haired girl on a broken bridge.

'You need to upgrade that ancient junk,' Steerpike scoffs, as he takes the emerald mindgem and tiny godbox from his pocket.

'Never!' says Fox, as he connects up the trusty old

298

godgem. 'Where would I be without this?'

The sizzling green curtains of the aurora tear apart. A pandemonium of colour rips through, erupting all around the airship, as if the universe has cracked open and a glorious chaos of tomorrows can't wait to tumble into today.

The world is full of tomorrows, thinks Fox.

And the world is all before him now.

ON A WING OF MAYBE

Mara shields her eyes against the sun, stalled mid-throw by what looks like a silver fish swimming across the blue ocean of sky. A shining shoal follows and she pauses to watch the fleet of airships flying up from the south.

The globe tingles in her hand, charged and ready. She feels dizzy, full of dread at what she must do. What's she waiting for? *Get rid of it, now*. Throw the globe, the whole cyberwizz, into the sea and be done with it all for good.

But Mara's fingers grip the globe as she feels the deep, raw tug inside that always leads her into trouble – and keeps her alive. It's the same impulse that once made her peer beyond the horizon and leap into the unknown – to the Weave where she first found Fox, then out on to the world's ocean where she lost almost everything. But the tug is her internal compass, always pointing to her true north. It brought her here to the top of the world, to a new life on a changed Earth. It's that same magnetic tug that must have brought Lily through the mountains to Ilira and led her, as it led Mara, to Fox.

None of it would have happened without the cyberwizz she is about to hurl into the ocean. Would she even be alive? She would never have known Fox and he would not have begun the revolution to save the future from the sky empire. Lily would never have been born.

Mara takes the halo and wand from her pocket. Barely thinking, barely able to breathe, she slips on the halo, flips open the globe.

Just once more. Just for a moment. Just to see.

The strange language of the cyberwizz is etched in her memory like ancient carvings on stone. Diving into the Weave is as easy as surfacing from the ocean and knowing how to breathe.

The real world fades.

The magnificent bridges and thundering waterfalls of Ilira all feel far, far away.

The wind of a homecoming tide wraps around Mara and seems to sweep her towards a broken bridge in a place where anything felt possible, once upon a time.

EXODUS

Julie Bertagna

A LOVE THAT COULD CHANGE THE FUTURE . . .

Mara's island home is drowning as the ice caps melt and Earth loses its land to the ocean. But one night, in the ruined virtual world of the Weave, Mara meets the mysterious Fox – a fiery-eyed boy who tells her of sky cities that rise from the sea. Mara sets sail on a daring journey to find a new life for herself and her friends – instead she discovers a love that threatens to tear her apart . . .

ZENITH

Julie Bertagna

CAN LOVE MEND A BROKEN WORLD?

As the ice caps melt and the world drowns Mara
stands at the bow of her ship, determined to believe
that somewhere there is land still. But a floating city is
about to throw her off course . . .

And in the ruins beneath the towers of a sky city, the
boy Mara loves plots a lonely revolution of his own and
hopes for the day when they will be together again.

GL◯W

AMY KATHLEEN RYAN

A SHIP HEADING FOR NEW EARTH IS HALFWAY THROUGH ITS INCREDIBLE JOURNEY ACROSS THE GALAXY.

ON BOARD, SIXTEEN-YEAR-OLDS WAVERLY AND KIERAN ARE PART OF THE FIRST GENERATION BORN IN SPACE.

THEY ARE IN LOVE.

THEY BELIEVE THEIR FUTURE IS WRITTEN IN THE STARS.

THEY HAVE NEVER SEEN A STRANGER BEFORE . . .

. . . UNTIL THE DAY THEY ARE WRENCHED APART AND SUDDENLY FIND THEMSELVES FIGHTING FOR THEIR LIVES.

SKY CHASERS

THE FIRST HEART-STOPPING ADVENTURE

Website Discount Offer

Purchase either of these Julie Bertagna titles
from www.panmacmillan.com for just £4.99

£1 postage and packaging costs to UK addresses, £2 for overseas

To buy the books with this special discount:

1. visit our website, www.panmacmillan.com

2. search by author or book title

3. add to your shopping basket

4. use the discount code **MARA** when you check out

≋ **panmacmillan.com**

NORTH LEAMINGTON SCHOOL